KEVIN B. HILLSTROM

Rainmaker Rainmaker

Cover painting: William H. Beard (American, 1824–1900), *His Majesty Receives*, 1885, oil on canvas, 18 x 24-1/8 in. (canvas); 23 x 29 in. (framed). Indianapolis Museum of Art at Newfields, James E. Roberts Fund, 76.13. Courtesy of the Indianapolis Museum of Art at Newfields.

Cover design by Matthew Jay Fleming.

First edition

ISBN (paperback): 979-8-99-461740-3
ISBN (hardcover): 979-8-99-461743-4
ISBN (digital): 979-8-99-461744-1

This book was professionally typeset on Reedsy.
Find out more at reedsy.com

For Mom and Dad and the stories they told

I

At eleven o-clock a boy went past,
With a rough-haired terrier following fast
The boy's sweet whistle and dog's quick yap
Woke the fox from out his nap.

He rose and stretched till the claws in his pads
Stuck hornily out like long black gads
He listened a while, and his nose went round
To catch the smell of the distant sound
—John Masefield

"Do you know," Peter asked,
"why swallows build in the eaves of houses?
It is to listen to the stories."
—J.M. Barrie

1

Gideon Starling made his grand entrance on April 1, 1936, though no one in Greenheart remembers his arrival on that day but me. April Fool's Day. A classic Gideon touch, as I'd come to learn. That day seems as good a place to start as any.

The morning dawned clear and blue and cloudless, which Mom declared to be a good omen. She knew I was nervous about what the morning held in store. Dad grunted something that might have been agreement with Mom's cheery observation if you wanted to give him the benefit of the doubt. Once we were away and down the road, though, Dad visibly relaxed. He asked me about school and teased me about girls. We talked about the Fosters' sickly new foal and speculated about the upcoming pennant races. With each passing mile the certainty grew in me that Mom had been right. It was going to be a good day.

Dad remained downright chatty until we made a final turn north onto the last of the ruler-straight roads that would take us to our destination for the day. He quieted then and I settled back in my seat and watched the telephone poles flash by. Their slanting shadows striped the road like railroad ties as far as I could see, and every time we passed through one of those columns of shadow the light from the climbing sun vanished from the cab for just an instant, as if the sun were blinking away the last of its slumbers on the other side of the world.

Clickity clack, clickity clack.

In my mind's eye our old Model A became a chugging locomotive, the dirt road beneath us the railbed of a towering trestle spanning a great mountain gorge. I imagined myself as the engineer of that spark-heeled Iron Horse, my hands steady and sure as I guided it across a jaw-dropping crescent of lumber and stone hoisted up between snowcapped peaks. I stared through the dust-clouded windshield and down into a timber-sloped abyss, the canyon air below us filled with floating hawks and darting songbirds. I imagined wise old owls presiding over it all from shadowy roosts deep in the trestle bridge's aging timbers, unperturbed by our violent passage overhead.

Clickity clack, clickity clack.

Clickity clack, clickity clack

And there I remained high in the mountains on that roaring train until a particularly jarring stretch of road gave the car a good rattle. I glanced guiltily at Dad and straightened in my seat, as if he might have sensed the storybook drift of my reveries. He thought I was prone to woolgathering. That I had the curse of an overactive imagination. That's why I never read my time-wasters around him anymore.

That's what Dad called the modest collection of *Argosy* and *Weird Tales* and *Doc Savage* pulp magazines I kept stacked on the lowest of my two bookshelves, each issue a fading relic from an earlier age of relative plenty. They resided on my little bedroom bookcase with a modest but carefully curated handful of hardbound volumes, mostly birthday and Christmas gifts from Mom and Dad or secondhand finds. *Treasure Island* and *Last of the Mohicans* and *Twenty Thousand Leagues Under the Sea* and *The Sketchbook of Geoffrey Crayon, Gent.* Miraculous tales of time machines and headless horsemen and boys raised by apes to become king of the jungle. I read them all many times over, in part because I could take them to other parts of the house without arousing Dad's ire. Their clothbound covers and embossed spines and evocative illustrations gave off an air of literary weight that inoculated them from the stink-eye Dad always gave my bedroom-exiled time wasters, even though they trafficked in many of the same wonders and miracles and monsters as their more celebrated shelf mates.

"Do you think Daniel will be there?"

I regretted the question as soon as it came out of my mouth. It was the first time I'd brought him up in Dad's earshot since he kicked Daniel and his father off our farm three weeks before. I had watched the two of them from our living room window as they lugged their meager belongings out of our barn and into the back of the beat-down truck Grant Ballantine had scrounged up for the day. They didn't have much but tying everything down took time and they had to patch a tire. Daniel and his dad didn't pull out onto the road until well past sundown, the borrowed truck's one working headlamp piercing the night's deepening gloom.

None of us went out to say good-bye that night. Not Dad, who spent the evening on chores that kept him away from the barn but within sight of the house and yard. Not Mom, who mended socks and clothes at the kitchen table with the radio turned up. And not me. Not even when they lugged out Grant Ballantine's steamer trunk of treasures from his diving days in the Navy.

Daniel and I had spent hours elbow-deep in that old chest, examining exotic and mysterious mementos his father had collected from what seemed like every corner of the world. Every time we opened the lid of that trunk I half expected to find the treasure map of Billy Bones himself inside. Every keepsake and curio hidden away in that steamer set my imagination afire; collectively, they made Daniel's father seem larger-than-life to me, like a character in a Jules Verne novel bursting with mad submariners and man-eating squids and gold-hoarding buccaneers. That feeling never entirely went away, not even after Grant Ballantine became a familiar sight in the barn and sitting on our tractor and drinking coffee at our kitchen table. As I watched them tie the steamer down it hit me I would never get to explore that vault of wonders again.

Yet even that fresh stab of loss failed to uproot me from my spot at the window. I felt paralyzed by a nebulous sense of blood allegiance, the certainty that I would cry if I set foot outside, and the enervating conviction that the world of grown-ups seethed with mysterious currents and agendas that I would never understand—let alone master—if I lived to be a thousand.

I worried my impulsive question about Daniel might turn Dad's eyes steely and distant but he took it in stride. "I expect Daniel will be at the drive, sure," he said evenly. "Just about every able-bodied boy your age and older will be there. Provided they can get a ride. All hands on deck, that's how everyone needs to think about it." I nodded agreeably and resolved to interpret his calm response as another auspicious augury for the day ahead.

"They had a drive in Kansas last year that got more than seven thousand rabbits," Dad continued. "How about that? That's a good day's work, son. I don't think we're going to beat that today but you never know."

I considered the long ax handles resting on the car seat between us and tried to imagine what a pile of seven thousand dead jackrabbits would look like. I recalled a grainy photograph I'd seen once, of a mountain of stark white buffalo skulls twice the height of a man. It had been taken somewhere out on the great fruited plains of America in 1871, when the slaughter of the continent's great herds was at its peak. I decided a pyramid of seven thousand rabbit bodies might look something like the obelisk of ghost skulls in that picture.

Dad was impressed by the turnout. What seemed like hundreds of cars and trucks lined the length of John and Myrtle Warwick's long hardpan driveway. A huge crowd milled around the front of their sun-bleached barn, a trio of grain silos arrayed in a row just beyond. A few hundred yards to the north of the barn an enormous rectangle of snow fencing had been erected, compliments of the King County Commissioners, as a holding pen for the hoped-for stampede of rabbits to come.

Dad parked the car and we walked up the driveway to the edge of the crowd. That's where we parted ways—him to find out where the organizers wanted to place us on the driving line and me in search of Daniel. I circled the outer reaches of the crowd, which was in a rambunctious state despite the early hour and chill morning air. Anticipation was high. Everyone was excited about the opportunity to do something other than worry and pray and fulminate about the unfairness of it all.

When a quick circuit of the crowd's perimeter didn't turn Daniel up I waded into the thick of it, sidling past red-faced men holding flasks of corn whiskey to their chests and twitchy boys comparing rabbit-killing fantasies like trading cards and small gray knots of women bundled up in their warmest scarves and coats. But I didn't run across Daniel or his dad and after a time I reluctantly returned to our car. Dad was in a good mood and I meant to keep it that way. He wouldn't be pleased if I kept him waiting.

It was possible Daniel wasn't even in Greenheart anymore. He hadn't been in school all week. For all we knew Daniel and his father had joined the swelling ranks of wanderers skipping like stones across America's hardpan heart. Maybe he and his dad were well and truly gone. They wouldn't be the first or last to leave Greenheart under cover of darkness without a word of goodbye to anyone. Just the tell-tale cough of an engine firing up in the middle of the night and slowly fading away. Some of those who left were flying blind. Most of them, perhaps. They just reached a point where they didn't have a choice. Where there wasn't anything left to hold on to that hadn't already been blown away.

Dad showed up at the car a few minutes later and we took our place among the motley caravan of dusty cars and sagging trucks that went rattling off from the Warwick farm to all four points of the compass. The commotion created fat rooster tails of dust that rose and drifted to the east, pulling apart like brown cotton candy in the cold morning air. I picked up one of the ax handles from the seat and hefted it. I wondered how it would feel when I slammed it into the bony, fur-covered ribs or hard skull of a terrified jackrabbit. The first tendril of disquiet about the day's agenda blossomed in my gut. I had shot rabbits before but this was going to be different. More brutish.

Dad brought us to a stop on the shoulder of Paint Road, four miles west of the Warwick farmhouse. Other trucks and cars pulled in behind and ahead of us, men and boys pouring out in a muffled flurry of shouted greetings and slamming doors.

"Don't lose that," said Dad, pointing at the ax handle in my hands. "I want it back. I'll see you down at the pen if we lose sight of each other during the drive. Listen for my whistle."

"Yes sir."

"Be careful."

"Yes sir."

We exited the car and crossed the road to join the growing line of people at the edge of the empty field. To our left stood a cluster of older men, hands buried deep in their coats against the morning cold. Baseball bats, oak table legs, and other crude weapons jutted from the crooks of their arms. People weren't allowed to use guns. Not because it wouldn't have been sporting but because the organizers didn't want anyone getting plugged.

In the other direction huddled our nearest neighbors, a man and woman with three young children. The two oldest—a boy and a girl, each nine or ten years old—were armed with pots and pans and long wooden spoons and exuded fidgety impatience. It was clear they had been placed under some sort of injunction to keep their instruments silent until the drive began. We watched the mother wipe the runny nose of the youngest child, a boy of three or four who kept fussing that he was cold because he had lost his hat somewhere. His mother looked like she was already down to her last nerve and the drive hadn't even started yet.

We must have waited a half hour or more, the family next to us growing more impatient and miserable with each passing moment, before the thin report of a distant gunshot finally reached our ears. The line immediately lurched forward into the field in a great clatter of shouts and whistles and banging pots. An assortment of trucks and tractors rattled across the fields behind us like tanks behind advancing infantry. The atmosphere up and down the line felt festive and surreal and thick with the promise of righteous violence. You could see it in the blazing eyes of the men around us. Their need for an outlet for all the sorrows and humiliations and sleepless nights and bouts of helpless rage they had suffered in the dust-choked world that had somehow become their existence.

The organizers had arranged everyone around the target area in a great square noose so as we kept walking forward the marchers on either side of us gradually drew closer. I heard the ripple of excitement through the men on our left when the first jacks came into view in the far distance, leaping around in a halting, zigzagging panic. We marched on, shouting and hooting and pounding our bats and table legs and iron pipes in the dirt, truck horns bleating behind us like rusty military bugles. And bit by bit, as if by magic, the barren fields in front of us filled with rabbits. My pulse quickened as I watched them flee.

One of the jacks abruptly reversed course and darted through an opening in the ranks of the men to our left. Caught flatfooted by the maneuver, they watched bleakly as the rabbit bounded off in the direction of the parked cars far behind us. The men grouched at each other over the breach but all was forgiven a few minutes later when a less fortunate rabbit—one without the escapee rabbit's nimbleness or element of surprise—tried the same maneuver. One of the men stepped forward and intercepted it, catching it in the hindquarters with a swing of his club that sent it spinning in the air like a top. The crippled rabbit landed at the feet of one of his companions, who promptly delivered the coup d'etat. The whole group sent up a cheer.

Several other rabbits tried the same thing up and down the line, as if they had been dragooned into some hellish version of Red Rover. Most didn't make it. Their grotesquely twisted forms were left behind in the dust as we continued our march. But a few slipped the steadily closing noose and each time I watched a rabbit hop away I felt something perilously close to gladness at its escape.

I knew the jackrabbits were a pestilence. Their populations had exploded after all the coyote and fox left for less drought-stricken hunting grounds. Now they were everywhere, gorging themselves on the meager crops and gardens we were still trying to coax out of the dirt. But the naked fear animating the flight of the animals was plain to see. I fell in a little behind Dad, hoping he wouldn't notice my dimming ardor for the task that awaited at the end of our march.

The noose continued to close and after a time I found myself walking virtually shoulder to shoulder with one of the men to our left. He was short and thick-necked, with specks of black blood that dotted his rosy-cheeked face like a pox. I looked away and far ahead, to the pen into which we were funneling the fleeing rabbits, the fencing finally visible in the distance. Beyond the fence I could see the far side of the inexorably closing noose. Sunlight glittered on the pots and pans and windshields interwoven in its thread. I could hear that far line too, their thin shouts and cries a jangle of scratches on the wind.

By the time we'd herded them all inside that pen it was wall-to-wall rabbits. Some of the creatures sprinted and darted around in frantic bursts or caromed off the fence planking. Others sat on their haunches in a near-catatonic state, long ears twitching as the alien cacophony of humankind on the other side of the fence poured down their ear canals and reverberated in their bones.

It was during that brief interlude, when everyone was waiting for permission to enter the pen and begin the slaughter, that I finally spotted Daniel. He saw me at the same instant and his face broke out in a smile of recognition. We made our way to each other through the jostling throng, his brown head bobbing at the same level as some of the men.

"Did you get any on the way in?" Daniel asked.

"Naw. You?"

"No," he said, turning his old baseball bat this way and that for my inspection. It was bone dry, unstained by blood or other bodily fluids. "Not so far. They knew better than to test me and old Widowmaker here." Daniel was acting as if nothing had changed between us. As if *my* dad hadn't just kicked *his* dad off our farm for getting too friendly with *my* mom. That's about all the two of us had been able to glean and it was more than enough. Once we realized the implosion of my parents' close friendship with Daniel's father had potential romantic or sexual dimensions we dropped the matter like a hot potato. That was a dark and mysterious wood through which neither of us wished to travel.

Dad's distinctive whistle pierced the air, twice, and I tracked him to the top step of Warwick's front porch. He appeared to be looking right at us but it was hard to tell because his face was hidden under the shadowed brim of his hat. He tipped his hat to us and leisurely stepped down into the crowd before I could wave back.

"Quite a crowd," Daniel observed after a beat, maintaining the charade that all was well. I couldn't tell whether Dad's appearance had spooked him or not. "Half the county must be here."

"Is your dad here?" I asked with forced casualness. I really wanted the answer to be no. I wasn't sure what would happen if our fathers ran into one another.

Daniel squinted into the sunlight slanting in from the east. "He's up in Washington right now, working that big dam they're building up there. The one on the Columbia? They say it's going to be the biggest dam in the world when it's done. Dad said there was dive work up there. Good pay."

That explained Daniel's absence from school. With his dad not around to watch him he was playing hooky. "When's he coming back? Or are you going up there?"

Daniel shrugged. "He's going to come get me once he gets the lay of the land. He needs to get established first, you know? He got us a room down at Bean's for now, but that's just temporary."

"Sure," I said, though I found this news unsettling. Bean's Billiards was Greenheart's last remaining pool hall and had a decidedly seedy reputation.

"Maybe Miss Wells is here," Daniel offered, changing the subject. He stood on his toes and lifted his chin performatively to take a long look above the scrum of people surrounding us, then lifted an imaginary spyglass to his eye and peered through the blur of faces.

The booty in Grant Ballantine's steamer included a rust-flecked but still handsome collapsible telescope that we treated like a holy relic. A faint cataract of ghosting in the eyepiece limited its usefulness for true reckoning but that shadowy imperfection gave everything that came into the spyglass's sight a gothic cast. More than eighteen inches long at full extension, the telescope's four tubes collapsed into a leather-clad artillery shell of polished brass that flickered with our distorted reflections. According to the brass plate on the front of the sturdy felt-lined storage box the spyglass had been crafted in Ealing, London in 1902 by W. Ottway but as far as I was concerned it might as well have come from the vest pocket of Neptune. Places like London and the North Sea were just as fantastical and beyond my reach as Neverland or Atlantis.

Daniel moved the invisible spyglass up and down and all around. "Don't worry, I'll find her," he said reassuringly. "You can kill a few rabbits together. Maybe if you kill enough of them, you can make her a fur coat with the pelts.

She can wear it on your honeymoon."

My face reddened, as it always did when Daniel started in on the subject of Miss Helen Wells, our eighth grade teacher. I had developed a hopeless crush on Miss Wells over the course of the school year and Daniel had a lot to say about it, none of it nice. He mocked me as a pervert for panting after older women and offered scathing assessments of Miss Wells' physical attributes. He said her chest was as flat as her blackboard. He said she wore underwear that smelled like chalk. He was mean about it. Perplexingly so, given that so far as I knew Daniel didn't give Miss Wells any trouble at school.

I didn't know how to deal with Daniel's persistent hostility on the subject. I had no idea what words would get him to stop and any fight between the two of us wouldn't end well for me. Daniel was strong and never seemed to get tired. And while he didn't go looking for trouble, he didn't back down. And when things reached that point he didn't care whether he got hurt as long as he hurt you worse. A few older boys around town learned that the hard way in those first few months after Daniel and his dad moved to Greenheart. So when Daniel started in on me about Miss Wells at the rabbit drive I did what I usually did. Curled into myself like a silent little self-loathing armadillo until he relented, which he usually did in pretty short order. And so it was that day.

Daniel got the hint and asked me how Buster was doing. Buster was a big-chested lab-terrier mix Mom got as a pup from someone at church. He kept me and Daniel company every day, no matter whether we were doing chores or field work or studying for school. Mom took to calling us the Three Musketeers and Daniel and I simultaneously declared that Buster was Porthos. In the evening Buster liked to push between us on the floor when we listened to baseball or the latest installment of *The Shadow* or *The Lone Ranger*. He thumped his muscular black tail against the floor so loudly when we scratched his belly that we only did it during the commercials.

Daniel had no way of knowing Buster was another sore subject.

"He ran off last week," I said, fighting through the sudden lump in my throat. "Dad thinks he was chasing planes and got himself lost again. Like he did last September, remember? When Mrs. Clute called to say he was all the way over there? Dad was so mad. He was only gone a few hours that time, though. Dad and Mom won't say it but I know they think he's lying in a ditch somewhere. Run over or shot or full of poison."

"You don't know that."

"Well I know where he's not."

Daniel looked stricken. "Damn. I'm really sorry. He's a smart dog, though, even with the plane chasing thing." He gave me an encouraging smile. "Don't give up is all I'm saying. He could turn up any day. Buster's got a good nose on him. I bet he finds his way back."

I nodded and looked away, not trusting myself to say anything more.

"Pastor Rosbourne's here," Daniel observed, pointing into the crowd. "How about that? You think he's going to get in there and kill some rabbits with the flock? Smite them with his Bible?"

Charles Rosbourne was swaddled in a heavy gray coat, deep in conversation with two other men I recognized from our church. I smiled at the absurd thought of our soft-spoken pastor swinging his Bible like a morningstar through the plague of rabbits we'd captured. My parents liked Rosbourne and I did too, but my thoughts wandered far afield during some of his sermons.

John Stagg was at the rabbit drive too. The crowd around us shifted and came back together again in a new shape and suddenly there he was. The Great Man himself, surrounded by his usual crowd of admirers. To judge by his fine coat and shining shoes and empty hands, though, he was attending in a strictly observational capacity.

Stagg was Greenheart's most prominent businessman and benefactor. He had arrived in Greenheart as a widower with young daughter Clara way back in 1912, when the town was but a fraction of its later size. The clean prairie air prescribed by his daughter's doctors ultimately failed to save her from the tuberculosis drowning her lungs, but Stagg buried her here nonetheless on a cold March morning in 1916 and never left. Mom said he laid his daughter to rest in Greenheart because of the happy memories they made in Clara's final years. Dad said Stagg saw the oceans of wheat sprouting up across King County and recognized financial opportunity when it was staring him in the face.

Whatever Stagg's reasons for staying, he quickly made his mark. He shunned elected office but his wealth and willingness to invest it or give it away made him the unofficial monarch of King County. Stagg had a philanthropic streak a mile wide. He opened his wallet to build a public library that a town five times Greenheart's size would have been proud to call its own. He was lenient with store credit when it came to widows and families who had lost their sons and brothers and fathers in the Great War. He stripped the old dance hall down to the studs and rebuilt it into a grand theatre festooned with golden drapes and sparkling chandeliers that attracted bands and vaudeville shows from Denver and Los Angeles and Kansas City. He built office buildings and garages, purchased and refurbished the Zephyr Hotel, bought and expanded the local tractor and combine dealership, and greased the legislative wheels (with help from the Denver and Rio Grande Western) for construction of a new train depot. Stagg even paid for the great bell that hung in the steeple of the church my family attended every Sunday morning.

And here Stagg was at the rabbit drive, a polite smile affixed to his square-jawed face as the men and women of Greenheart crowded around him. He said something to the man standing to his left and everyone around him laughed like it was the funniest thing they had ever heard.

We surveyed other faces in the crowd with studied nonchalance, gossiping about the people we knew—classmates and adults both—and speculating about the backstories of those we didn't. Everywhere we looked, poor folk one duster away from being blown out of Colorado once and for all stood with neighbors whose roots were still planted deep in Greenheart's powdered soil, at least to all appearances. Tenant farmers making do in tarpaper shacks were standing shoulder to shoulder with men and women still hanging on to the framed farmhouses and bungalows they built back in the twenties, when seas of Turkey Red winter wheat surrounded Greenheart as far as the eye could see.

I felt a surge of civic pride well up inside me as I looked around us. Yes, Greenheart was going through hard times but it wasn't going down without a fight. The turnout for the rabbit drive was proof of that. We had gathered together in common cause, every face shining with pride and resolve and grit, to defend land bequeathed to us by pioneering parents and grandparents and great-grandparents who had defied wolves and Indians and white-out blizzards and tornadoes and prairie fires and subzero winters and plow-busting rocks and deceitful land speculators to carve something great and enduring out of this world of tall grasses and empty horizons and relentless wind.

A pistol shot rang out somewhere behind us, making us both jump, and an instant later men and boys began pouring into the rabbit-filled pen like an army of club-wielding Gullivers. Some of the boys—as well as several men who had gotten liquored up over the course of the day—attacked the jacks in a pent-up frenzy of wild jabs and hurried swings. But the ranks of participants also included men who had survived gas-steeped trenches and cannonades of enemy rifle fire. A rabbit drive wasn't going to get their blood up. Those men took a more methodical approach, scything like metronomes as they waded through the sea of jackrabbits at their feet, the spray from their weapons turning their lower trouser legs crimson.

I, on the other hand, was so keyed up that when the pistol sounded I shouldered Daniel aside to beat him into the pen. I waded along the inside edge of the fence, taking short savage swings at every darting, bounding jackrabbit within reach. Every time I connected I felt the crunching impact run all the way up my arm and into my suddenly boiling heart. The rabbits were everywhere. For each one that lay motionless, five or ten still leaped about, their red-rimmed eyes darting and rolling in their furry brown skulls. It was as if the rabbits were sprouting out of the ground on unseen conveyor belts.

A bolt of white-hot pain lanced through the back of my skull and I staggered back against the fence. I clutched at my head with my free hand, dimly aware that I had been clipped by the backswing of a stout man to my left. I stared at the man's broad, slope-shouldered back with watery, murderous eyes but he never even looked in my direction. He just kept whaling away at the bounding jacks with his blood-smeared oak table leg.

There was a hunger in the way he prowled the pen, a savagery to his aspect. Everyone was giving him a wide berth.

In truth, though, the man had done me a favor. The thunderbolt of pain from his blow punctured the throbbing red mist of violence in which I had become enveloped. It was as if my ears had popped. Noises that had been a faint radio broadcast from a distant open window suddenly rushed blaring into my ears. I flinched as I heard for the first time how the rabbits were screaming all around me, the sound uncannily like that of crying human babies.

I let the heavy ax handle fall to my side and looked around me, trying to make sense of the sky above my head. When the gates of the pen had closed the sky over our heads had been a clear cerulean blue but it was a canvas of gray scudding clouds now. The air had a faint rust-colored tint to it and I felt the familiar taste of dust on my tongue.

How long had I been in the pen?

Blinking away the grit floating in the air, my gaze passed blearily over the seething, dust-kicking crowd. Back at Warwick's farm, before the drive, there had been a good number of women and girls about. But the faces lining the fence now were mostly old men and young boys. Some of them were talking to each other through handkerchiefs and Red Cross masks, their faces turned anxiously to the skies to the west. Behind me I could hear a stranded wife trying to convince her husband to leave but he was having none of it. *I am not running home every time there's a little dust in the air,* he said in a low angry hiss. *Do you hear me? We're not leaving until it's done.*

Further down the fence line I spotted the little girl from the family that had lined up next to us on the road earlier that morning. The little metal pot and wooden spoon she had been using to help drive the rabbits to their deaths lay at her feet. Her eyes were red but she was all cried out now to judge by her thousand-yard stare.

I was still rubbing my head and looking at that blank-eyed little girl when Gideon Starling spoke to me for the first time.

"Are you all right, son?"

He didn't raise his voice to be heard above the surrounding din, but it cut through the noise as if he had leaned over and whispered right in my ear.

That wasn't the strangest part, though. The strangest part was what happened when Gideon spoke. I was looking into the blood-slicked heart of the pen when Gideon's question came floating over my shoulder and into my ear and it seemed to me that when he spoke, every rabbit still alive paused for the briefest of instants to turn their bulging eyes in his direction. It was an eerie display of synchronization that made my skin break out in gooseflesh.

"Did you hear me, son?"

I turned to get a good look at the man standing on the other side of the fencing. I had never seen him before. He was tall and trimly built, dressed in an expensive-looking oxblood coat that reached below his knees. The coat had a collar of dense fur that rippled in the rising wind. Affixed to his lapel was a half dollar-sized pin of white ivory inlaid in a flat round frame of sterling silver. Etched on the ivory surface was a finely detailed rendering of a ram's horn nestled in a sweep of leaves.

The stranger tipped his wide-brimmed homburg hat in greeting when our eyes met. His russet-colored hair was going to silver but he still had most of it and his formidable widow's peak was neatly slicked back from his broad forehead. The lines on his face were not as numerous or deeply etched as the hieroglyphics of sun and wind and worry that marked the faces of the people I knew. He could have been forty or a well-preserved sixty, it was impossible to tell.

"Did you hear me, son?" The stranger frowned in concern. "That fool rung your bell pretty good."

"Yes sir," I said. I felt my head and checked my fingers once more to make sure I wasn't bleeding. "I'm fine, thank you."

The man's lips peeled back from his teeth to reveal a gleaming white smile. His eyeteeth were prominent, bishops in a line of pawns. "Glad to hear it. You're going to be sporting a pretty good lump there, though. My advice? Think up a good story for when people ask you how you got it. Give it a little flair. Dress it up a bit." He gave me a conspiratorial wink and I couldn't help but smile in return. "Blame it on brigands and thieves."

1

"Yes sir."

"You don't have much time to come up with something, though," he observed. "Looks like things are winding down. If you want to add to your tally you'd better hurry."

I turned back to survey the interior of the pen. Some men and boys were throwing dead rabbits in sacks and baskets, tossing their slack bodies in by their long ears or legs. Others stood around in groups of two or three or four, smoking and talking as they watched the arm-weary diehards stalk around the pen, finishing off the last stragglers. The man who had hit me was moving among them.

"That's okay," I said. "They can have the rest." I hefted my ax handle so that he could see the gory business end of it. "I got my licks in."

"So you did. Very impressive, young man. Truly, this whole affair has been inspiring to witness. You and your compatriots certainly put all these rabbits in their place. I'm curious: Did they owe you money? Were they cheating at cards? Stealing from the register?"

I drew back at the unexpected note of mockery in his voice but his words found the mark nonetheless. I looked around the pen with what I imagined to be the stranger's eyes and felt my pride in the day's events evaporate. He was right. We looked ridiculous. We *were* ridiculous. Why did we even bother? Killing all these rabbits wasn't going to make it rain, and the jacks would be back in even greater numbers in six months given that nothing ever went our way anymore. Everyone around us suddenly looked low and mean. Even Dad, who was standing down at the far end of the pen with a few other men, their backs hunched against the dust-tinged wind like a row of cows as they smoked their cigarettes and pipes.

The corners of the man's eyes crinkled in amusement. "Ah, there I go again, getting carried away with the ribbing. I can see you're a lad who's proud of where he comes from." He gave me an approving nod. "I respect that. I meant no offense. To the contrary, son, I'm genuinely impressed with what I've seen here today. Gatherings such as this show the fortitude of communities. It shows they have what it takes to survive. Hope or despair, which is it going to be? I know what I would choose. Looks like the people around here have made the same choice."

"Thank you, sir." I didn't know whether his praise was sincere but I wanted it to be and that was good enough.

The man told me his name was Gideon Starling and that he had business in King County and that he was going to be staying in Greenheart for a while. He said he had taken a room down at the Zephyr Hotel and was in need of an enterprising boy to run errands for him and show him around town. Would I be interested in performing such duties? In exchange for a fair wage, of course?

How could I say no?

And that's how it began, with a handshake over the fence as I stood ankle deep in dead rabbits. Then he tipped his hat to me once more and disappeared into the crowd from whence he came, leaving me alone under an orange sky aglow like the tip of a cigarette burning in God's mouth.

2

Mom and Dad were dubious about my arrangement with Starling, to put it mildly. Dad didn't even know who I was talking about when I described him, which I found almost impossible to believe. The man had looked like a new baseball in a crate of red apples. A bayonet in a drawer of butter knives. How had Dad not noticed him?

An uneasy look passed between my parents when I described my conversation with Gideon, followed by a barrage of skeptical questions. What was Starling's business in Greenheart? Why had he come? Where was he from? They took turns interrogating me, the unspoken truce between them holding strong as they gathered information. Was Starling a vulture come to pick at the foreclosed bones of our fields and tractors and barns? One of FDR's pencil pushers, looking for pigs and cows to kill for pennies on the hoof? What did he *really* want? What was he *really* after? And what about my chores? If I was going to be Starling's errand boy after school, was I prepared to ride my bicycle home from town in the dark? The sun was still setting pretty early in April. And I was needed in the morning and on the weekends around the farm, especially with the loss of the Ballantines. Did I understand that the needs of the farm always came first?

But I had girded myself for the conversation, and as they bombarded me with their questions I silently congratulated myself on anticipating all potential avenues of attack. I walked them through my plans for getting my chores and homework done and emphasized that Gideon had volunteered to drop me off if I was ever looking at a bike ride home in the dark. Still, it was touch and go until I told them my starting hourly wage. That's when they looked at each other and fell silent. That's when I knew I had won.

When school let out on Monday I made a beeline for the Zephyr Hotel, pedaling my bike for all I was worth. My heart pounded a little harder when I turned down Main Street and took in the Zephyr's big-shouldered three-story edifice on the left. The hotel took up the entire block. I pondered again, as I had on several occasions during the interminable school day, whether Gideon carried a gun hidden on his person in an ankle or shoulder holster like Dick Tracy wore. The man had a hint of that kind of dangerous glamour. Was he a G-Man or private detective on a secret assignment? A rich movie director or brilliant lawyer? The possibilities seemed endless and none of them were mundane.

I had never set foot inside the Zephyr before and if my folks did they never said. I hadn't the faintest notion, then, that the hotel was still so grand. It was a cool, leafy oasis in a sunbaked desert. The lobby was a plush seabed of thick carpeting and gleaming brass and dark mahogany punctuated with tasteful splashes of warm light and vibrant greenery. An autopiano was playing in the corner, its revolving calliope of sound casting moving flakes of shimmering light across the room's high ceiling. For a moment I felt as if I was swimming in deep water, looking up through fathoms of sun-dappled aquamarine.

I found Starling right where he said he would be, at the far end of the lobby reading a *Denver Post.* He was wearing the same oxblood leather coat he had been sporting at the rabbit drive. I noticed for the first time how its furred collar complimented his brilliantined hair. He smiled as I approached, grabbed his homburg from the side table, and rose to greet me.

"Right on time," he said approvingly as we shook hands. His grip was firm, his fingers big and callused. "I knew I chose wisely."

My face flushed at the compliment. "It's good to see you again, sir."

"Call me Gideon. Although it is true that I am technically your employer, I want us to pass these next weeks as friends. It will be more pleasant for both of us that way, don't you think?"

"Yes sir—I mean, Gideon," I said, cursing myself for the nervousness in my voice. I had hoped that once I saw him, the out-of-body sensation that was dogging me would subside. But his confident familiarity and the lobby's glamorous trappings had me feeling unsteady on my pins.

Gideon's grin widened and he gave me a nudge on the shoulder. "That's a lad." He tilted his head toward the door. "Well, there's no time like the present and sunlight's a-wasting. Shall we get this show on the road?"

I nodded and fell in step next to him as he led us through the lobby to the front desk, where he stopped and gave the counter a friendly rap of the knuckles.

"Yes sir?" said the clerk, stepping forward with alacrity. The man's face looked familiar and after a moment's puzzlement I placed him. It was Donny Ellery, one of the many once-prosperous Greenheart farmers who had lost everything over the last few years. I used to see him at church all the time but not anymore. The bank foreclosed on him back in thirty-two. Dad said the ones who overextended themselves during the boom times were going to be the first to go and he had been mostly right.

"Your guest in room 203 has checked out, yes?"

Ellery consulted the register, his lips moving as he read silently. "Yes sir," he said.

Gideon turned to me. "A snorer," he explained in a stage whisper. "He kept me up all night. It was like listening to a grizzly bear fall down a flight of stairs for eight hours."

Ellery made an apologetic face. "I'm sorry, sir."

"It's fine. So there's no one else staying on the second floor now? Besides myself I mean? No other grizzly bears on the premises?"

"No sir. I mean yes sir. He's gone, sir, and we have no other guests or reservations for the second floor at the moment." Ellery glanced my way for the first time and his face reddened in recognition.

"Let's keep it that way." Gideon pulled a black leather billfold out of his coat.

We walked out of the hotel together a few minutes later, my mind still processing what I had just witnessed. Gideon had reserved the entire second floor for himself for the next month. Every room. And he had handed over his money as casually as if he was buying a sack of flour or a roll of barbed wire.

I scrambled to keep up with Gideon's loping strides, feeling like a string of tin cans tied to the bumper of a honeymoon car. I could feel the attention of passersby linger on us as we passed, their footsteps slowing as they turned to look at us. The dapper stranger in their midst was the primary focus of their attention, but I felt sure at least a few of them had to be wondering what Tom Thorpe's son was doing at his side. I liked feeling mysterious, even if only by association.

He took me to a parking garage a few blocks over from the hotel. Our footsteps echoed in the dim interior as the noises of the street faded away. Amid the broken-down trucks and automobiles and motorcycles scattered in the shadows sat the ghost of an automobile. A long, sleek car-sized form draped in a silky white shroud.

I helped Gideon remove the covering, my hands marveling at the soft texture of the material, to reveal a glossy Lincoln Roadster V-12 convertible, jet black with gleaming whitewall tires. Every inch looked as if it had just rolled off the assembly line, from its shining grille to its swooping metal shell and soft leather cowling. It was a species of car rarely seen around our parts except on the big screen down at the Greenheart Theatre. The only other automobile in King County that could remotely compare was John Stagg's Pierce Arrow sedan, but Gideon's car seemed far grander to me.

Gideon placed his big hand on my shoulder. "What do you say, Will? Shall we take it for a spin?"

We spent the next couple hours driving up and down a handful of the rough, ruler-straight country roads that connected Greenheart to the southern end of King County. We stayed out until the molten sun was cut in half by the horizon line, talking and laughing as I stroked the soft leather of the upholstered seat between us and luxuriated in the roadster's powerful thrum. It felt like being inside a great mechanical shark with headlamps for eyes, gliding through the deep ocean in search of prey. When Gideon finally dropped me off at the foot of our porch with a smile and a wave, I was already counting the hours until I would see him again.

We drove around in that big fine car almost every day for the next two weeks, and I spent nearly every minute of that time in a state of dazed happiness. Gideon had been everywhere in the world or so it seemed, and he had a dozen stories for every stop along the way. At first I thought he was pulling my leg. Spinning harmless yarns and passing them off as biography. Or at the very least, taking considerable dramatic license in the re-telling. I couldn't imagine how he could have lived in or visited all the places he described in a single lifetime—let alone met all the famous people he name-dropped.

Gideon said he had been on the floor of the New York Stock Exchange on Black Friday and snagged front-row seats at the Hippodrome for Harry Houdini. He told me he bought William Jennings Bryan an ice cream cone in Dayton, Tennessee and shared a scene with Lillian Gish as a blackfaced extra in *Birth of a Nation.* One night he told me about hunting ibex in Spain's *Sierra de Gredos* mountains with fiery revolutionaries from Havana and Mexico City, the next he told me about a dinner party at which he had been seated next to Amelia Earhart.

Gideon also knew more about all sorts of strange and esoteric subjects than anyone I had ever met before. He spoke with an archeologist's authority about the pillaging ways of the Vikings and enthused like a gourmet chef about the finest restaurants in Paris and Tokyo and Monaco. He taught me about the diabolical and ecstatic meanings of the Major and Minor Arcana and the remarkable physiology of camels and salamanders and the torments and visions of Grigori Rasputin and Edgar Allen Poe and the pagan rituals of Samhain. One night he performed what he said was a lost-to-time soliloquy for *Othello* penned by Shakespeare himself.

He instructed me in the belief systems of ancient Romans and Babylonians who studied the still-warm livers and gall bladders of slaughtered sheep for insights into the will of the gods. He held me spellbound with stories of assassins who used *Amanita phalloides*—death cap mushrooms—to poison emperors and popes and business rivals and shrewish wives. He told me John Dillinger's nickname was Jackrabbit because he was no nimble and quick on his feet when he was a kid. One chilly afternoon he told me about whalers who cut open the bellies of sperm whales and found squid beaks the size of cannonballs inside. Beaks impervious to the digestive juices that dissolved the rest of the creature. Some of the slaughtered whales carried dozens of beaks inside their bellies, each one a memento of a successful hunt. The image haunted me for days, I couldn't shake it. All those squid beaks clacking against one another in the black wet dark as the whales roamed the seven seas, year after year after year.

Some of the stories Gideon told revolved around baubles he had tucked away in his vest pockets. Every couple days he'd tweeze something out of one of those pockets with his fingers—a button or pipestem or earring or ticket or bullet—and launch into another captivating yarn. Like the treasures squirreled away in Grant Ballantine's steamer, each item in Gideon's hand was drenched in fantastical, romantic history. Sometimes he spoke about the keepsake of the day in a register of reverence or melancholy. Other times he opened his hand and cackled like a thieving magpie as he related how the item resting on his palm had come to be his.

Were the stories true? Was the sturdy toothpick he kept in a tiny leather sheath really carved out of the ivory of a woolly mammoth tusk found poking out of the muddy bank of a Siberian river? Did a banana-skirted Josephine Baker really toss him one her earrings from the stage of the Folies Bergère? Was the wedge of cork he fished out of his coat pocket really used to stopper the barrel that carried Annie Edson Taylor over the mist-shrouded cataracts of Niagara Falls? Or was Gideon just telling tall tales?

I didn't much care, not back then. Not when every story was a magic carpet ride to faraway worlds that throbbed with exotic characters and spellbinding adventures. Gideon's yarns were time-wasters of an ilk I felt sure even Dad would find irresistible.

What I didn't know at the time was that all those jaw-dropping stories and uproarious anecdotes came at a price. A steep one I felt duty-bound to pay.

The bill came due for the first time about three weeks into our "excursions," as Gideon had taken to calling our jaunts around King County. He introduced a practice that became part of our regular routine. Whenever a farmhouse appeared in the distance Gideon would take his foot off the gas pedal and ask me who lived there and what I knew about them.

But he wanted to know more than just how big the family was, or how much wheat or alfalfa or sugar beets they grew before all their topsoil blew away. That information was of interest to Gideon but he wanted more. He wanted to know which men drank too much and which ones hit their wives. He wanted to know which families had lost children or parents or spouses to cancer or polio or the Great War. He wanted to know who attended the foreclosure auctions, picking over the bones of neighbors for bargains. He wanted to know who listened to Father Coughlin on the radio and who was still putting their full tithe in the collection plate.

I felt bad about some of the things I told him. I knew my parents would be furious—and crushingly disappointed in me—if they ever found out. On that they would still be united. But then another lonely farmhouse would float into view and Gideon would take his foot off the gas and the roadster would quiet to a purr, as if it too was eager to hear my report, and I'd find myself pouring out another rich draught of secrets and gossip for Starling.

He could have picked any boy in Greenheart and he had chosen me.

I was in his debt.

I wanted him to like me.

I wanted Gideon to like me so that he would keep taking me on his long drives around King County and telling me stories of other places and worlds and times and lives, each one a million times more interesting and exotic than my own. I wanted us to be friends, like Gideon had promised that first golden afternoon I met him down at the Zephyr.

One night he drove us over to John Stagg's house at the north end of town. We sat in the dark at the curb, looking up a curving flagstone driveway to the hulking silhouette of the Great Man's house. It was dark but for a single glowing window on the second floor.

Gideon poured a cup of steaming coffee out of the red metal thermos he always brought along on our travels. He sipped from it thoughtfully as he settled back into his seat and nodded in the direction of Stagg's house.

"So what's this fella's story?"

"What?"

"You know the drill, give me the backstory." He raised his eyebrows in the direction of Stagg's mansion as he took a sip from his steaming thermos cup. "I've been saving this one."

I shifted uncomfortably. Talking about John Stagg behind his back felt particularly disloyal given everything he had done for Greenheart. But at that point Gideon wasn't the only one sitting in the car with me. Not anymore. All the neighbors and families from church and kids at school whose secret shames and heartaches and vanities I had shared with Gideon over the previous few weeks were sitting with us too. They crowded around me, their breath hot on the back of my neck. *Why won't you tell him Stagg's story? You told him all of ours.*

So I folded my hands in my lap and watched John Stagg's big bright window floating out there in the dark and told Gideon everything I knew about the life and times of Greenheart's Great Man.

3

good number of the secrets I shared with Gideon came from years of eavesdropping on conversations between Mom and Dad at home. I often overheard them talking in the kitchen about their friends' trials and tribulations, long after they thought I was asleep. They used to talk for hours, their voices drifting under my closed door and into my curious ears.

I was no more than four or five years old when I first realized Tom and Emily Thorpe—my very own parents—were held in high regard around Greenheart. That was no small thing because the town was fresh-faced with vitality and ambition in those gold rush years. My father was someone from whom other men regularly sought counsel even during those years of record harvests and global wheat shortages; he became even more in demand after the Depression settled on America's midsection like a ten-thousand-pound anvil. Tom Thorpe was keeping his family's head above water in heavy seas that were swamping other boats left and right and he was doing it without fanfare—and with a still-pretty wife by his side. Who in his right mind wouldn't care what he had to say?

Mom was held in similarly high regard by the ladies around town. She was always getting taken aside by other women down at the grocery store or after church, where she was a prominent organizer of bake sales, holiday pageants, Sunday school classes, and the like. Once in a while they came to the house and I'd see them out on the front porch talking as I went about my chores. At least our telephone wasn't ringing off the hook with calls.

We were on a party line and you never knew who else might be listening. I wasn't above eavesdropping myself when I could get away with it. That's not to say there weren't women in Greenheart who remained hopeful or who set a perpetually brave face to the world. There were some of them too, even in thirty-six. But they weren't the ones taking Mom away by the elbow to pour their hearts out.

Gideon and I drove up and down what felt like every road in King County, some of them several times over. Gideon poured himself cup after cup of delicious-smelling coffee from his thermos as he asked me about the people living in the houses we passed by. Once in a while—usually after I'd told him something particularly sad or scandalous or odd about someone—he'd give a little m-hm of appreciation. Whenever I looked over at him, though, he just raised his cup to me and smiled. "Nothing like a good cup of coffee, Will."

Gideon had me wait in the car whenever he decided to stop in and say hello to someone. He put a whimsical spin on it, as if he was beset with uncontrollable impulses to be friendly. He did that with increasing frequency as the days lengthened and the weather warmed. He liked it best when he saw them sweating and swearing over broken-down tractors or chalky fields or wilting kitchen gardens, far from the distractions of other people or livestock. On those occasions he would park the roadster in whatever meager shade he could find for me, then tramp out to them with a wave and a big friendly hello. They'd see Gideon coming and put their hands on their hips and watch him approach, their postures radiating wariness. Strangers rarely brought good news. Gideon had a knack for setting them at ease, though. He could get most of them smiling and talking in no time at all.

If he didn't see anyone out in the fields or around the barn or hanging clothes on the line Gideon would walk up right to the farmhouse door, big leather satchel in hand. *You can't take more than five or ten minutes when you are interrupting their work outside. Bad form. You need to let those ones ferment for a while. When I'm at the kitchen table with a cup of tea or coffee, or a thermos full of ice-cold lemonade to share? And the lady of the house is secretly or not so secretly thrilled to have an excuse to step away from whatever's breaking her back on that particular day? That's a different situation entirely. That's when I can take my time. Get to know them a little better. See what makes them tick.*

Gideon disappeared inside some houses for an hour or more. One afternoon I waited for him outside the house of our church organist, Mrs. Brennan, for nearly two hours. Other times he'd return to the car in ten or fifteen minutes. No matter how long he was inside, though, the folks he was visiting with came out onto the porch to wave goodbye as we rolled off to our next stop, Gideon waving and turning the wheel to get away.

It must have been like shooting fish in a barrel for him. Everywhere we went they swooned for him. It didn't matter whether he was sitting in the meager shade of a tarpaper shack or shooting the breeze with the regulars down at Emerson Fingle's five and dime or helping snap peas on someone's front porch. Sometimes he was quiet and comforting, attentive to the outbursts of grief and mutters of impotent fury he heard. Other times he held court, talking and laughing and patting shoulders reassuringly and generally carrying on as if he was Will Rogers himself. He always seemed to know what the moment called for.

Within six weeks of Gideon's arrival it felt like he had introduced himself to every farmer, rancher, waitress, silo operator, secretary, store owner, and feedstore clerk in King County—and thanks to me, he knew the skeletons hidden in the closets of a fair number of them. I never asked him how he applied that information when he visited with any of those people. I tried not to think about it.

Gideon was driving me home at the end of one particularly visit-filled day when he asked if I aimed to make any of the girls from school or church my sweetheart. I batted his teasing away with a smile. "No one special. My teacher's pretty," I added with forced casualness. "Miss Wells."

"Miss Wells, Miss Wells. . . OK, fill me in, don't be shy, what's she look like?" he asked after a beat, as if his mind had been elsewhere and he was only inquiring to be polite. But the hairs on the back of my neck prickled up in the strangest way when Gideon said her name. Something new was coiled in the air between us. I could feel it. An invisible mine shaft in the conversation, breathing morgue-cold air.

"Is she a blonde or a brunette?" Gideon prodded playfully. "She's not a redhead, is she? Don't tell me she's a redhead, Will. Redheads are trouble, take it from me." I kept silent, staring self-consciously out the window at fields gone fallow. I felt him shift and straighten in his seat and he went silent himself. An unwanted vision of Gideon passionately kissing Miss Wells—and of her kissing him back with the same ardor—snaked into my mind. I pushed the disgusting image away but it kept capering at the margins of my thoughts. My face grew hot as the silence between us lengthened.

It was the first time I was ready for one of our excursions to end.

I remember Gideon's low chuckle when he took his foot off the gas. We coasted down the center of the empty road, his left forearm perched lazily on the steering wheel as the world outside my window slowed and resolved itself into barren fields and sagging fence lines choked with Russian thistle. Further down the road a lone windmill stood, two blades missing, motionless against the tangerine sky.

"Is she pretty pretty?" He was trying to sound playful but I could hear the pique in his voice. "Jean Harlow pretty? Lily Elsie pretty? Or just pretty? Young Will, what beauties are the people of Greenheart hiding out here on the prairie?"

"I don't know," I said finally. The curled up armadillo strategy I employed when Daniel brought up Miss Wells wasn't going to work with Gideon. He wouldn't relent until I responded. "I just think she's pretty."

I felt him looking at my burning face as we slowed to a stop in the middle of the dusty road. In the field to our left stood a headless scarecrow, corn husk limbs rattling in the evening breeze. Gideon set the brake, heaved himself out of his seat, strode to the back of the roadster, and took a long, arcing piss that darkened the middle of the road. I could see him in the side mirror, his figure dimly lit by the brake lights. It looked like he was writing in the dirt with his stream. The scent of his urine filled the air, foul and acrid. A moment later he was back in the car, smiling and shaking his head in admiration.

"Well, pretty clear to me that I'm not going to get anything more from you on the subject of Helen Wells!" He nudged my shoulder. "Turns out you can keep a secret after all. Good for you. A man's entitled to keep some things to himself, especially when they concern matters of the heart."

And then he started up the car and we roared down the road for home, Gideon whistling an aimless tune as if nothing had happened at all.

4

I watched from the window as Gideon stepped off our porch and strolled to his big shining car waiting for him out there in the moonlight. He turned and gave me a final friendly wave, then folded himself neatly into the driver's seat and rumbled off down the road in the direction of town.

"I admit it," Dad said from the kitchen table. "I misjudged him. Yes, I did." He turned his head lazily in Mom's direction and cleared his throat. "I was just as skeptical as you about Gideon but not half as closeminded. Isn't it funny how things turn out sometimes?"

When Mom didn't say anything in response, Dad left his seat at the table and began moving around the kitchen. I watched his reflection as it passed back and forth in the dark window glass, circling behind the sink over which Mom stood.

"He was more plainspoken than I expected," Dad said, continuing to stare at her back. "Smart too. Sounded to *me* like he knows his business. Like he deserves the courtesy of a fair-minded listen from people around here."

Mom continued cleaning up, giving her back to us both. "Will?" she called over her shoulder. "Go check on Amos and Andy."

"Yes ma'am." I didn't need to be told twice. She was issuing a storm warning. Urging me to take shelter. I could see the black thunderheads of Dad's mood on the horizon as well as she could. I left my station at the window and walked briskly to the door, grateful for the gift of an excuse to get out of there.

But Dad pinned me at the door with his voice as I was reaching for my jacket. "Sounds like you've been a big help to him, Will. You've been closer to him than any of us. At his side every day, showing him around. I guess since he's your employer and he's treated you nothing but well you'd probably like people in King County to keep an open mind about him, wouldn't you?" I could see that Dad was intent on taking advantage of the realignments of allegiance that the evening had laid bare. Even if the allegiances were only temporary. Maybe even especially if they were.

I felt Buster's absence more than ever in that moment. He had always been a comfort when Mom and Dad were fighting. Or when they were studiously ignoring each other, which was almost worse somehow. Buster and I would retreat to the porch or the barn or my small bedroom at the back of the house and I would put my arm around him and scratch his ears and read him stories from *Weird Tales* or tell him about my favorite baseball players or Miss Wells or the barn cats that had come and gone over the years. *Remember Slouch? Boy, that cat hated you. Not like Puff. Now* that *was a good barn cat. What a mouser.* I kept up a steady monologue to drown out the caustic laughter and bitter accusations that came shuddering through the closed door on the worst nights. Goblin sounds, impossible to reconcile with the voices of the two people I thought I knew best in the whole wide world. There had been three such blowups since Dad kicked Grant and Daniel Ballantine off our farm and every one of them had sounded uglier in my ears than the last. The worst part was that I could tell they were getting used to talking to one another that way.

"Have you seen what Starling hauls around for this cloud-seeding program he was talking about?" Dad asked me.

I hung my coat back up and stepped into the light of the room. I wasn't going anywhere, at least for the moment. "No sir. He hasn't shown me."

"And you don't know where he keeps all of this equipment he uses? All these cloud-seeding chemicals and rockets and whatnot?"

"No sir. Maybe down at the garage where he keeps his car?"

"Did you know that Starling studied meteorology in Europe? You never told us that."

"No sir. He never told me. He's told lots of stories about being in Europe but he never said that."

"What was that university he mentioned? The one in Germany."

"Groningen?"

Dad snapped his fingers and turned back to Mom. "That's it. That's pretty impressive, I'd say. All that school and he still talks like a normal person."

Mom kept scrubbing at the dishes, her face hidden by long strands of hair that had fallen out of the tortoise-shell barrette she only wore on special occasions. It was her pride and joy, the first birthday present she received from Dad when he was courting her. She had worn it that night as a goodwill gesture to Dad because she knew he would notice.

Dad pulled back a chair and sat at the table but never stopped looking at Mom's back. "I said Starling is smart," he repeated, his voice flat and hard.

"I heard you the first time, Tom," she said over her shoulder, her scrubbing never slowing.

"You were rude to him, Emily."

Mom dropped the plate she was washing in the sink and turned to face him with a heavy sigh. "No, I wasn't."

"Yes you were."

"No. Stop saying that. That's not what I was doing. I was just asking him the questions I kept waiting for you to ask. And waiting. And waiting."

"Oh sure, not at first," Dad said, as if she hadn't said anything at all. "You were all sweetness and light when he gave you the flowers. When he kept complimenting the meal. But after supper? That was embarrassing. Will was embarrassed, I can tell you that. Gideon must think I married a harpy."

"I wonder what he thinks I married."

Dad's face darkened. "You embarrassed both of us," he repeated, louder this time. "He's your son's *employer*, for God's sake. You know what he pays Daniel. Do you want him to find another boy? Do you want the bank to take our house? Why couldn't you just leave off of him? What's *wrong* with you?"

Mom's defiant expression crumpled into one of pure misery, her mask of composure finally slipping—as it always did when she and Dad argued. I felt badly for her but in truth, my sympathies that night were with Dad.

Why did she have to go and spoil everything?

* * *

I had felt downright giddy in the immediate aftermath of Gideon's enthusiastic acceptance of my parents' supper invitation. I remained in that exhilarated state until an hour or so before his scheduled arrival, when the first whispers of doubt about the wisdom of the whole enterprise came sidling in. I found myself wondering what Gideon would think of our chipped dinnerware and dusty floorboards and sagging porch, and whether he would notice how faded Mom's best dress had become. I wondered what he would think when he smelled the sweat wafting off my father and saw the grime caking his neck after a hard day of farmwork. Or maybe they would embarrass me in other ways. Would Dad get the same mottled look on his face when Mom and Gideon started talking to each other that I glimpsed a few days before he kicked Grant Ballantine and his son off our farm?

Even as the nightmare scenarios piled up on top of one another, though, I never really wavered in my desire to see it through. The prospect of having Gideon and Mom and Dad all orbiting around me for one starry night was just too irresistible. I told myself that my parents would find Gideon's company just as exhilarating and delightful as I did. How could they not?

But as it turned out I was only half-right on that score.

The evening started out well enough. Within seconds of crossing the threshold of our home Gideon reached into the large leather satchel he was carrying and withdrew a bouquet of wildflowers. He presented it to Mom with a flourish, as if he was a magician or a gentleman come a-courtin'. Begonias and black-eyed Susans and mariposa lilies and other flowers I'd never seen before, all bound together by a thin ribbon of supple black leather. The bouquet practically glowed in the lamplight, as if the flowers had been plucked from some secret mossy stream in the earth's powdered hide only minutes earlier.

"Well forevermore," said Mom as she took the spray of flowers in her hands, a faint smile of remembrance crossing her lips. She told us that they were the kind of flowers that had carpeted the rugged foothills of her childhood home outside Colorado Springs, where she had grown up surrounded by a pantheon of relatives I knew only from stories that sounded like folktales to my half-listening ears.

Mom retrieved a serviceable vase tucked deep in the cupboards, wiped the dust off the scratched glass, carefully tucked the stems into the vase's narrow neck, and placed the flowers in the center of the table. When she asked Gideon where he had found them he only smiled and said he was pleased she liked them.

Supper unfolded as if I had choreographed it myself. Mom blushed prettily at Gideon's many compliments about the food, which was good and hot and plentiful. Gideon brought his appetite and happily accepted seconds of everything as he listened to Dad talk about Greenheart's trials and tribulations and the breadlines in the cities and the great churning troubles of the world at large.

Gideon brightened the mood by speaking warmly and at length about my agreeable temperament and punctuality and good manners. Mom gave me a proud smile and Dad reached over and tousled my hair, a once-familiar gesture of affection from my childhood. It was strange to feel his big, callused hand rubbing on my scalp again after all those years and when he withdrew his hand I felt a sharp, unexpected pang of loss.

Gideon and Dad spent a fair amount of time exchanging observations about my various quirks—usually in the form of mildly embarrassing stories from my younger days that got all of us laughing, including Mom. She was busy attending to one supper preparation task or another in the kitchen but I could see her listening and smiling as the men talked.

Gideon told a couple of stories too. He gave us an eyewitness account of the chaotic scene in Sam Riddle's owner's box when his Man O' War defeated Sir Barton in the "Race of the Age" in Ontario in 1920. He described the swelling red-faced roar of the crowd when that magnificent, angry horse came thundering down the homestretch in a way that made all our arms stipple out in gooseflesh. He was that good a storyteller. An hour later he was explaining to us how the etymology of the word "sinister" was rooted in a Latin word for the "left-handed" side, which the majority-right-handed Romans decided was a mark of misfortune, depravity, or unsavory associations with the devil. *You don't have to worry about me, though, I'm ambidextrous,* he added, which elicited Dad's first outright laugh of the night.

Gideon never monopolized the conversation. He guided it, though, and made sure everyone felt included. Thanks to him, the night was going just as I had dreamed it would.

Things didn't start going south until after I helped Mom clear the table of the last remnants of the apple pie she had made special for the occasion. That's when Dad pushed the vase of flowers to the side and Gideon pulled a sheaf of rolled-up papers out of his satchel. He placed the papers on the table right in front of where I was seated and unscrolled them to reveal a dizzying succession of colorful maps and charts, each sheet mortared together with intricate diagrams and bricks of closely spaced words written in dense, florid cursive. I felt as if I was looking at . . . not a treasure map exactly. More like a blueprint for the scaffolding and gearworks *beneath* the treasure map.

Gideon and Dad leaned in to study the papers from either side of my chair. They blotted out the lamplight until I felt as if I were peering from the entrance of a cozy little cave. I watched raptly as Gideon explained the hieroglyphics laid out on the table before us. He paused at each cluster of diagrams and equations and instructions, briskly explaining each step and answering Dad's questions before moving on. I sat contently in the shelter of my cave, watching their shadows advance and retreat across the table with their every movement.

That's when I first noticed Mom standing at the far end of the kitchen, clean dishes gleaming on the counter behind her. She wore the aspect of someone who had been watching us for a while and I felt a jolt of self-consciousness. Her expression was unreadable but I recognized it immediately for what it was: the first discordant note in the evening.

Gideon and Dad had not waited for her. They had either forgotten her or dismissed her as unimportant to the proceedings.

"That is a lovely pin," Mom said, her gaze fixed on Gideon's chest. I twisted my head around so I could study the ivory pin affixed to the lapel of his suit. "I've found my eye returning to it all night. Is that a crown tangled in a lion's mane?"

"Why yes it is," he said. "You have a very discerning eye, Emily."

I looked more closely at the pin. The mane was shaped like a great wreath, its dense weave nearly swallowing the crown's gem-encrusted spearpoints. The image was rendered in the same extraordinary detail as the ram's horn pin Gideon had been wearing the day of the rabbit drive.

"It's beautiful. Is it a family heirloom?" Mom asked. "It must have a fascinating history."

"No, nothing like that. Just a bauble I picked up on my travels. Will can tell you that I'm a bit of a souvenir collector. And far too impulsive with my spending! I can't recall exactly where I obtained this particular pin. It is lovely, though, I quite agree." He flashed Mom an indulgent smile and turned his attention back to the papers on the table. Dad and I followed suit, eager to hear more about the scientific principles upon which his "rain generation" process was based.

But Mom wasn't done.

"Where are your people, Mr. Starling?" she asked.

"Ma'am? And please, call me Gideon."

"Your people. Your family. Do you have any children? A wife somewhere? Brothers or sisters? Are either of your parents still with us?"

"Alas, no woman has claimed my heart, Emily. And my vocation has a nomadic aspect to it that makes it hard to tend to home fires with the requisite constancy. You understand, I'm sure. I have some distant family back in California, America's land of milk and honey. A few cousins I haven't seen in years."

"California," Dad repeated reverentially, as if Gideon's bonds to that fabled land over the mountains said something essential about our guest.

"My great granddaddy worked on the transcontinental railroad," Gideon continued. "He was a foreman with the Central Pacific, had three crews of Chinamen under his charge. He was there at Promontory in sixty nine when they drove the last spike."

"So California's where you grew up?" Mom asked, redirecting the conversation back to the subject of Gideon.

"That's right." Gideon came around from behind my chair and strolled into view from my right. "I was born in a little town called Burnett, Emily," he said, his manner slipping into one of performative patience. "Old Modoc territory up on the Klamath. The town sprouted up from a mining camp, finally got big enough they decided it needed a proper name and named it after some governor or senator or railroad baron up there, I don't exactly recall. He was probably all three."

"What did your father do?"

Dad appeared in my field of vision to my left, on the other side of the table from Gideon. His face was flushed. He looked embarrassed by Mom but I wasn't sure why. The questions she was asking seemed reasonable. I was curious to hear the answers myself.

"This ain't a courtroom, Emily," Dad said. "None of this family history nonsense has much to do with the matter at hand and as I hope you can see Gideon has a lot of ground to cover."

"No, Tom, I don't mind," Gideon said, raising a mollifying hand. "My provenance is a legitimate line of inquiry, all things considered. Hmmm, where to begin. Well my father was a logger. Giant of a man, or so it seemed to me whenever I gazed upon him with my little boy eyes. A regular Paul Bunyan. If he had come home one day with a big blue ox trotting behind him it wouldn't have surprised me. Pops worked on crews in Washington and Idaho and northern California. Mother and I followed him everywhere. We were timber gypsies."

"What camps did he work?" Mom asked. "My Uncle Gary worked up in Washington as a timber cruiser for a good number of years. My mother's youngest brother."

Gideon looked up at the ceiling thoughtfully. "I don't recall exactly. Pops met his maker when a donkey puncher exploded in his face. I was seven years old. My memory doesn't go back much before that. I couldn't tell you the specific camps."

Mom paled at the sudden dark turn in Gideon's childhood history. "I'm sorry," she said. "How awful. I didn't mean to open old wounds."

"Not at all. My life should be an open book, Emily. We all understand that, don't we Tom? You are simply doing your due diligence. After all, I am asking you and your husband and the rest of the fine people of Greenheart to put your faith in me, aren't I? And young Will here too! There should be no secrets. So where was I? Oh yes. I was recalling my idyllic childhood in the towering emerald forests of the Pacific Northwest. Would you like to know how long it took after Pops died for my mother to start whoring herself out, just to keep a roof over our heads and food on our plates?"

Mom jerked back as if Gideon had reached over the table and slapped her across the face. "Oh goodness no," she said in a flustered rush, "I didn't mean—"

"Now don't be too hard on my dear old mother." Gideon gave us a calm smile. "Some of the jacks my daddy worked with became some of her steadiest clients. Let he who is without sin cast the first stone, isn't that what they say? You have to admit she was in a bit of a pickle after dad went and got himself killed. Between the devil and the deep blue sea is what she was. But she was pretty, for a while. That helped. Not that we had a room at the Ritz or anything. We always lived downwind of the mills, it didn't matter whether we were in Tacoma or Everett or Grays Harbor. Sometimes I can still taste the poisonous clouds that came drifting down from those mills on my tongue. But not tonight, thanks to that wonderful feast you prepared for us! Once again, Emily, I can't thank you enough. I've been dying for a delicious home-cooked meal and this was just what the doctor ordered."

Gideon's eyes danced away from Mom and locked on Dad. "The point I'm making here, Tom, in sharing my own personal trials and tragedies is to let you know that you and your fine family aren't the only ones who have experienced hardship in this life. We all have our crosses to bear, isn't that what the Good Book says? Chasms that open up at our feet with no warning, leaving us teetering on the abyss. Disasters that you never see coming, like black blizzards that take your topsoil and drop it on the decks of passenger ships halfway across the Atlantic. Everyone has trials, Tom. Everyone gets knocked down. And I've found that the key to surviving those trials is to recognize which hand is outstretched to help you back up—and which hand is just reaching for your wallet. Your wife here is just taking a close look under my fingernails."

"It's not what's under your fingernails I'm concerned with, Mr. Starling."

"Please, call me Gideon."

"It's what's in your heart, Mr. Starling. Because what you're asking of us? Of everyone in Greenheart from the sounds of it? That sounds like a lot of money. Maybe not back in California or wherever you're from but it is around here. And I don't know you. Neither does Tom. And you don't know us."

"Well, that's why I'm here," he countered smoothly. "Isn't that why you invited me? So that we could get to know each other?"

"That's why we invited you, Mr. Starling. I don't know that's why you came."

Gideon left five minutes later.

* * *

"He's a grifter looking for his next score, Tom. "He's selling snake oil, plain and simple. He wants to use us. He wants to use *you.* Can't you see that? That's why he came tonight. He knows your opinion carries weight around here. People listen to you."

"What about those testimonials he showed us? Those affidavits, he called them. Firsthand accounts from satisfied customers. What about those?"

Mom's eyes widened in disbelief at what she was hearing. "Oh my God," she said. "He could have hired anyone to write those. He could have written them *himself.* How would we know?"

Why did Mom have to be so suspicious? Gideon had a horrible childhood. No wonder he didn't like to talk about it. And it wasn't like she was going to win an argument with Dad anyway. She never won so what was the point? Dad always wore Mom down, sooner or later. They would argue and argue until Mom finally reached a point where she just laid down her arms and withdrew from the battle, wordlessly conceding the field so that Dad could have the last word. They both knew the argument would never end otherwise. He outlasted her every time.

But Mom wasn't ready to concede yet. "I don't want Will working for that man anymore."

"So what? I do. Because even if you don't care about keeping this farm my parents left for us I still do. So does Will." Dad sat back in his chair and cocked his head at her. "Wait, I get it now. Sorry, it took me a while but I guess that's the point, isn't it? That I'm slow on the uptake? Like the time with the tornado?"

"Stop it."

"Am I imagining things, Emily? Am I easily deceived? Is that what you think? Well, you should know."

Mom stiffened at the insinuation, her eyes going wide then shuttering cold, but she didn't say a word in reply. Was it guilt that kept her silent? Rage at the injustice of the accusation? Or sorrow that I was there, bearing witness to their ugly flailing?

They sent me to bed then but I lay awake for a long time that night, playing the evening's events over and over in my head. I wished I had never invited Gideon to supper. I wanted to go back in a time machine and change things back to how they were before, when Gideon and my parents existed on opposite ends of my boyhood universe. But it was too late. They were in each other's gravitational pull now, their orbits forever fixed to one another. All if took was one night.

I awoke an hour before dawn, still bleary from a fitful night of tossing and turning. Morning chores made no allowances for restless nights. I walked into the kitchen, rubbing away the last of the film of dust that had settled over my closed lids as I slept. When I opened my eyes again I saw what remained of Gideon's wildflower bouquet.

A circle of dead petals and leaves lay on the tabletop around the scratched glass base, every one leached of all but the faintest hint of its once-vibrant color. The water in the vase was swampy and clouded, the stems brittle and black. The decayed remains of the flowerheads had curled into little gray fists, every petal floured in dust. The bouquet looked as if it had been dragged out of the cobwebbed corner of a long-forgotten mausoleum.

I turned to Mom, who was looking at me hard from the stove, where she was stirring a steaming pot of oatmeal.

"What happened to the flowers?"

"I told you," she said. "I told both of you."

I pretended not to notice the frustrated anger in her voice. "Has Dad seen them yet? Maybe he knows."

"Oh I'm sure he does. He has all the answers. Why don't you go find him and ask him?" Mom said as she doled out baseball-sized clumps of hot oatmeal into three bowls. "And tell him his breakfast is getting cold."

$$5$$

I was a month shy of my tenth birthday the day the tornado came. It was the scariest thing I ever saw until the black dusters. But the tornado was a different kind of scary than the dusters because it moved like it had a mind of its own. As if it was sentient. Everyone who grows up on the Great Plains knows what a tornado can do to a farm or neighborhood. But for generations of residents of Greenheart it remained secondhand knowledge filtered through dramatic radio reports and newsreels and letters from relatives living elsewhere on the dust-hazed billiard table of America's central plains. I remember thanking God in my nighttime prayers that we didn't live further east, where towns and farms and ranches were lined up like nine-pins and all anyone could do was hope the Great Bowler in the sky didn't pitch his wrecking ball down your lane. Because what do you do if He does? How do you find the strength to sort through the shattered wreckage of your former life and salvage what you can and get back on your feet again? To recover from that astonishing punishment for who knows what sin? To wonder if maybe God is out to get you?

The tornado was still miles away when we saw it, barely visible on the horizon. You can see a long way out on the Plains. Sound carries too. That's what drew our eyes to it: the howling white noise roar it made, even all those miles away. I remember standing outside with my parents and watching the tornado's long black snout sniff the ground like an evil bee looking for a flower to suck dry.

After a while Mom got worried. She thought the tornado was turning toward us. It's getting louder, she kept saying. It's coming this way.

No it's not, Dad kept saying in reply. It's passing to the north.

Mom was persistent about it, though, and after a while her certainty got Dad kind of unsettled. He kept watching the twister, noncommittal about Mom's assertions until the wind turned and gusted right in our faces and a moment later the distant freight train roar grew louder. He began to believe her then. The tornado was coming for us. The Great Bowler in the sky had chosen our lane.

I remember how his face drained of color when the realization sank in. His expression warped from one of rigid self-control to a sort of exultant rage. All their years of hard work and sacrifice, obliterated in the space of an afternoon. We would never recover. He began laughing but it sounded like he was vomiting. His face turned deep red. I felt Mom's hand tighten on mine as we watched Dad howl and curse at the twister bearing down on us.

Only it wasn't.

The tornado never hit us. It spun away to the north of us just as Dad said it would, thickening and blackening and becoming more malevolent with each passing mile. We never even had to go down in the storm cellar, though we stood by its open door for most of that afternoon. When we were finally sure we had been spared we looked at each other with raw, stunned eyes and waited for our insides to unclench. We tried to rearrange ourselves back into some semblance of normalcy, but I don't know that we ever got there. Not that day. Maybe not ever.

I walked for the rest of that surreal day on legs that didn't quite work right. Mom spent the afternoon on the porch, darning socks and patching pants and studying the empty horizon. Dad went into town and didn't come home until supper, which he ate in silence. Then he excused himself and went out to the barn, where he worked late into the night.

Looking back on it now, I don't think Dad ever forgave Mom for making him think the tornado was coming for us. For seeing him carry on the way he did and for making him doubt his own senses. I know he never forgot it.

Gideon ended up being proof of that.

6

I kept working for Gideon, of course. Mom didn't win that argument either. But she watched me like a hawk when it came to my homework and chores. I felt as if I had betrayed her in some hazy way that I couldn't articulate, even to myself. Which made me feel all the more guilty, as if my inability to put a label on my crime was just another way in which I was failing her.

I was pretty anxious about where I stood with Gideon after his dust-up with Mom. But when I met him down at the Zephyr the following morning he gave no indication he was harboring any grudges or hurt feelings. To the contrary, he praised Mom's fabulous cooking and clean house and recalled the evening's "spirited" conversation with such enthusiasm that I came to believe he meant it. Gideon called Dad a straight shooter and said Mom's skeptical line of questioning had been the perfect after-dinner cognac. He told me to thank my lucky stars I had such good and capable parents. Then he grinned and mussed my hair and we were off once again, sallying forth in search of hands to shake and ears to bend.

We spent most of that week roaming the more sparsely populated northern end of the county, where foreclosures loomed everywhere and the few cattle we saw were gaunt and spindled. It was slow going down those bleak roads and I didn't know the business of hardly anyone up there. It was a relief not to know any secrets or rumors about them—and to have Gideon take all of my "I don't knows" to his questions in stride.

One day he drove us in a great loop over into Baca County and down into the Oklahoma panhandle before circling back to Greenheart. We drove for hours and somehow we never had to stop to refuel. That was when it dawned on me that for all our endless driving around, I had never seen Gideon refill his gas tank or patch a flat or have any car trouble at all. His roadster truly was a marvel of modern engineering. Our rickety Model A might as well have been a Conestoga wagon.

We were just a mile or two from our farm at the end of that long day of driving when Gideon pulled over to the shoulder and turned the car off. We sat there in silence, listening to the wind and the ticking engine. I felt as if I had spent the afternoon on carnival rides. My face was flushed, reddened by the sun and the wind and the exhilaration of speeding down country roads in a fine automobile with the top down.

Off to my right, the setting sun cast the undercarriage of a blanket of clouds in garish smears of garnet and gold. An endless tabletop of empty fields glowed below, the dirt still dark from a brief rain shower that had passed through earlier in the evening.

King County had received a few such tantalizing showers that spring, and some around Greenheart seized on those short bursts of rain as if they were Holy Writ. They said the rain was returning and the crops were going to grow again and soon they would be crying for their wheat in the cities again. God had finally exacted His pound of flesh for whatever offenses we had committed or harbored in our hearts. He was ready to extend mercy to our long-suffering community and take His boot off our necks. The rest of us listened and waited, hoping the optimists were right but ready to savage them for jinxing us if the spate of showers ended or the dusters returned.

Gideon had been in a storytelling mood that day, as he so often was. He liked to mix things up. One day he would keep me spellbound with riveting stories culled from *One Thousand and One Nights,* the next he'd regale me with the exploits of Rikki-Tikki-Tavi or Br'er Rabbit or King Arthur and his legendary retinue. Once he told me the entire plot of William Makepeace Thackeray's *Vanity Fair,* speaking with open admiration of comely Becky Sharp and her audacious striving for money and privilege in Victorian-era England. The next afternoon he told me macabre tales of Huay Chivo, a shapeshifting sorcerer with a taste for goat meat who was the scourge of the Yucatan Peninsula back in Mayan times. He followed that up by recounting a long-ago visit to the Musical Woods, a forest in Italy's Fiemme Valley where Stradivari and other Renaissance luthiers harvested the spruce they used to make their famous violins and cellos. He could sing too, and often did. Every couple of days he'd break into song, warbling Appalachian murder ballads and rollicking sea shanties with equal gusto. One morning he sang a cowboy song with about a million verses about bowlegged women who got around and by the end I was blushing six kinds of red.

Gideon alternated these performances with vividly rendered history lessons full of snow-cloaked mountains and vast oceans and blood-drenched battlefields and the beauties and terrors of life lived to its heart-swelling limits. He told me about Marco Polo's epic travels on the Great Silk Road and Edward Shackleton's triumph over the long Arctic night and Admiral Nelson's exploits in the Napoleonic Wars. He described the forty-foot waves that battered Sir Francis Drake and his ships turned the corner of Cape Horn at the bottom of the world as if he had seen them himself. He told me stories of Joan of Arc and Genghis Khan and Galileo and David Livingstone and Buffalo Bill Cody. I learned all about people I'd never heard of before. People like Charles the Bad, the conniving king of a place called Navarre back in the Middle Ages. To hear Gideon tell it Charles earned his nickname a thousand times over, most memorably by double-crossing allies at several critical junctures of the Hundred Years War. It was a wonder to me that other European monarchs kept falling for his treacheries but fall for them they did, at least in Gideon's droll retelling. Until a physician got the bright idea of wrapping the king in brandy-soaked linens to ward off a fever and someone else with a candle got too close. That was it for Charles the Bad, who went up like a kerosene-drenched torch in his own palatial bedchambers.

Other times Gideon told stories from his own life experiences. Straight from the horse's mouth, or so he always insisted—but with a wink that always left me wondering if he was putting me on. Stories of gluttonous feasts and tumultuous love affairs and harrowing games of chance and decadent midnight carousing, all unfurling against the shimmering backdrop of cities that might as well have existed on the other side of the galaxy. There was the night he won a pet civet from a famous French perfumer in a Berlin cabaret. The journey he made to a remote Trappist monastery for the sole purpose of sampling the monks' exquisite rose petal jam. The afternoon he instigated a fistfight with Ernest Hemingway outside Madrid's Plaza de Toros over a woman. The sweltering Atlanta recording studio where he watched Blind Willie McTell lay down "Statesboro Blues." The morning he went cliff diving with the clavadistas of Acapulco and the night he played Whist in a leper house in Romania until dawn. He had a million stories, each one more astounding than the last. I felt like breaking into applause every time he finished one.

When he stopped the car on the shoulder that evening I thought he was going to launch into a final story or song before dropping me off at home. He did that sometimes, to squeeze just a little more enjoyment out of an already fine day.

But that night he asked me a question instead.

"Do you dream much, Will?"

"I guess so. Compared to who? I don't know if I have any more or less than other people do."

"Are they good dreams?"

I blushed, thinking of a recent one in which Miss Wells had featured prominently. "Some of them."

Gideon smiled and raised an eyebrow as if he could read my mind. "Do you remember them the next morning?"

"Some. Not as many as I used to, I don't think. And I don't remember them as long either. They disappear with the morning dew when you get older. That's what Mom says."

A gibbous moon peeked out from a far scrum of clouds in the day's dying light, its reflection a ghostly shimmer on the black hood of the roadster.

"I have a lot of dreams," Gideon said, his expression crinkling into one of fond remembrance as he unscrewed his thermos and poured himself a cup of cold lemonade. "Most of them are grand."

I looked down dolefully at the milk-clouded bottle of water wedged between my feet. I kept it down there because I didn't like feeling its clammy glass, the surface all sweaty from the well water inside, up against my bare skin. In all the time we spent together in that car Gideon never offered me a sip of lemonade or coffee, although I saw him offer countless cups to other people. He was strange that way. He told me early on that I was responsible for my own hydration, a word I had to go home and look up in the dictionary Mom and Dad gave me when I was in third grade.

"What about nightmares? Do you have them too?"

"Sure. Everyone has nightmares." I thought about the question. "But they don't bother me much. I've only had one or two that were really bad. Mom and Dad say I had a nightmare once that was so scary I woke them up with my hollering and crying but I don't remember that. I was just a kid."

Gideon shifted in his seat to face me and assumed a posture of confidentiality. "I've never had a nightmare, Will. At least I don't think I have. I've never remembered one at any rate. I've never woken up with anything but a smile on my face. I find it very vexing. They sound so interesting."

I didn't know what to say to that. I watched silently as Gideon poured himself another cup of lemonade. He tossed it back, then cleared his throat and spat in a long arc out onto the road.

"Gideon?" The question was right there on the tip of my tongue. One of many I'd been trying to work up the nerve to ask.

"Yes, Will?"

"Why did you pick Greenheart? Out of all the towns out here that are hurting, I mean? Some hurting even worse than us to hear some people tell it. Why us?"

A slow grin spread across Gideon's face. "Well to be honest I was attracted to the name, Will. It was really that simple. I just liked the name." He put his hands out before him as if framing a shot for a movie scene. "Greenheart!" he said with mock reverence, then laughed and started up the roadster to take me home. "I love the hubris of it."

7

As the weeks passed I came to feel more like Gideon's traveling companion than his tour guide. That was partly due to the fact that he was such a quick study. Within a month of his arrival it felt like he knew King County better than I did. Yet he was keeping me around and paying me good money to do so.

I was perfectly happy to be his sidekick. It was a fine thing to be. I didn't have to do anything except laugh at his uproariously funny jokes and listen to his unfailingly riveting stories and compliment his excellent whistling and singing and remember to pack one or two of my time-wasters or *Count of Monte Cristo* to pass the time he spent visiting.

One afternoon we didn't even leave the Zephyr, the second floor of which Gideon reserved on a rolling weekly basis after his month-long reservation ended. We played checkers and took turns riding my bicycle up and down the hallway, timing each other. On several occasions I glimpsed Mr. Ellery staring up at me through the flashing balusters of the banister and each time I waved to him, then laughed out loud at his befuddled expression. Afterwards Gideon took me down to the Kress five and dime for burgers and chocolate shakes. As I sat there at the counter sucking down the last dregs of milkshake and listening to Gideon flirt with the waitresses I decided that I couldn't remember the last time I had so much fun.

Gideon was almost always in good spirits. Day after day we rolled up and down the dirt roads of King County, his big beautiful black roadster humming under our feet and kicking up contrails of dust that lingered in

51

the air for minutes after our passing. The spring winds remained docile in a way that nobody trusted but everyone savored. Once in a while the sky turned a faint but ominous hue of rusty orange, as it had done the day of the rabbit drive. But the rolling walls of dust that had tormented us in previous springs never materialized. The soil was staying put. The planting was done. Now we just needed rain. More than we were getting from the occasional light showers we were experiencing.

When spring gave way to the first days of summer, though, my excursions with Gideon trailed off to one or two a week. He never told me what he was doing with the rest of his time and I didn't ask, curious as I was. I figured he was probably cashing in on some of the innumerable supper invitations he had received since his arrival. Either that or tomcatting around Greenheart. I knew he wasn't lacking for invitations on that score either, to judge by the roguish smile he didn't bother to hide after many of his interactions with "the fairer sex," as he sometimes called them.

Back in the early days our travels had felt audaciously aimless. Every night the roads Gideon took and the ones he ignored seemed dictated entirely by whimsy. As our excursions dropped off to two or three a week, though, I realized he wasn't operating that way anymore. Instead we were systematically rotating through the same dozen or so farms and ranches and homes in town. Mayor Sipe's house was part of the circuit, as were the homes of Greenheart's most popular doctor and three city councilmen. I saw the same eight or nine cars at every one of these low-key gatherings. Cars owned by men like King County Commissioner Lake Morgan and Javier Ramos, who ran things down at the Grange Hall and was hands-down Greenheart's best tractor mechanic.

And my dad. Our old Model A was usually there too.

I never had much to do on those evenings except sit in the car and read. At the time I didn't understand why Gideon was bringing me along. It was only later that I understood he wanted me to know Dad was there too. Gideon wanted to show me whose side he was on.

Stagg's place wasn't part of the route. Gideon and I never returned to his house after the night he quizzed me about him. I sensed that Stagg's absence from these gatherings —his Pierce Arrow was never among the other cars at any rate—was significant. But I didn't necessarily want to know why. That was the business of adults and I wanted no part of any of that.

At the end of one of those later excursions Gideon surprised me by pulling up outside our church. It was the finest one in town, a broad-shouldered edifice of stone and timber with twin rows of stained-glass lancet windows arrayed along the flanks of the sanctuary. Their Biblical tableaus of saints and apostles and burning bushes glowed orange and red and yellow and blue in the gloaming. The sound of the church organ wafted faintly over us. Mrs. Brennan was inside, practicing for Sunday. I sat quietly and listened to the engine tick as I peered up at the great bell tower John Stagg's money had bought.

I wondered why we were there.

"This is quite a church, Will," Gideon observed, breaking the silence. "A town five times Greenheart's size would be proud to harbor such a fine house of worship. Look at those windows! And I've heard that bell several Sunday mornings now, you can hear that thing for miles."

"We're not that small," I said. "Greenheart's not. Seven thousand four hundred back in 1930 said the Census, and we had a lot more than that a few years later."

"And now?" he said gently.

"I don't know," I said defensively. "I'm just saying Greenheart's a pretty big town."

"Whoa, settle down there, mister mayor," Gideon said.

I smiled. He was good at that when he wanted to be. Teasing me in a way that was fun, not mean.

Gideon poured himself a cup of cold lemonade. "You go to this church, don't you? You and your folks?"

"Yes."

"How's the choir?" Gideon tilted his head back and polished off the cup's contents in two prodigious gulps, his throat moving like a boa constrictor in the pooled shadows of the cab.

"The choir?" My thoughts instantly went to Miss Wells, who sang in the choir's front row.

"Yes, the choir. I can't remember the last time I heard music that wasn't coming out of a box or a phonograph. And the nearest radio station must be a million miles away."

"We had one. A radio station right here in Greenheart. KFEW, up on the north end of town. It closed a couple years back. Mr. Stagg bought it last year when no one else even took a sniff. Remember? I told you about that. People say he's going to get it up and running again."

"Yes, I remember." Gideon sniffed and rubbed his chin thoughtfully. "The industrious Mister Stagg. I do like his estate, though. A regular Maleperduys of the Plains. Though it probably lacks the requisite passageways of escape. But where would you go anyway? To another pancake-flat wasteland baking in the sun a dozen miles away? Hardly seems worth the effort, does it?"

"What?" Gideon had totally lost me.

"Never mind."

I cleared my throat. "He's in the choir."

"Who is?"

"Mr. Stagg."

Gideon screwed the cup back onto the top of his thermos. "Of course he is. He's probably a baritone."

"I'm not sure," I said uncertainly, and decided to change the subject. "We have a good pastor. Reverend Rosbourne. He's nice. Mom and Dad like him."

"How are his sermons?"

"How long are they, do you mean?"

Gideon chuckled. "No. Are they fire and brimstone? You know, believe in the Lord, because raining fire down on your head is God's way of showing you He cares? Is that his racket?"

"Uh, I don't know. He . . . tries to comfort us, I guess? He mostly tells us to take care of one another. Extend grace to one another, he says that a lot. He organizes a lot of events. Potluck dinners, baseball games, that sort of thing. He has a pretty good glove—a lot better than you'd think just looking at him—but he hardly ever gets to play."

"Why's that?"

"Everyone wants him to call the balls and strikes."

"Probably cuts down on the arguing."

"Do you go to church?" I asked impulsively. "It must be hard to get to church, traveling all the time the way you do."

"Oh, I get by," Gideon said. "I've been pretty busy since I got to Greenheart, as you know. But I've been thinking I should come have a listen to John Stagg and his merry band of carolers. Sounds like I should hear this preacher man of yours too."

"Really? This Sunday?"

"No commitments. But soon. I can't wait. Maybe someone will speak in tongues for me."

8

Gideon's promise to come to one of our church services had an odd effect on me. Or perhaps not so odd, given the still-vivid memories of Gideon's visit to our home. My stomach hurt when I thought about how Mom's eyes would harden over if she saw him in our church sanctuary. But I was more preoccupied with trying to game out what Gideon would think of *us*. By which I mean our church.

I found myself wishing Gideon could have seen the church as it had been when I was a young child, back before this age of blight. Back when every pew was full of worshippers and we filled the tall rafters with songs and prayers of gratitude to God for His mercy and our many blessings.

We were a confident bunch back then. We had come to tame the frontier and bend the prairie to our will and we had done it. The Great War was over and we won that too. And the fruits of that sacrifice and labor were plain to see. Head ten miles out of Greenheart in any direction on the day I was born and you would have beheld the same tableau: shimmering fields of wheat, alfalfa, sugar beets, and barley crawling with combines and tractors and trucks that moved like clanking beetles.

Downtown Greenheart filled up with wheat money too. Women and girls dipped in and out of shops like colorful swallows, sharing the sidewalk with men heading to or from work at the flour mill or the district courthouse or one of the town's two banks. Families from the panhandle and southwest Kansas started coming to Greenheart to see our Fourth of July Parade and shop at Christmastime.

The Crash back East didn't shake us. Not at first. The stories Dad read to us out of the newspaper sounded like dispatches from an alternative universe where lurid plots from my time wasters had come to life. Food riots in the cities. Millionaires-turned-paupers flinging themselves off tall buildings. Glittering flappers turned into disease-wracked cautionary tales. Muggers in the alleys and hoboes on the rails, drifting like tumbleweeds themselves, their ears filled day and night with the train's rhythmic gallop. Mobsters spraying each other with machine guns to sort out the post-Prohibition pecking order. Unemployed clerks and factory workers and salesmen and secretaries shuffling through bread lines that snaked for blocks.

We told ourselves we were made of sturdier stuff. We thought we could ride it out. Until our crops started piling up and moldering at the train station when the price of wheat dropped like an anvil. Until the rain stopped coming and the crops stopped growing and the topsoil started blowing away and we started waking up with dust on our faces and in our noses and on our toothbrushes and in the bottom of our coffee cups.

That's when we remembered how vulnerable we were under that infinite canvas of sky. It was like we awoke with epic hangovers from a long night of drinking from a magnum bottle of Manifest Destiny. How had we ended up out here in the middle of a desert? What had we been thinking? In the 1910s and 1920s we had anointed ourselves the new lords of the plains. By 1936 new parents had to drape wet linens over cradles at night to keep their babies safe from dust pneumonia.

Some people snicker at the thought that when disasters big or small come crashing down on us—floods and earthquakes and shipwrecks and cancers and business failures and infidelities and limb-maiming work accidents— those tragedies might just be God smiting us for our wicked ways. They scoff at the idea that any of that smoking heartbreak and sorrow and devastation can be placed at the feet of a God with murder in His eye. When some people hear that sort of thing they turn to each other and confidently deconstruct the social and familial forces that could have produced such a superstitious creature.

All I can say to those people is *you weren't there.*

You weren't there when centipedes and black widow spiders and tarantulas exploded like a witch's curse in our houses and sheds and barns and coops. You weren't there when great swarms of grasshoppers chewed away at our fence posts and porches, the sound a throbbing drone of unreality. You never wore goggles and Red Cross masks to keep the dust out of your lungs and eyes.

You weren't there when the wild birds and animals disappeared, leaving only the jacks and the creepy crawlies behind. You weren't there when brown snow came falling out of the evening sky like ash from a distant charnel house. You never saw the crackling bolt of pale blue light that shot out of the topmost blade of our windmill and into the night sky when static electricity charged the air. You weren't there, experiencing all of that, in a town that ten years earlier had been puffing its chest out with confidence that it was going to be the next great city of the West. You didn't endure the sickening, terrifying plummet from those halcyon days. You never wondered when you were going to stop falling.

What had we done? Had we been too proud? Too gluttonous or covetous or proud? I overheard my parents talking about a lot of things that our neighbors and fellow parishioners had done or were thinking of doing. Messy, sad, awful things. Heartless and selfish and desperate things. Maybe I wasn't the only one eavesdropping on those stories. Maybe God finally decided He had heard enough and it was time for the belt.

That's what some people thought, at any rate. One of the virtues of casting one's lot with an Old Testament God is that it gives all the suffering some meaning. He might be a hard God, but at least He isn't a howling void of nothingness.

Some embraced the lassitude of fatalism, going limp in the implacable current of God's will. Others fled with middle fingers stabbing at the heavens, spitting and snarling and cursing His name. And some took a third path, one that heralded coming days of judgment and a recommitment to God's Holy Word.

Fire and brimstone was not Reverend Rosbourne's style. He had been a professor of literature or history or something like that before he switched gears and it sometimes showed in his sermons, which Mom and Dad both thought could get a little wordy. But they approved of the basic thrust of his weekly meditations. Sundays came and Sundays went and Rosbourne's message never wavered. Do not despair. Be of good courage. Stick together. The only way we were going to come out the other side intact was to persevere, to be generous in heart and spirit with one another, and to reject the creeping fear that God had forsaken us. I envied Rosbourne's relationship with God. The certainty of purpose that it seemed to give him.

Rosbourne's favorite scripture reading was from the seventh and eighth verses of the seventeenth book of Jeremiah. He often used it as his closing benediction, reciting it from memory with head bowed down and hand raised in blessing.

Blessed is the man who trusts in the Lord, whose trust is the Lord.
   He is like a tree planted by water, that sends out its roots by the stream,
   and does not fear when heat comes, for its leaves remain green,
   and is not anxious in the year of drought,
   for it does not cease to bear fruit.

That was always my favorite part of church. Besides watching Miss Wells sing, that is. But those weren't the words that some people wanted to hear. So they left in search of a messenger more attuned to the panicked pounding of their hearts.

9

I rode my bicycle into town to meet up with Gideon at the Zephyr but he stood me up. Again. It had happened three times now and never with any advance notice, although he always paid me for the day. Every time I lingered in town before heading back home. I was in no hurry to return to the façade of normalcy that my parents contrived for every mealtime.

The first time Gideon was a no-show I rode my bicycle a few streets south of the square to the street where I knew Miss Wells lived, but I only did it the one time because it was too depressing. The house she was renting sat on a street down by the railroad yard that was honeycombed with abandoned homes. Skeins of sand stretched across the yards of some of the houses. Fenceposts and mailboxes like pilings in a harbor of powdery swells.

I took a long, slow stroll around the town square, walking my bike as I peered in each dusty shop window I passed. I kept an eye out for Miss Wells's car among the ones parked around the square, both hoping for and fearing an actual encounter. The prospect of such a meeting was nerve-wracking, but by the time I completed my circuit of the square I felt besotted anew with my desire for her. The ache made me miserable but I luxuriated in it too.

That's when I spotted Daniel walking past the bandshell in the center of the square. I hailed him and after a minute or two of chatter he invited me over to the room his dad had rented for them above the pool hall. I eagerly accepted the offer, excited at the prospect of entering the inner sanctum of one of Greenheart's more mysterious business enterprises.

But the seedy glory I expected was nowhere to be found inside. The place was nearly empty except for a half-dozen faded green billiards tables in two rows of three, the worn felt of each one filmed over in a pollen-like coating of dust and cigarette ash. Two men were playing at the furthest table in desultory fashion, smoking silently as they circled the table and lined up their shots. The air inside was stale and foul, redolent of cigarette smoke and old sweat.

We took a back stairway that smelled of beer and clomped down a dimly-lit hallway past a community bathroom that reeked of sulfur. The bathroom door had been removed from its frame and I glanced inside as we passed, just long enough to glimpse a straw-haired man with a half-shaved face staring back at me through a mirror bolted to the wall above one of the sinks.

By the time Daniel brought us to the last door at the end of the hall I thoroughly regretted having taken him up on his offer. The room at the back of our barn where Daniel and his father bunked had been far from a palace but it hadn't been a hovel either. The room had an old coal-burning stove for warmth and a big basin for washing up, and Dad and Daniel's father had lined the outer walls with dense blocks of straw for insulation. The room was clean and had a south-facing window that provided a big slanted block of natural light that Buster loved to lay in. My parents even scrounged up a twin bed for Daniel's dad and a sturdy canvas army cot that Daniel used. He kept all his clothes under there along with a modest stack of personal possessions. The stack was topped by a small wooden box with a faded image of a fly fisherman casting down a tree-lined stream on the lid. That's where he kept pictures of his Mom along with several letters she had written to her six-year-old son in the weeks before her death. He let me read one of them and by the end I was wiping tears from my eyes. It was filled with words of love and hope and encouragement and hard-won wisdom she would never get to share with her son in the years to come.

Daniel locked the door behind us as soon as we were inside. The room looked and felt nothing like the cozy one at the back of our barn. Most of their possessions were still crammed into beat-up suitcases and boxes lined up against one dingy wall, next to a battered dresser with two missing drawer handles and a small chair with the cane seat busted through. Daniel's familiar brown sweater with the blue elbow patches was draped over the metal footboard of the far bed, looking alien and out of place in that room of cinderblock walls. The only comforting sight sat at the foot of his father's unused, neatly made bed: the big steamer trunk of treasures from Grant Ballantine's glory days in the Navy.

I walked over to the trunk and rubbed my hand over the rough lid. I knew the stories behind every trinket and curio inside. Every conch shell and matchbook and poker chip and postcard. There was the finely polished Japanese puzzle box from Hakone. That was a Daniel favorite because he knew the long sequence of moves that opened the intricately patterned wooden box—his father sometimes left pieces of hard candy inside for us to find—and I couldn't figure it out. The teacup with the silhouette of a fanning peacock at the bottom. An ashtray from a Honolulu restaurant called *The House Without a Key*. Every piece was a message in a bottle, a totem of oceans and mountains and people that existed far beyond the borders of the forgotten, used-up land to which we had been exiled. The only thing we weren't allowed to touch was his father's dress whites, tightly packed in butcher paper and mothballs at the very bottom of the trunk.

Everything else was fair game, including a small stack of photographs neatly wrapped in an old linen napkin banded with twine. Daniel's father kept them tucked under a framed certification of graduation from the U.S. Navy Diving School in Newport, Rhode Island. Inside the napkin were black and white pictures of a much younger Grant Ballantine against backdrops of palm trees and oceans and warships and freighters that loomed behind him like walled cities. One of the photographs was a blurry shot of him with his parents—Daniel's grandparents—on a nameless street in Braintree, Massachusetts, where Grant Ballantine had been born and raised. He was twelve years old in the picture according to the writing on the back.

Our favorite photograph was a grainy one of Daniel's father in a bulky Mark V diving suit at New York Harbor, the skyscrapers of mid-1920s Gotham glittering behind him. His gleaming helmet is cradled in the crook of one big arm as he points down with the other at a nautical chart held open for inspection by two serious-looking Navy officers, one on either side of him. It was a postcard from the world that existed before Daniel or I came on the scene. A world in which our parents were young and strong and without children. Confident in the life they were forging together. Destined for happiness and prosperity.

None of those curios or photographs fired up our imaginations the way Grant Ballantine's old diving gear did, though. An old diving weight belt, blanched nearly white from hours of salt water immersion. Heavy binoculars tucked away in a scuffed black leather case. The antique spyglass his father bought in Southampton.

Daniel's dad even kept an old diving helmet from his days at the Navy Yard, though it took up nearly half of the steamer's packing space and its fifty-five pound weight made the trunk a beast to carry. Daniel said that when he was little his parents used to decorate it with garlands and flickering candles for Christmas.

The previous New Year's Eve Daniel's father had brought it out for everyone to try on as part of the festivities. He hauled the helmet out of their room at the back of the barn and set it in the middle of the cleared-off kitchen table. An odd sensation of ceremony took hold as he prepared a thick yoke of twisted rags and seed bags to place around our necks. Otherwise the heavy breastplate of copper and brass would cut into our knobby shoulders and leave our skin bruised and bloody.

Mom went first. She sat straight in her chair and took a deep breath as our fathers gently lowered the helmet down over her head. When the weight of the breastplate had fully settled on the cloth yoke circling her neck she smiled through the glass at us as if she was having a delightful time. She turned her head to look through the glass plates at either side of the helmet. Then she said okay get me out of here in a muffled underwater way that made all of us laugh and they quickly brought the helmet back up, releasing her head from captivity.

Daniel went next. He promised to breathe really hard so that I would smell his breath when it was my turn. His dad transferred the yoke of seed bags and rags to his shoulders and they lowered the diving helmet down over his head, Mom grimacing nervously as she watched.

Daniel loved it. He didn't want to take it off. His dad opened the glass plate at the front of the helmet so that Daniel could breathe freely and he spent the next twenty minutes wearing it at the kitchen table. He only agreed to relinquish it after Mom brought out a hand mirror so that he could see what he looked like with the helmet on. His grin was a mile wide the entire time. For days afterward he talked about what it would have been like to walk with his father on the bottom of the East River. He imagined the two of them running their thick rubber-gloved fingers along the cold pewter skin of the warships and cargoes at rest in the harbor, then flying together afterward through New York City's glittering, tumultuous streets. Togged to the bricks, racing through every dance hall and jazz club and tree-shaded park they could find, then spending the last hours before dawn riding elevators suspended like diving bells inside the oily throats of skyscrapers. Daniel had never been in an elevator and was keen to give one a try.

I hated the helmet. As soon as they put it on me I felt as if my head was encased in a hatbox-sized sarcophagus. The circle of glass two inches from my nose was already filmed over with Daniel's condensed breath and I couldn't see a thing out of the side plates either. I closed my eyes and told myself that I only had to wear it for a minute to immunize myself from any mockery. I didn't last nearly that long. A seizure of claustrophobia ran through me and an instant later my hands were frantically pushing on the front lip of the breastplate, eyes wide with panic behind the glass. An animal sound came boiling out of me that was something between a moan and a scream, setting off a monstrous babel of echoes inside the helmet. And then the torture device was off my shoulders and I was taking great gulping breaths of air, not caring in the least that everyone was staring down at me in varying shades of pity, concern, and disappointment.

Perhaps that unsettling experience accounted for my belief that the steamer's greatest treasure was actually Grant Ballantine's old set of blue and white semaphore flags. When Daniel and I held them close to our noses we told each other we could still smell the ocean air in the fabric, even over the mothballs. His father taught us the flag positions for each letter of the alphabet and Mom dug up some threadbare canvas swatches that we converted into a rough pair of flags for me to use and that's all we needed.

My hand-dyed semaphore flags were much less impressive than Daniel's authentic ones but I didn't mind. I liked watching him make those colorful pennants snap and flutter in the distance, creating words out of thin air. Daniel's flags were visible long after mine had been leached of form and meaning by the evening's gathering gloom.

So how had father and son Ballantine ended up in Greenheart of all places? I put it together piece by piece over the course of the fourteen months they lived on our farm. When Daniel's mom died of scarlet fever in 1928, his dad decided to leave the Navy behind and seek a new life for himself and his son in the American West. He fled the haunted places and faces that he was certain would remind him of the wife and life that had been taken from him. Go West, young man, and take your broken heart and motherless son with you.

And so it was that Grant Ballantine found himself tenant farming for an unfriendly old Scotch-Irish widower named McDonald, our neighbor to the north, on fields that started cracking from thirst a year after Daniel's dad signed on the dotted line. Or so I overheard Dad tell Mom one night after supper, his voice thick with sympathy. Dad said that Daniel's father had been unlucky.

When the bank foreclosed on McDonald—he was one of the first people we knew who left—Grant Ballantine lost everything too. He had to sell what little farm equipment he had for pennies. But Dad saw how hard Daniel's father had worked to make a go of it—and how good he was with a wrench— so he took him on as a farm hand, offering room and board to both him and his son.

In practically no time at all I came to feel as if I had been gifted a brother and I knew Daniel felt the same. His loyalty to me was so fierce that the older boys who had occasionally bothered me at school took note and drifted away. He helped Mom make my birthday cake when I turned fourteen; she told me the next day that he beamed the whole time. We were inseparable.

* * *

"What's he like?" Daniel asked.

"Who?" I said, though I knew who he meant.

"Gideon Starling. Maybe you've heard of him? Some people are saying he can make it rain. Turn water into wine. Something like that." He gave me a crooked smile. "It has to do with water, I know that. Everyone says you're showing him around."

"A little," I said. "Not that much anymore, he's a pretty quick study."

"Uh huh. So what's his angle? What's he like?"

I considered the question. I wasn't quite sure what to tell him. Gideon had been very good to me, no two ways about it, and he was spectacularly entertaining. He was relentlessly cheerful and a born raconteur, full of rich and buttery storytelling confections that always left me hungry for more. And I knew I wasn't the only one in Greenheart who felt that way. Whatever he was telling people in his little heart-to-heart chats, they sure seemed to like it. He knew people were talking about him and he liked that too.

But the memories of Gideon's disastrous visit to our home—and the ways in which that evening had redrawn and hardened the battle lines between my parents—gave me pause. As did the image of Gideon's angry roadside piss when I refused to tell him anything about Miss Wells.

But what made me hesitate most in answering Daniel's question—*what was Gideon like?*—was an unsettling turn of events that had occurred on our last excursion. Two days earlier I had joined him for a drive out to Ed Wagner's place. Six hundred and forty acres of sandbox that had been producing bumper crops of Turkey Red as far as the eye could see a decade before. Wagner was holding on but his German blood was still held against him by some—Gideon knew the names of people who called him a Kraut behind his back thanks to me.

When Gideon slowed to turn into Wagner's long dirt driveway I warned him that the man owned two famously vicious dogs that practically had the run of the place. I related how Dad and I had once driven out there on some errand and been forced to sit in the truck for five minutes as those hackled-up half-wild dogs circled us, snarling and barking like they wanted to tear us limb from limb. Even after Wagner called them off they watched us balefully, murder in their eyes. Neither dog was particularly big—sixty or seventy pounds, tops—but they looked made out of teeth, gristle, sinew, and rope. They were very mean and very territorial dogs.

When we pulled up to the Wagner house in our usual cloud of dust, though, those dogs were nowhere to be seen. Gideon parked in the shade of the sagging barn and walked right up the porch steps to Ed Wagner, who was looking around the yard as if he too was puzzling over the absence of his hellhounds. I dared to hope that they were both dead.

Gideon and Wagner emerged from the house onto the front porch a half hour or so later, deep in conversation. Gideon gave him a vigorous handshake, then stepped lightly down the steps and strolled over to the car. He paused as he opened the door to give a friendly shout that I couldn't quite make out. Whatever he said it made Wagner's dour features break out in a broad grin. I'd never seen the man crack a smile before.

As Gideon turned the car around to leave, I saw both dogs come slinking out from behind the far side of the house, tails tucked low between their legs. The dogs froze, statue-like, when they saw me staring out at them and a shiver of memory snapped into place. Of that hallucinatory moment when Gideon spoke and all those terrified rabbits turned as one to his voice.

What do the animals know about Gideon that we don't?

I was still pondering that question when Daniel turned away with a dismissive wave and opened the heavy lid of the steamer. "If you don't want to talk about him just say so," he said. "No skin off my nose. I don't really care. I was just making conversation."

Chastened, I joined him at the foot of the open trunk. Together we began liberating his father's old gear and souvenirs from the confines of the steamer. We tried to make it feel like old times. We took up the semaphore flags in our hands, seeking comfort in their familiar weight and texture and colors. Sniffing the fabric for the scent of the sea I once swore was there. I would have given anything in that moment to be transported from that cell-like room back to our windswept fields, barren as they were, and watch his flags flash and dance in the day's dying light one more time. But it felt like our flag-waving days were over.

I had just reached in for the diving helmet when Daniel cleared his throat. "For the record, my dad never did nothin' with your mom." His voice was thick and aggrieved.

I froze across the front of that open steamer trunk as the words hung in the air. I could tell he had been wanting to say those words for a long time but I didn't know what to say in response. All I could think about was how much I didn't want to talk about it. So I pulled the gleaming helmet out of the trunk, grunting with the exertion. I held the helmet toward him, pretending I hadn't heard his declaration. "Here," I said, my arms trembling under the heavy weight. "Take it. Put it on. But we need a towel or something for your shoulders."

* * *

Ten minutes later I was back on the sidewalk outside the pool hall, blinking against the bright afternoon sunlight as I savaged myself for my stupidity.

I had ruined everything.

When Daniel refused to accept the diving helmet I turned and tossed it on his bed in a sudden rush of righteous anger. Why couldn't Daniel just shut up and let sleeping dogs lie? I didn't want to talk about our parents or the secret appetites and motivations and desires that drove them to do the things they did. I didn't want to think about whether Mom had cheated on Dad, or what might have driven her to do it.

We watched silently as the helmet bounced and rolled on the thin mattress like the decapitated head of some alien monarch from outer space. The edge of the copper breastplate cut a white divot in the gray plaster above Daniel's bed before coming to rest in a slanting square of sunlight from the small room's only window. The glass ports of the helmet glittered in the sun behind their grids of steel bars, stamping a latticework of black and gold on the far wall.

I glanced sideways at Daniel and was shocked to find him furiously blinking away hot tears. I had never seen him cry before, not even about his mom. He was waiting for me to say something. But I didn't know what to say to him. I didn't know what to do. All I could think about was how hard my heart was pounding and how much I wanted to get out of that room. When I told him I needed to use the bathroom he stared disbelievingly at me. "There's the door, figure out the rest."

I hurried out of the room, closed the door behind me, and walked nervously down the hall to the sulfurous communal bathroom. I was grateful beyond measure to find it empty. The straw-haired man who had been shaving earlier was nowhere in sight.

I stared into the cracked mirror over the sink for what felt like a long time, listening to the pipes clank fitfully behind the walls. I gave my hands and face a good washing, even though there wasn't any soap and the water from the faucet smelled bad. I dragged myself back down the short hallway to Daniel's room until I was facing the closed door. I felt feverish with misery but knew I couldn't go home without telling him I was leaving. I couldn't just run away. I turned the knob, swung the door open, and found Daniel sitting on the bed in mid-conversation with his father. Grant Ballantine was standing in the center of the room with the diving helmet cradled in his big, callused hands. The helmet didn't dwarf his hands like it did ours.

He hefted the helmet thoughtfully, as if he were considering throwing it at me. His eyes locked on mine and I did my best not to look away because I was desperate for reassurance that everything was somehow still okay. I wanted him to restore the bonds of brotherhood with his son that had unraveled before my eyes. But his eyes were cold and hard and Daniel refused to look at me at all. They didn't have to say a word. I knew where I stood. They were casting me out, just as Dad had done to them.

* * *

"Will, are you all right?"

I turned in the direction of the voice, squinting against the sun. It was Miss Wells, looking slim and kind and heartbreakingly-pretty in the golden afternoon light. She leaned in closer so that she could get a good look at me, using her hand to shield her eyes from the sun. "Will? Are you okay, Will?" she asked, her voice cutting so hard with its sweetness. And then she touched my arm and I burst into tears and she hugged me for a long, long time.

II

At Tencombe Rings near the Manor Linney
His foot made the great black stallion whinny,
And the stallion's whinny aroused the stable
And the bloodhound bitches stretched their cable. . .

The red-wattled black cock hot from Spain
Crowed from his perch for dawn again,
His breast-puft hens, one-legged on perched,
Gurgled, beak-down, like men in church,
They crooned in the dark, lifting one red eye
In the raftered roost as the fox went by.
—John Masefield

Somehow you strayed and lost your way,
And now there'll be no time to play,
No time for joy, no time for friends
—Not even time to make amends
—Lewis Carroll

10

John Stagg and my Uncle Leonard died on the same day. May 15, 1936. Three days after my friendship with Daniel had shattered into a million pieces over at the pool hall. It was a Tuesday.

The news of the Great Man's peaceful passing in his sleep was a deeply unsettling shocker for everyone in Greenheart. Not only because he had seemed so healthy and vigorous and *permanent* in a way that few things remained in this world but also because his death was bound to have significant economic ripple effects across King County.

The death of Uncle Leonard, mom's oldest brother, caused less of a stir. He died of a heart attack on his way to work downtown, where he had been a postman for nearly fifteen years. Aside from the date of the funeral and the offer of a room to stay in, that's about all we knew from Aunt Ruth's telegram. Mom tried to call her a few times but could never get through.

I thought Dad might try to keep Mom from going. It was less than 150 miles to Colorado Springs as the crow flies but the train schedule options were unworkable and the roads leading to my aunt's house were stippled with desperate gasoline gypsies and interminable WPA road construction projects. Gasoline was expensive too. And if she traveled to Colorado Springs she would miss Stagg's funeral, which was shaping up as a very big deal. But Dad offered only a single half-hearted protest when Mom declared that she was going to Uncle Leonard's funeral whether he was or not. Uncle Leonard was her older brother and that's all there was to it.

Dad also readily agreed when Mom said she wanted to take me with her.

She probably had a whole speech prepared but there was no need. Dad said he would have suggested it if she hadn't. He said it was fine with him as long as Gideon could spare me for the week we'd be gone. He didn't trust the truck to make the trip but we could take the Model A. He gave us refresher courses on patching and changing a flat and checking the oil and packing the gas cans and water jugs. Like most farm kids I'd been driving for a couple years by then so he reminded Mom that I could take a shift behind the wheel if she got tired. He went over the roadmap with us and made sure I packed the right bullets for the secondhand Winchester .22 he stowed behind the front seat. It was a gun suited for small game, rabbits and the like. It wouldn't put the same hole in you as Dad's Savage 99 but I still wouldn't want to get shot with one. Just before we left Dad took me aside and looked at me very seriously. *Take good care of your mom.* I said I would.

An escape from Greenheart—even a temporary one—sounded like an excellent idea to me. The memory of my breakdown in front of Miss Wells outside Bean's Billiards was a constant torment. I had revealed myself to be nothing but a callow schoolboy in her eyes. A blubbering crybaby. And when I wasn't beating myself up about falling apart in front of Miss Wells I was replaying how Daniel and his father had turned me out. The way they had looked at me.

Grant Ballantine had come back for his son, just as he had promised. The two of them were probably halfway to Washington by now. Gone forever from my life. Already they felt like apparitions.

Mom's mood was somber when we left the following morning, but her own excitement at escaping Greenheart's miseries and discouragements bubbled to the surface as we put the miles behind us. By midday she was not bothering to hide her high spirits and neither was I. We filled the car with conversation as we puttered across the dust-caked plains of southern Colorado. We didn't talk about Dad or Buster or Daniel and I was grateful for that.

We didn't talk about Gideon either—until I brought him up myself.

Mom had packed some food in a dented little icebox for us to eat along the way but I convinced her to splurge on a little roadside diner for supper by divulging a secret that had been gnawing at me for several days.

"Gideon gave me a bonus last week. And the week before that too,"

"He did? How much?"

Mom's mouth dropped open when I told her. "I'm sorry I didn't tell you or Dad. I wanted to. But Gideon said he'd take back the money if I told you and . . . well we need it, right?"

It was true. Both bonuses exceeded my already generous weekly pay. But they had come with the same stern warning attached: I couldn't tell my parents. But how could I explain the money otherwise? How could I put it to good use without them knowing? *That's for you to figure out,* he had replied.

Mom kept her eyes on the road but when she spoke her voice was tight with anger. "But why? Why would he do that? What does that—that—never mind. OK, fill me in."

"On what?"

"On everything. Including why you waited until now to tell either one of us. You should have told us, honey."

"I'm sorry. I didn't tell you about the money because I was worried he'd find out if I told you. Somehow." I already regretted telling her. I never should have accepted the bonuses in the first place, not with those kinds of strings attached. Gideon caught me off-guard with them. He had the advantage of surprise and the dictatorial authority of the gift-giver—the architect of time and place and setting and circumstance for every such ceremony—and before I knew it Gideon had extracted a solemn promise that I would never tell my parents of his secret largesse.

Maybe it had been a test. One he knew I'd fail. Maybe Gideon told me the bonus payments had to be a secret because he knew I couldn't keep secrets. He knew he'd get the money back.

The full implications of my impulsive confession pressed down on me. I slumped against the car door and stared out the window. I imagined returning home from Colorado Springs in a week and opening the lid of the pencil box in which I had stashed Gideon's bonus money to find it empty but for a small colony of death cap mushrooms, luminous in a pale bed of nightshade.

"I shouldn't have told you," I said dolefully, placing my head in my hands. "Oh God. Mom, you've got to promise not to tell anyone. Not even Dad. That's the only way we'll be able to keep the money. Gideon will find out if Dad knows."

"What good is the money if we can't use it?" She squared her shoulders to the wheel. "No, that's not the right way to think about it. That's a good little nest egg for you, make sure you don't lose it. Keep it close but somewhere you don't have to check on it all the time for peace of mind." She looked at me to make sure I was listening. "A shovel and a landmark is about all you need. Make sure no one follows you. Don't tell us where it is. Either one of us."

"Okay. But you have to promise not to tell Dad about any of this. Gideon will find out for sure."

Mom sighed and took a long look at me. "I promise," she said finally, shaking her head at the words coming out of her mouth. And then her face broke into a big smile. "Well Daddy Warbucks, if you're still buying we might as well have someone cook *me* a decent meal for once in my life."

Twenty minutes later Mom pulled us into a roadside diner on the northern outskirts of Pueblo. We chose a scuffed but sturdy booth over seats at the long counter and as we waited for our food Mom told me stories about Uncle Leonard and other characters from her eventful childhood. Some were funny, some were sad, all made Mom's eyes sparkle in the telling. One or two of them came with a good deal of eye-rolling, as if she could not believe the foolishness of her family. But even those stories were leavened with a sort of exasperated affection. Uncle Leonard and Aunt Ruth and the rest of Mom's side of the family sounded larger than life.

I told Mom a few stories too, mostly from school. She listened attentively as I brought her up to speed on various dramas at school, nodding and smiling and asking occasional questions as she sipped her coffee. We didn't talk about Gideon anymore. It was grand.

As was the week that followed. Colorado Springs was high arid country, its downtown district nearly as flat as ours. But the foothills and mountains of the southern Rockies were arrayed to the west and what a sight for sore eyes they were for this child of the flatlands.

It wasn't just the land that was different. From the moment we arrived at Aunt Ruth's modest but comfortable home the place swarmed with cousins and uncles and aunts and a parade of other relatives and family friends. They were gruff and boisterous and sentimental and every one of them seemed to have missed Mom something fierce.

I received a good amount of reflected glory from her light. Everyone was predisposed to like me. All I had to do was not make a total ass of myself and I would remain in everyone's good graces. I managed to do so, and at the end of the week Aunt Ruth called me "a good sport," which I had come to recognize as a compliment of the highest order in the Cochrane tribe.

My older cousins immediately took me in as one of their own. There were seven of them in all, boys and girls in their mid- to late teens who had all grown up together. I was a year younger than Katherine, the next youngest at fifteen. I was as self-conscious about my age as I was about everything else the day I met them but within an hour I had a formal invitation to go camping with them in the mountains. They were leaving the next morning with the intention of squeezing in two nights of sleeping under the stars before the funeral. I jumped at the offer and spent most of the next two days following them through a head-spinning wonderland of deep green forests and tumbling streams and vertical rock faces.

They took me to the Garden of the Gods, where jagged spines of ancient red stone thrust out of the forested hills like the dorsal fins of a breaching sea serpent. Everywhere I looked, earth and sky joined and sheared off at jaw-dropping angles, heaving up gaudy geometries in infinite combinations of stone and earth and air and water and forest. It was a joy to watch my cousins Morgan and Fred patiently work their way down a cold blue stream, filling their creels with bucking silver-scaled fish that they fried up for supper that night. We spent the second night tucked deep in the mountains, as far from the real world as we could get. Just the eight of us, talking and singing around a crackling campfire, serenaded by owls and crickets. The next morning Katherine said she heard coyotes late, long after everyone else was asleep. She said they were far away but howled for a long time.

When we returned to Aunt Ruth's the eight of us ate supper and cleaned up with everyone else, but each of the next two nights we found an hour or two to ourselves. One night we played Billy Whiskers in the parlor while the sounds of Gene Autry and Benny Goodman washed over us from Aunt Ruth's radio. The next evening we brought Uncle Leonard's old phonograph player out to the kitchen and put on half a dozen records Morgan found in the top drawer of an old bedroom dresser marooned in the parlor. We played the music low and tried to be quiet, but the small kitchen echoed with our hushed singing and half-stifled laughter. I felt sure that Aunt Ruth or Mom or their cousin Lois would come down and yell at us but no one ever did. It was after midnight before my cousins finally scattered into the dark, shivering in their jackets as they made their way to their beds.

My cousins were taking temporary sanctuary among family just as we were. Savoring a final interlude of warmth and safety and order before venturing out into a world strangling on dust and pink slips. Every one of them was standing at a crossroads of one sort or another.

Fred and Morgan were leaving two days after the funeral for a CCC camp north of Fort Collins. Morgan turned eighteen seven months before Fred, but he had waited for his cousin before signing up to go plant trees and build bridges and fire towers.

Sarah Erin was leaving too. Off to Boulder in August to work as a switchboard operator for the university up there, the job arranged by a faceless benefactor orbiting somewhere in the outermost reaches of the family's constellation of friends and associates.

Their imminent departures loomed as crossroads for those left behind too. Like the twins, Stephen and Robin, who would miss Morgan terribly when he was gone. Their older brother was the one who knew how to keep the peace between their parents—or at least keep things from spiraling out of control. He was the peacekeeper. Every day would be harder for them after Morgan was gone.

Life would also be different for Katherine, with whom I became hopelessly smitten over the course of that week. She was Aunt Eunice's daughter from her first marriage. Both she and her brother Fred had been absorbed into the Cochrane family as small children when Eunice married Frank, Mom's middle brother. Katherine was pretty and liked to read and had an infectious laugh that made everyone smile, me most of all. She was quieter than the rest of my rambunctious cousins but a master of the clever retort, as her sputtering older brother rediscovered time after time.

Katherine wanted to know all about my life. She wanted to know how it felt to sit through plagues of dusters and tornados and sub-freezing winter nights, and if it was true that we dragged chains behind our trucks and automobiles to keep the static electricity packed in those dust storms from shorting our engines out. She wanted to know what we planted in our vegetable garden and if I could remember the last time I had seen our fields get a good solid soaking. She wanted to know if I wished I had a brother or a sister and whether my parents got along. She wanted to know what my favorite school subjects and least favorite chores were. She asked me my favorite Christmas song and when I said *Silent Night* she smiled shyly and said that was her favorite song to hear but that her favorite to sing was *O Come O Come Emmanuel*.

I answered all those questions and many more besides. I told her about how Greenheart had been forced to turn on all the street lamps at noontime on Black Friday, and how I got to thinking that the storm was just going to keep coming and coming and never stop until we vanished like a ship going down in a heaving sea of dust. I told her I got in a bad fight with my best friend just before he moved away, probably forever. I told her I was scared we were going to lose our farm and that my parents' marriage was falling apart and that my dog was likely dead and that everyone in Greenheart was mourning John Stagg and praying for rain.

But I didn't tell Katherine about Gideon.

I was sorely tempted but each time the urge struck I fought it into submission. I didn't want to do anything to jinx the magic of those days. I didn't want to think about him at all. It was as if uttering Gideon's name might cause him to appear, like some malevolent fairy tale witch or underworld demon. I wasn't taking any chances.

10

The Cochrane men weren't around as much except for the day of the funeral. Most of them were gone from dawn to dusk—or dusk to dawn in the case of Mom's Uncle Earl, who worked the night shift at one of the TB sanitariums outside of town. Everyone was clutching their jobs tight to them or trying to hunt one to ground.

The morning of the funeral, though, the men were all present and accounted for and wearing their Sunday best. They clustered together in little knots just like the women they dismissed as "gossips." Because they had things to talk about too. Advice to share and forebodings to confess and condolences to extend and memories to refashion into encouragements and admonitions and warnings. Plans gone sideways to dissect and ruminate over.

The day dawned gusty and gray. Everyone wondered whether the rain would hold off until the service was over. Far off to the west, Pikes Peak and her front range sisters huddled together like a second procession of mourners, shrouded in curtains of shadow and rain. No one carried on much at the service. Everyone took their lead from Aunt Ruth, who sat in stoic silence behind her black veil.

When we got back to Aunt Ruth's all the women congregated in the kitchen to prepare supper while the men happily exiled themselves to the front porch and side yard. They talked and smoked and drank bottles of beer and frowned at the stone-colored clouds churning by overhead. They strolled up and down the street in twos and threes like dukes and viceroys at a garden party.

The rain held off until nightfall, by which time supper was ready. No one had any money and yet we feasted that night. Everyone had plundered their stocks of preserves and pulled whatever they could out of gardens and root cellars and ovens. I ate like a starveling and basked in the feeling of being cocooned in the house's warm and raucous din. At one point a peal of thunder shook the lamps and plates and Mom said there's Uncle Leonard saying hello and everyone laughed.

It was the one night when the whole Cochrane clan was together so my older cousins were much in demand. Everyone wanted to know the details of the new lives upon which they were about to embark, and to wish them Godspeed. Finally left to our own devices, Katherine and I drifted in and out of the crowded rooms and up and down the dark street, speculating about what everyone's lives would look like in ten years. I joked that I would probably be a train-jumping hobo by then and Katherine became very serious and said that she couldn't bear to imagine me that way.

We had the street mostly to ourselves even though the rain had stopped. The wet flanks of the parked cars and trucks gleamed with the reflection of lonely porch lights and bright living rooms. Water dripped from the trees under which we passed and the eaves of the closely packed houses lining the street. I thought about how much joy such a rainfall would have brought back home. I wondered if Greenheart even got a drop.

At one point we saw the dark silhouette of a lean dog or coyote padding leisurely across the far end of the street. It trotted through a pool of moonlight before vanishing into pitch-black shadow. We waited for another glimpse but it never reappeared. I pictured the animal sitting on its haunches in the dark, watching us with unblinking eyes.

It felt like a night for spying. We crept through the shadows along the side of Aunt Ruth's garage and eavesdropped like children on two men out smoking on the back stoop. Both of them had hitched their stars to our family through marriage. Katherine and I grinned at each other as we huddled together in the dark, savoring the sensation of being accomplices in a mischievous but harmless lark. But our smiles faded as we listen to them inveigh about the economic and political forces working against them and the shortcomings of their wives and in-laws in voices. We watched them wreath their faces in cigarette smoke painted bone-white by the glare of the back porch light. After a while they stopped talking and just watched the fireflies blink their way across Aunt Ruth's small backyard.

Katherine put her hand on my forearm and we silently withdrew, moving through the night back to Aunt Ruth's front yard. We stood in the grass in the great square of light cast by her living room window and let it wash away the chill of our eavesdropping. From there we moved to the old but sturdy swing suspended from the ceiling at the far end of the front porch.

We rocked back and forth with our shoulders touching, leaning into one another so that we could hear each other over the babble of conversation and clattering dishes drifting out from Aunt Ruth's open parlor window. Our thighs touched as the swing took us into and out of the light and I'll never forget how that felt. Or the way her dark hair framed her face and spilled down around her shoulders. I remember how my heart thudded when I saw how she was looking at me on that porch swing. I wondered if she had ever kissed a boy before. I wasn't sure what I wanted the answer to be since I had never kissed a girl.

And then Fred poked his head out the open window and told us to come inside and help clean up.

* * *

Katherine and I spent the next hour in that crowded kitchen exchanging furtive smiles whenever we brushed past one another. The clean-up effort seemed endless. I rushed through each chore only to be handed another. But even that was all right because Katherine was dashing in and out of my sight all the while, her cheeks flushed with the knowledge of what we had been about to do on that porch swing.

And then the chores were done and Stephen called for one last game of Billy Whiskers. Katherine and I raced to the parlor with the rest of our cousins but Aunt Eunice stepped in and put a stop to that right quick, ignoring our protests. She told Katherine and Fred to get their coats and five minutes later they were out the front door, the rest of the cousins not far behind. Katherine turned and waved goodbye to us all on her way out, but her eyes were on me. I'm sorry, she mouthed. Or maybe I imagined it. And then she was out the door, her parents following after like a pair of hulking bodyguards.

11

We left Colorado Springs the morning after the funeral with the rising sun shining in our eyes. Most everyone who had come for Uncle Leonard's funeral had already left for home or work so not many people were around to say goodbye. I prayed for Aunt Eunice to pull up with Katherine in tow but my aunt was alone when she pulled up fifteen minutes before we were scheduled to leave. I overheard her tell Aunt Ruth that Katherine had been left behind because she had chores to catch up on and I felt a quick stab of hatred for Aunt Eunice in my heart. In that instant I didn't care that she lost her first husband in a barn fire and that her left arm was withered due to a childhood bout with polio and that she had treated me with gruff affection throughout our stay. My anger at Aunt Eunice guttered out as quickly as it had flared to life but my longing for her stepdaughter remained. Would I ever see Katherine again? Did I have to hope for another family funeral? Our star-crossed circumstances seemed monumentally unfair and tragic to me.

Mom got a little teary-eyed when we left. So did Aunt Ruth, a marked departure from her calm and collected demeanor the day of the funeral. Mom said it's different when you say goodbye to the living. She honked into her handkerchief for about five minutes at the end of Aunt Ruth's street and didn't say a word the first hour we were on the road. We were both feeling pretty blue.

We passed the diner outside Pueblo at which we had eaten less than a week before. The squat building looked half-abandoned in the glare of the morning sun, as if twenty years had passed since we had slipped into one of the booths inside. It was lunch hour but the lot was completely empty of cars. I watched the diner recede behind us, still not trusting myself to talk.

After a while Mom asked me if I wanted to drive for a spell and I said sure. She pulled over, we switched places, and I pulled the car back onto the road. It was a good day for driving, the sky empty and blue. I watched in the rearview mirror as the distant peaks of the front range receded and then vanished altogether. By the time we stopped to eat a late roadside lunch of leftovers the horizon line to the west had been sanded down to a straight line again.

Mom resumed driving duties after lunch and we forged on, rarely speaking. I flipped through my memories of the just-concluded week as if they were baseball cards, lingering especially over the ones that made my heart ache and my eyes blur. I considered the ones of Katherine with particular care, conjuring up absurd coincidences or feats of trickery that might somehow bring her back into my life again. I didn't know until that day how much it was possible to miss a girl.

Stranded vehicles dotted the shoulders of the roadway at regular intervals. Some had been picked clean days or weeks before, their rusted truck beds and sun-bleached interiors already filled with dirt. Others had only recently expired to judge by the welter of worldly possessions still roped to their backs. Clots of castaways sometimes milled around the latter, men and women and boys and girls, all terrified for their futures. We stopped a few times to give people water and food and encouragement but Dad had warned us to be careful about stopping and we were. The ones for whom we didn't stop—larger groups mostly—watched us pass with furious or vacant or beseeching eyes. I kept imagining that one of them was going to jump in front of our car and make us crash. I was glad for the .22, which we kept in the front seat with us.

Mom and I pushed onward, stopping only to refill the gas tank and take bathroom breaks. We polished off the last of Aunt Ruth's leftovers as we drove. Sunset gave way to a darkness that turned everything fifteen degrees colder in less than an hour and still we drove on. Dad had warned against traveling at night but Mom was anxious to get home. Jackrabbits darted in and out of the lights as we pressed on and it occurred to me that in all the times Gideon and I had driven around after dark I had never seen a rabbit in his headlights. Or any other animal for that matter.

I felt unready to return to my real life back in Greenheart, with all its worries and fears and suspicions and sadnesses. Memories I had been able to keep at bay in Colorado Springs came sidling back into my thoughts with each passing mile. Of my awful last encounter with Daniel and his father. Of Mom and Dad's sullen silences and Miss Wells's words of pity and Ed Wagner's petrified dogs and all the days and nights I'd spent whispering in Gideon's ear about our friends and neighbors. But the darkest riptides in those memories—the ones that pulled at me the strongest—swirled around Gideon and his enigmatic ways.

After another hour's travel we found ourselves riding down roadways freshly silted in dust, evidence of a recently passed duster. How long ago had the storm passed through? Would the roads get worse the further we drove? We had no way of knowing. The radio was a fog of crackling static wherever I turned the dial. We could have been driving on the moon.

Mom slowed down repeatedly to maneuver past serpentine dunes of dirt drifted over the road like brown snow. I found myself wishing we had stopped somewhere and just slept in the car. If we got stuck it would be a long time until anyone came by who could pull us out.

During our final approach to Greenheart—the last fifteen miles home took us more than two hours—a parade of nightmarish apparitions materialized in the watery light of our headlamps before disappearing again. Abandoned trucks and automobiles and tractors buried to their axles in flour-soft dunes of sparkling dust. The stiff-legged carcass of a gaunt cow, its open mouth half-filled with dirt. Lanterns floating unmoored deep in the night, twinkling like ships at sea. There were exhausted men and women and children shoveling and sweeping and hacking their lungs out under those lights.

That's when I turned to Mom and told her that I didn't want to work for Gideon anymore.

She didn't say anything for a minute. Then she asked me if I was sure about that and I said yes. She reached out and tousled my hair.

"I'm glad," she said. "I guess you know that. He's as crooked as a dog's leg, Will. He's not a rainmaker, he's a carnival barker. A snake oil salesman."

I looked out the window into the darkness. "I don't know what he is."

12

We were less than an hour from home when I finally fell asleep, slumped against the door under an old blanket, and fell into a strange and terrifying dream. I had the same unsettling nightmare five or six times over the next several weeks. It still returns on occasion, all these years later. And when it does I always wake up feeling the same way I did the first time: limp with relief at having clawed out of its witching-hour grip.

The nightmare always begins the same way, with me standing upon a vast and empty plain that looks untouched by human hands. Not even a rock cairn to point the way across the blighted land before me, let alone a road or path or signpost. It looks like a world where rain has never fallen. I look up into a fast-darkening sky, half-expecting to see Earth floating up in heaven where the moon should be. To the west an orange sun sits one finger high over the horizon, spilling molten light across armadas of fast-moving clouds. When the wind stills I can hear the steady inferno roar of that star echoing faintly across the cosmos. Nightfall is coming on fast and I don't want to be out there all alone. The need to find shelter feels essential. But I don't move because I'm waiting for someone in that trackless emptiness. Is it a friend? An enemy? I don't know but I am rooted to the spot until I find out.

I sense movement far off to the west, accompanied by a gust of hot wind that knocks me back a half step. I turn my face toward that fiery sun as it flares against the deepening dark, the wind ratcheting up another notch. My eyes stream with scalding tears, my squinting eyelids turning the sun into a horizontal blade of searing light, but I force myself to look because someone is emerging from that incandescent blast furnace of light. The figure looms larger as it approaches, the silhouette blocking out more and more of the dying sun as it coalesces into a striding black form. I am desperate to know who it is.

As the stranger closes the distance between us I see he is wearing an old diver's suit. It looks even older than the one worn by Grant Ballantine in those photographs from his Navy days. The diver's broad shoulders are armored in dust and his weighted diving belt sags with overflowing sand. It looks as if it spent the last century hanging in the back of a barn. Yet the diver's great brass and copper helmet shines eerily in the half-light, as if electrified from within.

And then the diver is standing before me, his chest heaving with exertion. His panting is loud in my ears. Long entrails of diving gear trail behind him, snarled in clots of dry seaweed and broken wheat stalks and rusted curls of barbed wire.

The diver's bellows-like breathing devolves into desperate gulps of labor and he throws his head back as if drowning. Something in the diver's movements strike a chord of memory and I realize that the man in the diving suit is someone I know. *Is it Grant Ballantine?* I ask myself. *Is it Dad? Is it Gideon?* My stomach knots into a kind of sick excitement at the latter thought. But it's impossible to tell. The darkness behind the face plate is absolute. Peering into that helmet feels like looking down into a pitch-black basement.

I jump forward and claw at the diver's helmet, frantically searching for a release so I can swing the big faceplate open, give him the air he so desperately needs, and reveal his identity once and for all. The diver's gargantuan head lolls and his chest convulses and his big arms hang loose and free at his sides, swaying uselessly like flanks of beef on hooks.

I can feel my fingertips mashing and bloodying on the hard edges of the faceplate. The metal bars protecting the helmet's windows are wrapped in old barbed wire, the blood-red tips quivering like wet rabbit ears. I peer into the faceplate for a hint of the diver's identity. A familiar curve of nose or jawline. But the moon came up when I wasn't looking and all I can see is its reflection in the glass. I keep telling the diver that it's going to be okay but I know he can hear the panic in my voice. I tell him I'm going to save him and though the pain makes me cry out and ribbons of blood race down my forearms I prod and pound and pry at the helmet's rusted and wire-snarled hinges with my ruined fingers until the plate finally opens somehow, as if it was on a timer all along.

Before I can glimpse inside, the diver pitches forward as if to rid himself of a bellyful of cold seawater. But it is topsoil and dust and bits of chaff from old Turkey Red that spills out of the open faceplate instead, a thick column that spills around my feet in a steady hiss. Black clouds of pulverized topsoil rise from the ground and glitter like fairy dust around our waists. And then finally the diver's violent bout of vomiting stops. He straightens to face me and the helmet's faceplate swings slowly open, giving me a long, deep look into the moonwashed emptiness within.

Mom said I woke up screaming just as we made the last turn for home.

13

The expression on Dad's face when we walked through the door was one of naked relief. He gave me a fierce hug as soon as I crossed over the threshold, then turned and gave Mom one that was softer but of considerably longer duration. She hugged him back with her eyes closed. Murmured *I missed you* in his ear. I felt a flicker of hope ignite in my heart as I watched them hug. Maybe returning to Greenheart wouldn't be all bad. Not if a week apart was what my parents needed to remember what was at stake—and resolve to make a fresh start.

It was well after midnight and the long drive home—especially its harrowing late stages—had worn us both down to the nub. But when Mom asked Dad about the duster that had passed through he warmed to the topic immediately and just kept talking. By the time he was done I wished he had waited until morning because what he told us kept me awake for another two hours.

The duster had blown through King County roughly thirty-six hours before our return. It rolled into Greenheart just as Stagg's funeral procession was setting out for the cemetery from our church, which had been packed to the gills. Dad said the weather was clear and calm when the service began. Blue skies as far as the eye could see. But by the time Rosbourne wrapped things up inside and everyone piled into their cars and trucks for the solemn three-mile procession to Greenheart's cemetery, the skies to the west had turned smudgy and black. And by the time the hearse carrying Stagg's body had taken its place at the front of the line and begun inching forward a banded smear of brown ink was stretched taut across the horizon. The duster came on like a slow-motion tidal wave. Everyone was trapped in their cars with no other recourse but to brace themselves.

The duster stampeded into the funeral procession two minutes later, plunging it into an otherworld of hissing darkness. Lamar Gunding ran the hearse off the road and into an empty field. Dad said Gunding had to sit there alone in the dark with Stagg's corpse for the better part of three hours before the duster finally subsided enough for him to escape and take refuge in another car. I thought about what those three hours must have been like for the funeral director. Listening to the storm moan and scratch at the windows as it ghosted past. Submerged in a darkness so complete you couldn't see the hand in front of your face, with a dead man as your only company.

Gunding left Stagg overnight in that hearse but no one blamed him. Most of the people who had turned out for Stagg's funeral couldn't stick around anyway. They had to get home and dig out and check on their livestock and otherwise see to their own affairs. No one with a working tractor was going to be available to pull Gunding's hearse out of the ditch that day, simple as that. And it wasn't like Stagg was going anywhere.

It took Dad and eight other men, two horses, and John Bentley's Farmall to pull the hearse out of the ditch the next morning. But the funeral car wouldn't start and every tow truck in King County was otherwise occupied so Dad and the other men grunted and groaned and heaved and swore in the rising sun until Stagg's enormous casket had finally been unearthed from its fetid, sunbaked hold. Dad and the other men pushed it onto the bed of a trailer hitched to the Farmall, then held the coffin in place on the trailer's warped, rattling floorboards as the tractor lurched its way to the gravesite. Bentley shut down his tractor and Dad and the others stepped forward to muscle the casket down into the patiently waiting hole. Only then was Reverend Rosbourne able to step forward and deliver his final graveside remarks.

And that's how Greenheart said goodbye to its Great Man.

"Was anyone hurt?" Mom asked. "Are Amos and Andy okay?"

"They're fine, mostly. Andy's a little off plumb, he's not eating again. He'll shake it off in a couple days, he always does. South of us caught the worst of it. Bert and Sally got hit pretty hard. Maybe you could go see her now that you're back. Bert says she talks to herself more than him these days. Cyrus Bellcomb lost half of what he had left of his herd, maybe more. He cut one of them open and he said the lungs looked like feedbags full of dirt."

"Anyone else?"

Dad sighed and shook his head. "The usual, mostly. Some people with breathing problems. Kids and old folks mostly. Someone had a heart attack; we don't know her. Richard Dereway broke his hip. Howard Traubeck caught him broadside with his truck. I swear to God, that man's a menace behind the wheel. The parking lot and road was blocked before I had time to blink. No one was going anywhere, cars were shorting out everywhere. Once it swallowed us up there was nothing to do but hunker down and take it. Thank God the two of you weren't with me like last time."

He was referencing a storm that hit Greenheart in late April 1933, back when the dusters still had a sinister novelty to them. The three of us were together that morning so we rode it out in the parking lot behind the feed store. I spent the entirety of that storm nestled between my parents in the front seat of our Model A, taking refuge in the reassuring firmness and warmth of their bodies close up against mine. I remembered how the abrading grit of the dust hissed over our Model A's metal skin like the legato drone of a thousand drum brushes. How the temperature in the cab's interior cooled as the duster blotted out the sun like a black cloth over a birdcage. How the storm made the car rock gently back and forth on its creaking axles as we sat there in the darkness.

Mom taught us to sing *Frère Jacques* to distract me and pass the time. Dad was grumbly about it at first but by the end he was singing just as loud as we were, even the parts in French. We sang that song for the longest time, varying the tempo, singing it as a tavern song and a lullaby and everything in between. It helped mask the sound of the duster hissing at the car windows.

After Dad filled us in about the debacle of Stagg's funeral he locked eyes with me. "I have a message for you from Gideon, Will. He wants you to go find him down at the Zephyr right away."

"Now?"

Dad rolled his eyes. "No, not now. It's the middle of the night, for God's sake. Tomorrow morning. After your morning chores."

"Yes sir." I could feel Mom looking at me. Wondering if I was going to tell Dad about my decision to quit then and there.

"You told Gideon you were going to be out of town, yeah?" Dad looked at me steadily. "I'm not sure how he's feeling about you being gone this last week, Will. He relies on you."

"It was my brother's funeral," Mom reminded him. "Leonard was his uncle."

"I know that," Dad snapped. "And that's what I told Gideon. I ran into him the day after you left and mentioned your trip to Colorado Springs for the funeral and he got this funny look on his face. He looked like a man hearing something for the first time."

"I left him a letter."

"A what? You left him a letter?"

"Yes sir. He wasn't at the hotel the last two times before we left for Aunt Ruth's. He never tells me when he's not going to be there."

"Does he pay you for those afternoons? Whether he's there or not?"

Dad already knew the answer to that question.

"Yes sir."

"Then you have nothing to complain about on that score."

"No sir. I went up to his room like usual and knocked on the door. I knocked a few times, Dad. I knocked hard. But Gideon never answered. I even tried the doorknob and it was locked. So I went down and left a note with Mr. Ellery at the front desk. He said he would make sure Gideon received it. I explained everything, Dad."

"You should have told me you left a note. Next time you ask him for time off, you ask to his face or you don't ask at all."

"Yes sir."

"When you see him you'd better be ready to make up for lost time. Gideon's a busy man these days. He reserved the theatre for a week from Saturday.

He has a whole program planned. It's all anyone wants to talk about. You should hear them down at the grange. It's going to be a full house."

"What kind of program?" I asked.

"How should I know? You work for him, not me. All he tells me is to hold on to my hat."

Mom started to say something but I cut her off. "I'll go down to see him right after breakfast, Dad."

"Glad to hear it."

14

I t was full dark outside my window when Dad rousted me out of bed early the next morning. One firm shove on my shoulder, a muttered "time to get up," and then his heavy footsteps echoing down the hall. When I came into the kitchen, though, it was Dad at the stove instead of Mom. It was a disorienting sight.

I took a seat at the table and Dad placed a bowl of oatmeal cut with corn syrup in front of me. He took a seat at the other side of the table with his own bowl and a cup of black coffee.

"Where's Mom?" I finally asked as I picked at the last of the oatmeal. Breakfast had chased the last vestiges of sleep from my mind and with wakefulness had come the dread of what awaited me later that morning. I didn't have any idea how I was going to tell Gideon I was quitting and Dad was going to hit the roof when he found out. I didn't have any illusions about that. But going behind his back was the only way I could cut myself free. If Dad caught wind of my intentions he would expressly forbid it. Which would shackle me to Gideon, outrage Mom, and light the fuse for an explosive renewal of marital hostilities.

"I let her sleep," he said. "Your Mom was pretty beat last night." Dad took a sip of his coffee. "She's not as young and spry as me, you know."

I smiled. Mom was a year older than Dad. He used to tease her about that. "Yes sir, I know."

"We've got some work to do on the coop when you get back, Will. Something got two of the chickens while you were gone. Coyote or fox."

"I thought they all lit out from these parts."

"Well, I guess one of them doesn't read the papers. Left tracks all around the coop, piles of feathers, and disappeared with two chickens. Lost them the night before the storm came through. I might borrow a couple traps from Howard."

Dad removed the napkin he had draped over his coffee cup and took a sip. He set the cup back down on the table, covered it again with the napkin, and sighed heavily.

"I think Gideon's pretty steamed at you, son."

"Yes sir," I said. "I told you I left a message—"

"Don't matter. What matters is that John Stagg is dead and gone and so is his money and every farm around here is drying up and blowing away including ours and Gideon Starling—your employer—is Greenheart's last chance. For rain like we used to see and wheat like we used to grow."

"Yes sir."

"OK. Off you go now. Get your chores taken care of and then you go see what Gideon wants. We can move some of your chores around if we need to. And never mind about the coop, I can take care of that myself. Make sure Gideon knows you're available any time for anything he needs. Make yourself useful."

"Yes sir." I walked out onto the front porch, lit the barn lantern, and crossed the yard, a bobbing ball of light in an ocean of pre-dawn black. I hung the lamp from its usual hook. Its hissing flame cast blocks of light and shadow across Amos and Andy's broad backs and up into the cobwebbed rafters and over the closed door behind which Grant and Daniel Ballantine had once slept. Miniature mounds of dirt marked where the planks met all along the foundation of the building's western wall.

I grunted and pushed and swore my way into the dark stalls to work my way around the horses. Their hulking forms wreathed me in rising clouds of steam as the usual barn smells of manure and urine and hay and feed washed over me. I fed what needed to be fed and pumped the water that needed to be pumped and swept and shoveled what needed to be swept and shoveled. I carried out my chores robotically, as though my body belonged to someone else. All I could think about was the man waiting for me down at the Zephyr Hotel when I was done.

Staying in Gideon's employ would be another betrayal of Mom, not to mention a betrayal of my own suddenly recoiling heart. But how could I ever face Dad again if I quit? He would be so disappointed in me. And furious. Would he ever forgive me? Ever? I didn't know how to tell him that if I ever hoped to be half the man I wanted to be—half the man *he* wanted me to be—I needed to cut ties with Gideon.

I was already in a lather from my chores by the time I found my bicycle under the barnacles of rope and harness it had acquired in my absence. I hauled the bike out of the barn's cobwebby shadows and into the light and looked it over for a moment, searching for some flaw in its construction or operation that would give me a plausible excuse to delay my visit to Gideon for another day. A busted chain, a flat tire, anything. But my bicycle was in perfect running order and I knew Dad was keeping tabs on me that morning so I headed into town on wobbly legs. I tried to calm myself but it was no use. My heart was a thudding drum by the time the Zephyr came into view.

I had lied to Dad about the note I left before we went to Colorado Springs. I *had* left one, I didn't lie about that part. But I hadn't gone up to Gideon's room beforehand to tell him I was going away. I never knocked on his door. I hadn't wanted to face him because then I would have had to pretend Wagner's dogs hadn't been petrified of him when we came calling. Or that I wasn't wracked with guilt over the secrets he'd pulled out of me as we crisscrossed the back roads of King County in his big black car. Or that the mountain flowers he had gifted to Mom hadn't withered into ashy husks after a single moonlit night on our kitchen table. Or that I hadn't seen how all the jacks in the killing pen turned their red eyes to Gideon when they heard his voice pierce the air.

"Hi Will," said Mr. Ellery. He was standing behind the front counter as usual. "My condolences, I was sorry to hear about your uncle. Condolences to your mother too."

"Thank you, sir. I'll tell her."

Mr. Ellery and I had become friendly with one another. I was dropping by the Zephyr a couple times a week and after a while we just got used to each other. We talked about baseball a lot. Turned out Mr. Ellery had been born and raised by his grandmother in Philadelphia so he still followed the Athletics. About once a week he told me he would never get used to seeing Jimmie Fox in a Red Sox uniform. He liked the Cardinals too, though, which was good because that was my team. His favorite player was Pepper Martin, mine was Dizzy Dean. We both hated the Giants.

"Hi, Mr. Ellery." I tried to keep my voice casual but the first thing I'd noticed when I walked into the lobby were the three suitcases sitting next to the front desk. Mr. Ellery was watching them like a hawk. I recognized them as Gideon's.

Could it be? Was Gideon moving on? I was giddy at the possibility that the decision to quit was being taken out of my hands—and with precisely the resolution I wanted. If Gideon was pulling up stakes I couldn't very well go with him. Maybe there was a God after all.

"Is Gideon leaving?"

Mr. Ellery scratched his head, his nails adding to the dusting of dandruff on the shoulders of his frayed black vest. "Leaving Greenheart?" he scoffed. "Not with his big show coming up, he's not. You heard about that, right?"

"Yes sir. Everyone's talking about it."

"Mr. Starling isn't leaving town but he *is* ending his stay with us here at the Zephyr. He just checked out. He went down to the garage to get his car. Boy that thing's a beauty, isn't it? I don't know how he keeps it looking so shiny and new all the time."

"I don't either."

"We're going to miss Mr. Starling around here, Will. He's had the entire second floor since he got here."

"Yes sir. I know."

"And now with Mr. Stagg gone, may he rest in peace, no one knows what's going to happen. Will any one from his family even want it? Whoever gets it, I hope they don't give up on the old girl. She just needs a little attention." He looked past me to take in the lobby and his face assumed a doleful aspect.

What was he talking about? The Zephyr was beautiful. I turned to follow his gaze and felt my face drain of blood at what I beheld. I couldn't make sense of it.

I had met Gideon in the lobby of the Zephyr dozens of times by then. And each time I relished that moment when I crossed the threshold and left the dusty red-rimmed world outside for the cool and verdant glade of the Zephyr Hotel lobby.

But the lobby wasn't a glade anymore. That morning the place looked as if it had aged a half-century overnight. How had I never before noticed the patches of threadbare carpeting? Or the sorry state of the uncomfortable highbacked chairs scattered around the room? How had I never seen that the wallpaper was peeling and the arms of the couches were pocked with cigarette burns?

I felt Gideon's presence behind me an instant before he spoke.

"Well as I live and breathe," intoned that familiar silky voice. "The prodigal son has returned."

I shoved my suddenly trembling hands deep in my pockets as I turned to face Gideon, who looked sleek and tall and confident standing there in his oxblood coat, unbothered by the rising morning heat. His slicked-back hair still gave off a wet sheen, and his grin was as wide and toothy as ever. The lapel pin he was sporting was new, though. It was identical to all the other pins in dimension, with the same filigree of silver and the same ivory face, but this one depicted a pyramid of small interlocking bones in the center of an ornate platter.

"Hi Gideon," I croaked. My throat felt as sun-bleached and gritty as the carpet on which we stood.

"Hello, Will. Your father told me you were called away suddenly."

"My Uncle Leonard died."

"My deepest condolences," Gideon said. "Your mother's older brother if I'm not mistaken?"

"Yes sir."

"Sir?" Gideon echoed, then smiled and wagged his finger at me in a tut-tut motion. "That's not how friends address each other, is it? You haven't called me that since the day I hired you."

"Sorry, Gideon."

He chuckled and looked me up and down, making a show of taking stock. "Gone a week and I swear you've gotten taller, Will. Your mother needs to take you shopping for some new clothes! Must be all that healthy mountain air. Rejuvenating! Is that your secret?"

"I don't know, si—Gideon."

"Or maybe something else has you bursting at the seams of your trousers." He winked and leaned in conspiratorially. "Did you get in her bloomers, Will? Tell me you did." He made a show of bringing his long fingers up to his nose and inhaling deeply. "There's no other scent like it in the world, son."

I took an involuntary step backward, frightened and revolted in equal measure. Gideon could draw blood with his tongue—I had seen him employ it against my own mother—but he always kept it sheathed with me. Not even after long days of gladhanding folks in their yards and barns and fields and parlors. Even when I could tell he was dog-tired. He always rallied for the long drive back to our house, filling the air with song and story. The only time he had ever displayed irritation or anger with me was the night I clammed up about Miss Wells—and even then he dropped the subject five minutes later and never brought her up again.

But today was a different day.

"Did your uncle die suddenly? Or did your mother only belatedly hear of the burial plans?" Gideon asked, his eyes widening in what I recognized as a mockery of confusion. He turned to Mr. Ellery, who clearly wanted to be somewhere else. "I only inquire because young Will's sudden departure was such a mystery to me. Initially, I mean. Before Will's father explained everything."

Gideon turned his attention back to me, eyes unblinking. "You and your lovely mother must have lit out like cats with their tails on fire when you heard the news about poor Uncle Leonard. No time to call, no time to come down and let me know you needed some time off—which I would have happily granted, given the circumstances. Although I guess you did find the time to scratch out a note and leave it here at the front desk with our friend Mr. Ellery here, didn't you?"

"Gideon—"

"No need to explain, Will. I understand the need to prioritize. You never know what old Uncle Leonard might have left for you and your fishwife mother after all. Smart to get out there lickety-split, just in case the vultures are already circling. I've heard tell of some families out in these parts, they'll grab the dearly departed by his ankles, haul him right out of his coffin and turn him upside down, just to make sure they're not burying him with any loose change. Do you belong to one of those families, Will? Did Uncle Leonard drop any quarters on the floor for you?"

Gideon looked at me expectantly, his eyes capering with glee. His gaze hollowed me out like a rusty post auger, twisting down deeper and deeper.

He knew everything. Everything I'd done in Colorado Springs. Every trail we hiked, every meal we ate, every song that came wafting out of Aunt Ruth's radio. He knew how much I wanted to kiss Katherine on the porch swing. He knew I didn't come up to his room at the Zephyr before I left town. He knew I didn't want to work for him anymore. He knew that I had come to dimly understand, whether through primordial instinct or some high angel's whisper of warning, that Gideon was different somehow. Different than the rest of us in some way I didn't yet understand.

I was the only one who saw behind the amiable mask that Gideon presented to the world. I was the only one who knew it *was* a mask. No, not the only one. Mom had known. She had sensed his amoral essence. A whisper of warning issuing from somewhere deep in her bones. We didn't listen when she told us he was the crow in the corn. The scorpion curled deep inside the boot, venom-beaded tail trembling with the desire to strike. Gideon's charm offensive hadn't worked on her and he hated her for it.

Just like he hated me now.

"I can't work for you anymore," I said. As soon as I said the words a sort of strange exultation came over me. My heart pounded as if I had thrown myself off a high bridge into a pitch-black canyon. I didn't know whether I was cannonballing toward the sanctuary waters of an unseen river or a boulder field that would burst me open like a melon but in that moment I didn't care because at least I was flying. At least I wasn't still up on the bridge with him.

"Is that right?" said Gideon.

"I'm—that's right. I'm sorry but I'm done working for you, Gideon." Mr. Ellery melted away from my peripheral vision and a moment later I heard the office door behind the front desk quietly close. It was just the two of us now.

"You can't quit," Gideon said flatly. "Don't be absurd. You're done when I say you're done."

I didn't know how to respond to that. In all of the scenarios of this moment I had played out in my head I never figured on one in which Gideon refused to accept my resignation. Could he do that? What did you even do in that case? A flutter of panic passed through me when I realized I had no idea.

"You're bringing coal to Newcastle, son. You can't quit when you've already been fired. And replaced." Gideon smiled unpleasantly and raised his voice. "Daniel, come in here, will you? An old friend of yours has dropped by to say hello."

Daniel walked in a few seconds later. He stopped short when he saw me and I watched his features harden into an expressionless mask. Daniel walked to Gideon's side and we stared at each other in silence.

"Life can be so serendipitous at times," Gideon said expansively, his eyes merry and bright. "Will, you'll be relieved to hear that your old pal Daniel here has ably filled the post you abandoned. When Grant Ballantine heard what I was offering his boy to stick around and work for me he decided to go back north without him. *Again.* And so here he is. With me. Little Orphan Danny."

Daniel remained blank-faced, refusing to rise to the bait of Gideon's mockery, but I knew it must have crushed him to wait week after week for his father's return, only to get left behind again. Were the dive wages for that dam really *that* good?

"Young Daniel here was slow to see the wisdom of the arrangement but fortunately his father was a sensible man. I was happy to take Daniel under my wing. Provide some much-needed direction to his life. He's become the son I never had. May I be blunt? I've found Daniel to be a much harder worker than you ever were, Will. Although I will admit he doesn't know the secrets you do. Of if he does he's not telling them. He's not the *sharer* that you were."

Gideon pondered the two of us for a moment, his expression gradually slipping from expectancy to boredom. He rolled his eyes and clapped his hands dismissively. "Well as delightful as this reunion has been, we have several important appointments this afternoon so we really must be off." He turned to Daniel. "Make yourself useful. Get the suitcases stowed in the boot."

Daniel lurched over to the three suitcases at the base of the counter as Gideon gave a final sardonic tip of his hat to me and walked outside. They were too big and heavy to take in one trip but Daniel tried anyway. He was in a hurry to get away from me.

I watched him struggle with the luggage, cursing under his breath. Without thinking I found myself stepping forward to pick up one of the suitcases.

He straightened and locked eyes with me. He opened his mouth as if he wanted to say something but the horn from Gideon's car blared outside. Three insistent, sustained honks. Gideon didn't like being kept waiting.

Daniel knew it. Whatever he might have been about to say died on his lips. Daniel turned without a word and lugged the other two suitcases outside to Gideon's idling car. As I followed him to the curb with the last suitcase I watched Gideon's silhouette in the driver's seat, his right hand casually draped over the steering wheel.

Daniel put the suitcases he was carrying inside the car's open trunk, placing them next to two rectangular wood crates. I recognized them as old ammunition boxes from the war but each one was outfitted with a new-looking padlock. Daniel stood aside, one hand on the trunk lid, as I placed the third suitcase inside. I wracked my brain for something to say but Daniel didn't give me a chance. He slammed the trunk as soon as I was clear and brushed past me without a word to join Gideon inside the car.

I watched Gideon ease the roadster into the street at a stately pace and drive away. I told myself I should be relieved at how it had all turned out. Watching them go, though, I felt more like someone who had booked passage on a grand and glittering ocean liner, only to be left stranded at the dock after losing his ticket to the wind.

15

Watching Miss Wells sing was my favorite part of church. She sang in the choir, third from the left in the front row. My parents were partial to the left side of the sanctuary, about two thirds of the way down. I was partial to that vantage point as well because it gave me an unobstructed view of Miss Wells in her choir loft perch, an ash blonde buoy bobbing in a sea of black robes.

And when the choir stood up to sing? Well, that brought a smile to everyone's face because we had a pretty good choir. Mrs. Brennan saw to that. She was the organist and pianist and she pretty much ran the show. The nominal director, Mrs. Croft, got more confused and forgetful every year but no one had the heart to ask her to step aside. So the choir operated with Mrs. Brennan as a form of shadow government, organizing and leading practices from behind her keyboards. Reverend Rosbourne played along with the charade and Mrs. Croft got to keep singing with all of her friends. It was a lovely arrangement, all in all.

Even among the members of our talented choir, though, Miss Wells stood out. Not for her singing voice, which was merely pleasant, but for the clear joy she took in the act of singing. Some people just love to sing and Miss Wells was one of them.

When Mom and Dad and I walked into church for Sunday services the morning after Gideon and I parted ways, I realized my feverish infatuation with Miss Wells had finally broken. A week in Katherine's company had seen to that. I wondered what I would feel when I saw Miss Wells file into the sanctuary with the rest of the choir. Would I still think she was pretty? Would I feel any of the longing that had been such a miserable, exciting torment to me through the past school year? I kind of hoped so. A twinge would be a nice keepsake.

But when the choir marched in and filled the loft at the front of the sanctuary Miss Wells was barely recognizable. She looked haggard and pale and her eyes were rimmed in red, as if she had just been crying. The women on either side of her exchanged glances of concern and one of them leaned in close to whisper in Miss Wells's ear. She shook her head firmly and made a visible effort to compose herself. A moment later she was gazing expressionlessly out over the heads of the assembled congregation. Whatever was troubling her, she intended to lock it away for the duration of the service.

People trickled into the pews around us, mouthing greetings to their neighbors as they scootched past, not even trying to be heard above Mrs. Brennan's stentorian organ prelude. The church was nearly full that day, which struck me right away as odd. It could have been Christmas Eve 1928 the way people were pouring in. That's when I felt it for the first time: an odd ripple of suppressed excitement moving through the fast-assembling congregation. I looked around me, the hair on my arms suddenly prickly with gooseflesh, as I studied the people in the surrounding pews. But I didn't see or hear anything untoward in the rows around us and after a time I gave up and settled back into my seat. Whatever had tickled my amygdala had disappeared like a gleaming shark fin in a moonlight-frosted sea.

Mrs. Brennan's last notes faded away and Reverend Rosbourne rose from his seat and stepped to the pulpit. He had just opened his mouth to speak when the back doors to the church clattered open, the noise echoing through the worship hall, followed by the sound of scuffing footsteps in the narthex. An excited ripple of murmuring washed over us from the back rows. I knew in that instant, well before Mom turned in her seat and stiffened, that Gideon Starling was making good on his promise to come to church. Rosbourne stood stone-faced as the congregation's hushed exclamations and whispered greetings to Gideon washed up to the chancel and swirled around the reverend's feet. I heard Gideon slide into a pew several rows behind us, everyone eagerly jostling and sliding down to make room.

Rosbourne waited what felt like a very long time after things had quieted down before he spoke. But when he issued the formal call to worship his voice was clear and strong, and from there the service settled into its usual rites and rhythms of understated pageantry, familiar and reassuring. I watched dust motes tumble through the vaporous columns of light pouring through the sanctuary's lancet windows as Rosbourne read off the weekly announcements. I rose to sing hymns with everyone else. I said my prayers and listened to the choir sing with everyone else. None of it settled me. I felt sure that Gideon was staring at the back of my neck the entire time. Pondering various and sundry options for breaking it.

I never really believed that Gideon would make good on his half-promise to come to church. I thought he was putting me on or being polite. But I had been wrong about that, as I had been about so many other things concerning Gideon. He had breached a fortress that I had always seen as an impregnable place of refuge. Gideon's presence both frightened me and left me feeling strangely piqued, as if he had violated some unspoken rule of engagement to which we had agreed.

The presence of my parents on either side of me added to my anxiety. On my left, Mom was following every step of the service with rigid attentiveness. She had a tight grip on the Bible in her lap, as if it were some wild thing that might otherwise wriggle free and disappear under the pews. Gideon's presence had her out of sorts too.

To my right sat my expressionless father, his big calloused hands resting atop the Bible in his own lap. He had not spoken to me since I returned home from the Zephyr and told him that Daniel had taken my job. He just glared at me from his workbench when I gave him the news, then shouldered past me and out of the barn without saying a word.

The church service didn't start to fall apart until Rosbourne gave the scripture readings—and let everyone know where he stood on the subject of Gideon Starling.

"The Old Testament reading this morning is from the book of Jeremiah, chapter fourteen verse fourteen," he said.

Then the Lord said unto me, 'The prophets prophesy lies in my name:
I sent them not, neither have I commanded them, neither spake unto them:
they prophesy unto you a false vision and divination, and a thing of nought,
and the deceit of their heart.'

Rosbourne raised his head from the page and looked out over his congregation, his unblinking gaze moving across our faces like a searchlight. A silence descended over the sanctuary, interrupted only by the usual subdued coughs from sandpapered lungs.

"The New Testament reading this morning is from Paul's Letter to the Ephesians. Chapter four, verses fourteen and fifteen."

That we henceforth *be no more children, tossed to and fro,*
and carried about with every wind of doctrine,
by the sleight of men, and cunning craftiness,
whereby they lie in wait to deceive;
But speaking the truth in love,
may grow up into him in all things,
which is the head, even *Christ*

Rosbourne shut the Bible and stared out into the pews, where a good amount of uneasy seat-shifting and coughing was taking place. "The grass withers and the flower fades," he pronounced. "But the word of God abides forever."

Rosbourne followed up the scripture readings with a sermon that was something of a stemwinder, at least for him. He stumbled out of the gate at first, following faint foot trails of sermonizing that petered out in brambles and vines. It looked to me like he had scrapped whatever sermon he had prepared and was flying by the seat of his pants.

He found his footing quickly, though. His voice gathered strength until it filled the worship hall. It was like listening to a train gather speed as it pulled out of the station and headed for the open plain. He reminded us of

Delilah's betrayal of Samson and Jacob's long ledger of deceit. He spoke of trickery and idolatry and greed, and of the plagues of grifters and confidence men and carnival barkers and bank robbers stalking our Depression-addled nation. He told us that the garments worn by such men were threaded with strands of fool's gold. Gideon's name was never mentioned but Rosbourne wasn't being subtle. Everyone knew who he was talking about.

Rosbourne didn't go off his rocker or anything like that. He was a shepherd, not a showman. But that morning Rosbourne was an angry shepherd. And when our dust-bleared congregation, already discombobulated by Gideon's entrance that morning, heard the iron in his voice? The whole place rocked back on its heels and hunkered down for the spiritual tongue-lashing that some had dreaded—and that folks such as Mom had surely yearned for.

She sat unmoving beside me throughout Rosbourne's sermon but I could feel the satisfaction and relief radiating off her. Satisfaction at having her own views of Gideon affirmed—and by the highly regarded pastor of the biggest church in town no less. And relief that Rosbourne was warning everyone to wake up before Gideon sank his claws any deeper into us. But if Rosbourne's words were a balm to Mom's troubled mind they had no apparent effect on Dad. He sat placidly throughout, hands folded neatly atop his Bible. It was like watching rain bounce off granite.

When Rosbourne brought his sermon to a close he cleared his throat and asked the congregation to stand and turn to page 171 of their hymnals. Mrs. Brennan played the hymn's introductory notes with her long, knobby fingers and the familiar ¾ time melody of "I'll Not Be Afraid" filled the air. The choir gathered itself and rose in response to her cue and a moment later the sanctuary filled with song, a shock to the system after Rosbourne's extended scolding. I felt it again, a prickle on my arms and the back of my neck. Something unseen was in the worship hall with us. Brushing its cold scales around our ankles in the dark beneath the pews. It wasn't God.

I'll not be afraid
  For the terror by night,

Nor the arrow that flieth by day

We weren't more than two stanzas into the first verse when I heard the first audible disruption in the flow of the song. It was Gideon. His voice rose above the congregation's traditional rendition of the hymn, reaching our ears at a different register somehow. He was singing the same lyrics as the rest of us, but in a melody that was jarringly at odds with Mrs. Brennan's stately piano accompaniment. Gideon's version was faster and punchier.

For the Lord whom I serve
  Is my shield and my light;
  He will guide and protect all the way.

Gideon had a singing voice like his laugh, rich and warm and inviting, a hearth fire over which you wanted to warm your hands. He sang the words of the hymn in perfect cadence with the mysterious score looping inside his head, swinging his voice like a wrecking ball through the song of praise the rest of us were singing. He was making an ass of himself, brawling through the song like he was.

I will trust Him alway
  Both by night and by day;
  He'll be with me forever, I know

Gideon's act struck me as a shocking act of self-sabotage. How would embarrassing himself in front of a packed church help his cause, whatever that mysterious cause might be? It didn't make any sense to me.

Until I heard other voices, pockets of dissonance, take up Gideon's strange canticle. Most of them were men with loud, blaring voices but not all of them. Dad, for instance. He didn't like to sing, and his voice that Sunday was as toneless as ever. But Mom and I both heard him veer away from our song and fall in behind Gideon's galloping version. He left us without a word in the middle of the hymn, like a man catching a ride on a passing trolley car.

He didn't even wave goodbye.

Gideon's voice grew louder and more insistent with the swell of accompaniment, eliciting a shudder of confusion and uneasiness through the rest of the congregation. Other voices peeled off and joined Gideon's strange, discordant melody and for the first time ever I heard Mrs. Brennan's piano falter and fall silent.

I'll not be afraid,
  Tho' the stormy winds blow,
  And the billows sweep over my soul

Rosbourne sang the original melody of the hymn as loudly as I'd ever heard him. He turned to the choir, exhorting them to raise their voices with his. But Gideon had agents in the choir loft too, and the choir broke into warring factions just as the congregation was doing. I looked for Miss Wells and found her, still singing to the original melody. Whenever she looked up from her hymnal she looked scared by what she was seeing out in the pews behind us. Mom and I exchanged a look and raised our voices, pledging our allegiance to the hymn's original, true melody. We sang as loud and as hard as we could. Dad's face darkened when he heard us and his own voice rose in retaliation.

The two factions bayed at each other until the clamor filled the church. Stray notes from Mrs. Brennan's piano tried to find footing in the original melody but were swept away again and again in the ugly din.

I'll not be afraid of the scorns of the world,
  Nor to tell of God's wonderful love;
  When from Satan's vile host fiery darts shall be hurled,
  I'll be strengthened with grace from above.

At the beginning of the third stanza Mrs. Brennan's piano fell in behind Gideon's version. Her notes provided vital support to his soaring voice, still somehow sharp and crystalline above the cacophony. It had been bad enough when Mrs. Brennan's piano fell silent. But when I heard those first flat, plinking notes come out again—only this time in fealty to Gideon's weird chanting gallop—a spasm of panic ran through me.

The number of people singing with us seemed to lessen with each line of hymn, and though the volume of Gideon's mob choir did not swell with many newly minted converts, his acolytes sang with growing confidence. Some of them began stomping their feet between the pews in time with the corrupted hymn, eyes twinkling then going dark as their bobbing heads passed in and out of the light pouring down through the sanctuary's leaded-glass windows.

I'll not be afraid when the grave I shall see,
Just beyond its dark shadow is rest;
And the welcome of angels is waiting for me,
When I enter those realms of the blest.

By the end only a few dozen of us were singing the hymn as its composer had scored it to be sung. Our voices were drowned out by the cresting roar of Gideon's tribe of congregants. His briskly paced perversion of the hymn took on a sprightly air in the last stanza, jumping into a reel-like gallop that filled the sanctuary.

I finally mustered the courage to look behind me. Gideon stood at the center of a pew five rows back. People were crowded all around him. Their mouths opened and closed like beached fish as they sang. He grinned at me from behind the upside-down hymnal he held in his big callused hands. Gideon was not done with me yet. Not nearly.

To Gideon's right stood Daniel, his own hymn book forgotten in his hands. I watched my former friend surveil the men and women in the pews around them with hooded eyes. He looked for all the world like Gideon's bodyguard. An image—I feared it was a vision—flashed across my mind of the two of them together in thirty years' time, dressed to the nines and out on the town, just as Daniel had always dreamed of doing with his father. I imagined them turning heads on every block, Daniel all grown up and angry-eyed and Gideon somehow looking just the same. Restless and on the prowl, sizing up everyone they met. Mobsters looking for a score.

I guessed Daniel was probably spending even more time with Gideon than I did. School was out, his dad was doing dive work on a dam that might as well have been on the moon, and he was living alone above a pool hall that felt more like a jail block. I would have hitched my star to Gideon too if I was him, no two ways about it. One big roll of the dice and live or die with the results. What did he have to lose?

When Gideon guided his version of the hymn to its braying end, most everyone who had joined in his profane rendition grinned and laughed, eyes shining with exhilaration. They looked at one another as if they had breathed new flesh onto the old bones of that hymn, just as Gideon was promising to breathe new life into Greenheart's played out dreams. A handful, though, just looked queasy about the whole affair. Unmanned by the wrenching tectonic shifts in their understanding of themselves that the hymn had laid bare.

Those of us still singing along to the original melody finished a full ten seconds behind Gideon and his crowd. There weren't many of us left by that point. Just a couple dozen tremulous voices rising from the pews and the choir loft into the stifling air. We sounded like birds trapped in the rafters, wings fluttering with fear.

All except for Rosbourne, whose voice never faltered, even after it was clear we had lost.

I'll not be afraid when the grave I shall see—
  Just beyond its dark shadow is rest;
  And the welcome of angels is waiting for me,
  When I enter those realms of the blest.

I don't know how Rosbourne found the strength to finish the service that Sunday morning. I don't know how he was able to raise his hand over our bowed heads and impart that farewell blessing meant to tide us over until the next time we gathered in good fellowship to praise God. Those words must have tasted like ash on his tongue. I opened my eyes and watched him intone the final lines. He looked gutted.

Something broke in our church that day. Maybe it was Rosbourne's heart.

16

Less than twenty-four hours after Gideon's awful visit to our church word got out about where he'd taken his bags after checking out of the Zephyr: John Stagg's mansion. The news that Gideon had somehow ensconced himself in Stagg's house less than two weeks after the Great Man's disastrous funeral march struck me as further confirmation, as if I needed any, that some mysterious but crucial inflection point had been reached in Gideon's sinister courtship of our town.

My parents certainly seemed to think so. The mere mention of Gideon was enough to set them both on edge. They watched each other warily across the yawning abyss between them, practicing avoidance except when the daily necessities and ceremonies of family forced them together. When we said grace before meals the words were recited by rote, the food consumed in virtual silence. On the rare occasions when Dad and Mom spoke to one another their brittle exchanges had all the warmth of penny-pinching telegrams. They never stayed up talking at the kitchen table anymore. The only thing I heard in the house most nights was the radio, which was suddenly on all the time. I imagined my parents lying in the bed they still shared after the radio was turned off. The unmoving wall of dead air between them as the night ticked by. They were no longer a balm in each other's lives but a grievance.

The end of each day gave me little relief from my troubled thoughts. The nightmare of the diver descended on me night after night, strange and foreboding like a dust-breathing ghost of Christmas Future. The diver came as a premonition, an emissary of grim tidings. Every one of his visitations left me filled with a nebulous but paralyzing certainty of doom. I spent hours staring up into the inky darkness of my bedroom ceiling, sluicing the nightmare's contents for anything that might glint of gold in the cold light of morning. The tiniest clue or insight in its twisted entrails. But every time I ransacked the nightmare for meaning I came up empty.

Gideon's triumphant vandalism of our church service, meanwhile, was the talk of the town. Awful memories from that morning rose up and jeered at me with every snippet of overheard conversation. The malevolent twinkle in Gideon's eye when he broke Rosbourne's shepherd's crook over his knee. The way my own father sang along with Gideon's blasphemous burlesque of a hymn. The grief-stricken expressions of Rosbourne and Miss Wells. Mom's tear-filled eyes when it was clear we had lost. The memory from church that sank its teeth deepest into me, though, was of Daniel standing sentinel by Gideon's side. Glaring like a Doberman, shoulders tensed, ready to throw himself at anyone who posed a threat to his owner and master.

Gideon was a great serpent coiled around Greenheart, constricting his muscled flanks so slowly that the town hadn't even noticed it was short of breath. I imagined what Greenheart would look like after Gideon was done squeezing. The town's sightless eyes rolled back in its head. Broken bones jutting out of its sun-bleached hide like grotesque flagpoles.

No one seemed to know exactly how Gideon had wormed his way into Stagg's empty mansion. When Mom first heard the news from one of her church friends she asked Dad how Gideon had pulled it off but he was tight-lipped about it. I couldn't tell whether it was because he didn't know or because he didn't want to tell us.

Mom didn't let it go. She said she didn't care what Gideon was paying in rent to stay at Stagg's place. No one had any idea whether Gideon was rich or not, but the suits he wore and the car he drove and the bills he ran up at the hotel suggested he could manage the cost. It was the *legality* of his occupancy that Mom kept chewing over. She said that settling an estate of Stagg's size would take months. His surviving family was all back east in Pennsylvania. So how could Gideon move in? Who gave him permission?

Who had the legal authority to broker or approve such an arrangement?

Dad batted all her questions away in a condescending tone that Mom found infuriating, which was why he used it. He just kept telling her the arrangement was temporary, as if that was the point. And a done deal so there was no use crying about it. Gideon lived in Stagg's house now and that was that and everyone might as well get on board with that, Mom most definitely included. The county sheriff sure wasn't going to try to drag Gideon out of there, not if he wanted to get re-elected. Dad told Mom she was the only one in Greenheart who even cared that Gideon had moved into Stagg's house and that pretty much seemed to be true.

Oh the rumors ran wild that week. Word spread that prior to his arrival in Greenheart, Gideon had rescued several towns gasping their last across South Dakota and Nebraska. Towns that sounded a lot like Greenheart from a distance. Towns that had revived like hardy desert flowers with the replenishing rains Gideon delivered. Farms that had seen their cisterns once again fill with rainwater and their fields once again fill with rustling seas of wheat and corn.

People said that when the phone lines got fixed from the last duster Mayor Sipe was going to call a bunch of folks to verify Gideon's bold claims. He also gave an interview to the local paper thanking everyone for their patience about the unexpected delays in getting the power back on and the telephones working. Apparently no one could figure out what the problem was, they were blaming it all on faulty equipment.

Dad boasted that Gideon's upcoming program would feature testimonials from several residents of those revitalized, financially blossoming towns on the northern plains. Grateful people eager to tell us about their experiences with Gideon—and to congratulate us on our impending deliverance from oblivion, so long as we were brave enough to reach for it.

Mom only got a rise out of Dad one time, when she asked him if Gideon planned to saw a lady in half at his show. Dad glared at Mom with a look of utter loathing and his right hand briefly closed into a fist before loosening again. I understood in that instant that he wanted to hit her. Mom saw it too. Her eyes widened and she went pale and a second later Dad pushed himself away from the table and stalked out the door, cursing under his breath. He stayed out in the garage until well after midnight. When he finally came in for the night he made a lot of noise, as if he didn't care in the least whether he woke us up.

It took me a long time to fall back asleep that night. But my last hours of slumber were undisturbed, and the next time I opened my eyes the eastern horizon was aglow with the approaching dawn.

The day of Gideon's big show was finally here.

17

I was taking bed sheets off the line later that morning when Daniel showed up at our house. I saw him out by the road in front, hoisting his dad's big steamer trunk out of the back of an idling pickup. I watched the driver get out and help Daniel carry the trunk over to our side of the road. Daniel gave the man a wave as he drove off, then dragged the heavy trunk down our dirt driveway in the direction of the porch. The corners of the trunk dug gouges into the hardpan as he pulled. Mom came out of the house and I watched the two of them talk for a minute before she helped him carry the steamer inside the house.

I didn't know what was going on but I didn't like what I was seeing. Daniel didn't belong at our house anymore and neither did his dad's shitty old steamer trunk.

Daniel reappeared on the porch and trained his gaze on me for a long moment, then trotted down the steps in my direction. His trousers and shirt were plain but clean and new. They fit his body. He had a canvas knapsack slung over his left shoulder, its bottom sagging with the weight of whatever he was carrying around inside. I busied myself folding another bed sheet as he approached. I didn't want to talk to him and didn't want to hear anything he had to say. He was with Gideon now.

"Hi Will."

I pulled another sheet off the line, pointedly ignoring him.

"Hi Will," he said again, but this time in a smirking drawl. He seemed more amused than chastened by my silent treatment.

"What do you want?" I snarled, turning on him. I was too mad at him to ignore him for long anyway. "What are you doing here?"

"Well I'm doing pretty good, thanks for asking. How about yourself?"

"I asked you a question."

"Touchy. I needed someplace to store Dad's steamer. Just for a couple weeks. Probably."

"Why didn't he take it with him this time?"

"He says he doesn't have a safe place for it."

"So he left it in your lap—again—and you thought it would be a good idea to bring it here."

"I didn't have a lot of options."

"Why not ask your new best friend to hold on to it for you? Plenty of room over at Stagg's place."

He rolled his eyes. "Listen—"

"Don't tell me to listen," I hissed and realized, appallingly, that I was on the verge of tears.

"Will, I know Gideon's pretty slick. I trust him about as far as I can throw him. And I know that you two have had your differences—"

"Yet there you are, standing by his side."

"It's not like that. Give me a chance—"

"Save your breath. I don't want to hear your excuses, Benedict Arnold."

Daniel's eyes widened in surprise, then hardened into a cold stare. I felt an odd shiver of uncertainty run through me. He wasn't acting how I expected. He wasn't acting guilty or ashamed of himself. At all.

"You're damned right I wanted to get back at you," Daniel said, biting off each word. His lip curled. "And Gideon offered good money. Ha, you know that better than anyone, right? Enough money for three squares a day for the first time since your Dad threw us out on the street. Enough to buy food I actually like. Enough to buy shoes that fit. Maybe you haven't noticed but I'm pretty much fending for myself at the moment."

"Cry me a river." I took savage pleasure in the hurt look that flashed across Daniel's face. "Gideon hates me now. He wants to hurt me, I can tell. He *plans* to hurt me. And yet there you are, standing by his side like Judas in the flesh. Nice shirt, by the way. You buy that with your thirty pieces of silver?"

Daniel's expression went blank in a dangerous way and for a second I thought he was going to slug me. "You think I should just keep wearing hand-me-downs with holes in them?" His kept his tone even but it trembled with leashed anger. "*Your* hand-me-downs? Like I don't deserve better? You think I should go to bed every night with an empty belly while you go to bed with a full one? Just because *you* and Gideon had a falling out over something that didn't have a damned thing to do with me?"

"You—"

"And who are you to call me a Judas anyway? To call *anyone* a Judas? Oh yeah, Gideon told me *all* about you."

If Daniel thought he could shame me into backing down he had another thing coming. "I did help him," I said evenly. "For a while. Until I knew better. Until I opened my eyes and saw what he was and quit."

Daniel sighed. "I didn't come here to argue with you, Will. I came here to—"

"What about church last Sunday?" I spat. "The service. The song Gideon had everyone singing."

"What about it?"

"You were standing right there with him. With Gideon. When he turned that hymn all wrong."

"Will, it was just a *song*. It doesn't matter."

"It doesn't *matter*?" My heart thundered in my chest. I felt as if I was going to explode in a thousand directions. "It matters a lot, Daniel. He took over our *church*. Maybe that suits you fine. I saw how you were in there. You were ready to take a swing at anyone who even looked at Gideon wrong. Gideon's little guard dog."

Daniel stared at me, his expression incredulous. "Are you out of your mind? You think I care if someone takes a run at Gideon? You can knock his block off yourself for all I care. Be my guest and good luck with that. He can take care of himself. I just wanted to be ready if someone took a run at *me*."

"He means to kill me, Daniel," I blurted. I knew he wouldn't believe me. I just had to say the words out loud to someone. "I can tell. He wants to do it,

I know it. He thinks I . . . spurned him or something and now he means to kill me before he goes. I know it."

"Wow. Come on, Will. Your Dad's right about one thing—you spend too much time reading those crazy magazines of yours. Yes, Gideon hired me because he knew it would hurt your feelings. I'm not an idiot. I took the job for the same reason. To get back at you. But come on. No, Gideon doesn't like you. That doesn't mean he's out to *kill* you."

"You don't understand," I said tonelessly.

Daniel frowned. "I'll tell you what I do understand. I understand that so far he hasn't asked me to do anything that's going to get me in trouble with the police or God or anyone else. And if he does? I guess I'll cross that bridge when I come to it."

"Oh you're going to come to it all right."

"Probably so. Because he's definitely cooking something up for Greenheart. Dad says he's a grifter. He thinks Gideon's some hustler who blew in with the tumbleweeds and that he's just hanging around until the heat dies down from his latest big-city score."

"That's what Mom thinks too, pretty much. But why bother messing around with us then? We're small potatoes out here in the middle of nowhere."

"Maybe he can't help himself. He sees a town full of marks and the gears in his head just naturally start turning. He's a predator and he smells prey. That's what Dad thinks."

"And your Dad is okay with that? With you working for him?"

"It's a payday, nothing more, nothing less. Dad says money makes the world go round and what's the difference between a grifter and a banker these days anyhow?"

I remembered Wagner's terrified dogs and the way the rabbits in the killing pen had stared Gideon's way when his voice first rang in their bloody ears. "He's more than just some grifter."

Daniel smiled. "I think so too. He's from New York or Philadelphia or Los Angeles or St. Louis or Detroit. Those places are full of men like him. If you cut open Gideon's ball sack a pair of dice would fall out. But what Dad doesn't know—what nobody in Greenheart knows except maybe you—is that's not *all* he is. He's got something special on the side. A *gift* that makes him different from all the other con men out there. More dangerous. Maybe that's what's got you so spooked."

"Daniel, I don't—"

"Don't you read the papers, Will? Don't you listen to the radio? The walls between our world and the next are paper thin. Some folks—spiritualists—have figured out how to talk to people from the great beyond. They can talk to the dead. And mind reading, there's folks out there that can do that too. All sorts of things like that. I think he's one of those kinds of people, Will. People with weird . . . abilities. Strange talents. They mostly live in London and New York, places like that."

"And Greenheart, according to you."

"He's not *moving* here." Daniel pressed on. "People who can bend nails with their minds or predict the future or learn all about a person's past just by touching something that belongs to them, like a handkerchief or a pocket watch."

"Fortune tellers." I was annoyed with him. He might have replaced me but he didn't know Gideon like I did. "You're talking about circus freaks and fortune tellers. Magicians. He's not like that. He's more than that."

"Over in Europe they call them . . . uh what's the word . . . clairvoyants. People with second sight. That's when you can see into the future. Or what's going on halfway around the world the same time it's happening. Wouldn't that be something? There's people out there that can move objects with their minds just by thinking about it. People who can see and talk to ghosts. They say women are better at talking to ghosts."

"Gideon isn't a ghost, either."

"Never said he was. But listen to this. Dad told me that when we lived in Brooklyn we had a neighbor who worked as a midwife. He said she delivered babies for the better part of sixty years and she always knew whether it was going to be a boy or a girl before it came out. Every damn time. She wasn't guessing, she just knew. Stillborns? She knew what they were too. Twins? It didn't matter. If it was a boy and a girl she knew which one was elbowing to the front of the line."

"How?"

"Who the hell knows? The point is she *knew.* Just because someone's powers are peculiar doesn't mean they're not real. I think Gideon is one of *those* kind of people. Like that lady back in Brooklyn. Sure, he's a world champion bullshitter who was born with his hand in the till. But he's *also* someone with a little something special in his hip pocket. A *gift* that the rest of us don't have. A little flask of second sight or something that he can take a nip from now and then to help grease the wheels of whatever con he's working."

"It's not a gift."

"Call it whatever you want. Call it a disease if that makes you happy. Call it a *condition* that all the doctors and scientists don't understand. And it don't even work on everyone, remember? You think everyone singing along with him on Sunday was under some kind of spell? Not me. I bet lots of people weren't. But that's how people are. Hard to tell the true believers from the scared ones sometimes. Not that it matters in the end. Not if you're all singing the same damned song. But at the end of the day it does get me to wondering, Will. Truly it does. It gets me to wondering if Gideon's special gift might be making it rain."

I sat with the idea for a minute. Daniel's theory had an oddly comforting pull because it posited that whatever else Gideon might do and be, he might yet also be the instrument of Greenheart's rebirth and renewal. I wanted so much to believe that. But I knew in my heart that whatever Gideon was, he wasn't Greenheart's savior. He had a different agenda.

Daniel turned to look at me, his eyes shining with a kind of wonder. "That's what I want to know. I want to know who Gideon *is.* Don't you? I want to know what Gideon can really *do.* I want to know where he's *from.* Don't you want to know any of that?"

"Of course I do."

Daniel smiled. "Good. Because I was thinking maybe you and me should go looking for some answers," he said. "Two can cover more ground than one, right?"

"What are you talking about? He's dangerous, Daniel. You know what it was like in church last Sunday. It was like there was something else in there with us. Something not God. And have you seen how dogs act around him?"

He gave me a startled look. "What?"

"Never mind."

He grabbed my arm. "No, what's this about dogs?"

The faint sound of cursing interrupted us. We rose our hands to block the sun and squinted out to a distant stretch of fence line, where Dad was resetting and rewiring a badly listing fence post. Our truck was parked next to him, caked in dust, a roll of rusty wire poking out of the back. Amos and Andy watched him too from their usual stations in the dusty paddock, their tails swishing like brooms on each other's flanks to keep the flies away. I had completely forgotten Dad was out there.

We heard a tapping on the window behind us. Mom, smiling dimly at us through the dust-clouded glass. We each gave her a dutiful little smile and wave and she waved back, relieved to see that Daniel and I had apparently patched things up. But when Daniel turned back to face me his expression turned somber again.

"When did Gideon first come to town? Do you remember?"

"April Fool's Day," I said promptly. "That's when I first met him at least. At the rabbit drive."

"The rabbit drive? Are you sure?"

"Yeah I'm sure. Trust me."

Daniel raised his hands in mock surrender. "OK. I believe you, geez. You met him at the rabbit drive. Got it. I just don't remember him being there at all and he doesn't exactly blend in to the scenery. The timing makes sense, though."

"Timing of what?"

Daniel took a deep breath, as if gathering himself. "Why did you ask me about dogs before? About how they act around Gideon?"

"Wagner's dogs were really scared of him. *Really* scared. You should have seen them."

"Those dogs? I hate those dogs."

"It was so weird. But then again not really. Daniel, no dogs *ever* barked when we came calling. Not once. Not a single dog ever ran out to even just give us a sniff. We must have stopped at two hundred houses and Wagner's dogs were the only ones I ever even saw."

"Huh."

"Daniel, I've never seen Gideon around any animals at all. No cows, no barn cats, and you should see the chickens hightail it. I never once saw him go into a barn or anywhere near a working horse out in a field."

Daniel looked away and down the empty road in the direction of town. "Well, he's got a dog now. Over at Stagg's place. He gave it a weird name. But Will? I can't quite be sure, and he sure doesn't act the same. It's like he's sick or something. But I swear to God it's Buster."

18

Ten minutes later Daniel and I were flying to John Stagg's house in our old Model A. Mom told us "just take the car" when we told her Gideon had Buster. I knew she wanted to go with us. Few things would have given her greater pleasure than calling Gideon a lowly dognapper to his face. And she was worried about us going over to Stagg's place alone. But Daniel assured her that Gideon would be down at the theatre all afternoon preparing for his big show. John Stagg's house would be empty. Even the staff was gone for the day. All we had to do was grab Buster and go.

She relented then, but only after extracting solemn promises that we would carry out our mission carefully and quickly—and that we would call it off if there were any signs that Gideon was about. Then she sighed and turned back to the hundred other things she had to do that day before beginning supper preparations. Because she was going to Gideon's show too, like everyone else still left in King County. It was all anyone was talking about. A looming question of the night was whether Mom was going to be able to stomach sitting next to Dad. Or maybe the question was whether he would let her sit next to him. That's how bad things had spiraled between them.

She said we didn't have to ask Dad for permission to use the car, that we could just take it. That's when I realized Mom didn't have any more idea than I did whether Dad would stop us if given the opportunity. I watched Dad out of the corner of my eye as I wheeled the car around and sped away,

126

making a beeline for town. I couldn't see his expression. He was too far away and the sweat-stained hat he wore against the sun cast his face into deep shadow. But I still remember how Dad straightened from his work, went still as a statue, and watched us leave. Bearing witness to my latest treachery.

Still and all, it felt good to roll down the windows and feel the warm rushing wind on our faces and know that Buster was alive and only minutes away. And to leave my unhappy home behind, if only for a while. It felt even better to have Daniel sitting on the car seat next to me. An unspoken truce had been forged between us. Whatever had transpired between my parents and his father didn't matter, not that afternoon. Buster was what mattered.

But if Gideon had Buster in his possession, that meant the dog was part of the game too. A pawn that Gideon would sacrifice without a moment's thought if he perceived advantage in doing so. We needed to be careful.

I asked Daniel if it was true that Gideon's presentation that evening was going to include guest appearances from folks he had saved from ruin up in South Dakota and Nebraska. He said two couples were coming in on the late afternoon train but didn't know anything more. Daniel asked me about Uncle Leonard's funeral and the next thing I knew I was telling him about Katherine. "I met a girl," I said, trying to sound casual about it. "Someone my age, you'll be happy to know."

Daniel gave me a knowing look. "I knew it. The two of you probably got that last duster started with all your wrestling around over there."

That was all the encouragement I needed. It felt so good to talk about her. To say her name out loud. I had never told another human being about how hard my heart was pounding when I was sitting on the porch swing with her, or the way her bright smile made me feel every time it turned my way. Mom had known that Katherine and I were sweet on each other, she wasn't blind. But she pretended otherwise and I couldn't have talked to her about how Katherine made me feel in a million years. It felt good to rave about how smart and funny and fearless and pretty and perfect she was.

"Thank God you're not mooning after Wells anymore," he said as we passed the Greenheart Theatre. PVBLIC MEETING 7 PM, announced the marquee, and underneath: PRESE TATION BY GIDEON STARL1NG.

"You were mean about that," I said, aggrieved. "About me liking Miss Wells. I couldn't help it."

"That was for your own good."

"Uh huh."

"Will, they almost caught on." Daniel's expression turned grave. "Conrad and Ralph and Oscar. Brenda too! She would have been worse than any of them." He gave a bewildered laugh. "Will, you were looking at Miss Wells like she was Ginger Rogers and you were Fred Estaire. Oh my God, you were ridiculous." His smile widened in remembrance.

"I was not."

Daniel looked over at me and laughed harder. "Oh yes. Yes you were. There were times I didn't know whether to laugh or cry."

"See? You're still being mean."

"Nah. I just knew they'd make your life miserable if they ever caught wind of it. And I'm not going to fight Brenda for you. I have my limits."

I hated to admit it but Daniel had a point. I had come to dread being called on by Miss Wells because of how the blood rushed to my cheeks whenever I was the focus of her attention. I remembered how strangely enlarged and unresponsive my tongue felt whenever she gave me one of her encouraging smiles. My inarticulate stammering whenever Miss Wells chose me to solve a problem at the blackboard. I pictured my classmates sniffing the air like blueticks, trying to place the scent of infatuation in the air.

"Well . . . if that's what you were doing, thanks," I said grudgingly. "I guess. You still didn't have to be so mean about it."

"It worked, didn't it? What really helped was she stopped calling on you when she saw how dewy-eyed you were getting."

I felt the blood drain from my face. "She knew?"

"Miss Wells? Of course she knew. She's not stupid. She didn't call you up to the board the whole last month of school! That was a switch. She always used to call on you whenever she needed someone who knew the answer so she could keep the lesson moving along. Nobody knows the answer? Ask Will, he knows! Those last weeks of school, though? Wells knew you'd swallow your tongue if she called on you. She's the one who saved you from yourself. You were too busy picking out engagement rings to listen to me."

I was still absorbing those revelations when we turned onto Hurley Boulevard, which would whisk us from downtown Greenheart to Stagg's park-like estate on the town's far northwest edge. Once upon a time the boulevard had been a six-block long promenade of green grass and carefully tended flowerbeds lit at night by sleek black streetlights that dropped great circles of bronze light on the street and cars passing below. The boulevard had been the centerpiece of every one of Greenheart's Fourth of July parades and Christmas pageants for as long as I could remember. But the flowerbeds were gone now, drifted in with dirt and chaff shoveled onto the median from the street.

At the end of the boulevard, though, Stagg's place looked like a postcard from a different world. One where dusters and drought were hypotheticals and the price of wheat never fell through the floor. Mature lindens and maples dotted the big yard, offering attractive pockets of shade. On the far western flank of the property sat a fat belt of wind-bent fir and spruce. A fringe of aspen skirted the far end of the pines, their leaves fluttering like little flags with every hint of breeze.

People used to say Stagg ordered his trees to be watered every day. That his staff poured gallon after gallon into the soil around their trunks but only at night, when no one could see. He didn't want his thirsty neighbors to know that he was emptying wagonloads of life-giving water onto the roots of a bunch of damn trees that didn't even provide the house with shade.

It was a nasty rumor—the only such kind I ever heard about Stagg— but I had dutifully passed the information along to Gideon along with everything else I had heard about the man. Gideon circled back to Stagg in our conversations a couple more times after that. He asked me about the staff too. Their names and circumstances. He had been probing for weakness. For chinks in the armor. Deciding how he was going to take Stagg out. And I had helped him do it.

"Those trees look nice, don't they," Daniel murmured. "You ever hear that story about how Stagg used to secretly water—"

"I've heard it."

I drove up the Great Man's looping white gravel drive and parked, feeling very much the interloper in our creaking dust-coated Model A. We sat there for a second and studied the empty yard and porch and windows. I pointed my chin in the direction of the knapsack sitting on the floorboards between Daniel's feet.

"What you got in there?"

"Mom's letters and a few things from the trunk. His Navy pictures and medals. That teacup with the peacock in the bottom. The flags and the spyglass. I didn't have room for that much."

"Why?"

Daniel kept looking out the windshield. "Because who knows how this is all going to turn out for me? I decided it might be good to have some of Dad's stuff with me in case I need to leave in a hurry."

"In case Gideon turns against you?"

"Or in case Gideon decides he wants me along wherever he goes next. He's keeping me on the dangle about that but if he makes the offer he won't give me long to decide."

"But he—"

"Hey, as long as he keeps paying what he's paying and doesn't ask me to kill anyone it's a possibility."

"What about your dad?"

"What about him? I'm here and he's not. At this point I don't think he gets a vote on anything I do."

We wandered through the empty stable and peered through the beveled glass windows of the garage, exchanging relieved smiles when we confirmed Gideon's car was absent from the premises. We called Buster's name as we walked what felt like every inch of Stagg's sprawling grounds, including the shelterbelt of heavy-shouldered pines arrayed along the property line to the west. Daniel and I pushed through narrow gaps in the trees, calling for Buster and peering into the caves of darkness beneath the lowest boughs as the branches scratched and poked at our bare forearms and exposed necks.

When we emerged Daniel suggested we try calling for Buster using the name Gideon used. Icegrin or Icegrim or something like that, Daniel wasn't sure. But no dog appeared in response to those names either.

"Where are the horses?" I asked. Usually there were three or four of them grazing out in the grassy paddock behind Stagg's big barn.

"They're all being stabled out at John Elmendorf's ranch. Gideon arranged for that before he even set foot on the place. Didn't want to deal with them, I guess. Shoot, he wouldn't even have to pay me to take care of those horses as long as I got to ride them too. Wouldn't it be something to have just one horse like that? If I had one I'd have a saddle on it all the time. Just me and my horse, riding the prairie and eating beans and playing duets with coyotes on the harmonica and sleeping under the stars."

"You and Gene Autry."

"And Champion."

"And the Tumbling Tumbleweeds."

"That doesn't sound so bad to me."

"You don't know how to play the harmonica."

"I'll learn."

We arrived at the base of the mansion's grand wraparound porch and looked at each other, both of us knowing that the next step was to go inside and pick up the search.

"Gideon gave Marie and Bernice the day off so we don't need to worry about them," Daniel reminded. "He told them to get themselves pretty for tonight and they laughed like a couple of schoolgirls. He gave Cal the day off too. Stagg's yardman. I guess he's Gideon's yardman now. I think he's just going to keep coming to work until someone tells him not to. Why not? He gets three squares a day from Marie and Bernice, even if he doesn't get paid. Hmm. He probably didn't want the day off now that I think about it. The other workmen are all gone, Gideon sent them away with big bonuses as soon as they finished cleaning out the stables and getting all of that closed down. He was pretty slick about it. They walked away thinking he was the cat's meow, just like everyone else around here."

We went around to the back of the house, Daniel adopting the easy saunter of a newspaper boy collecting payments on his route. I followed behind dumbly, my heart running at an adrenalized gallop that somehow made my legs feel only distantly connected to the rest of my body.

Daniel held up a shiny key when we reached the door. "Gideon never gave me a house key but I nabbed this off Bernice the other day. She doesn't need it anyway. Her and Marie come to work together every day and Marie's still got a key. Bernice keeps hoping the key will turn up so she's keeping her mouth shut about it. Because if Gideon's staying on here for a while . . . well, they want to stay on too, right? Can't blame 'em for that. Where else they going to go? Marie's been cooking up a storm for him. Gideon always tells her how delicious everything is—which it is, don't get me wrong—and she just basks in it. I dunno, I don't like how he talks to her."

"How does he talk to her?"

Daniel inserted the key and turned the deadbolt to unlock the door. "Like she's his pet."

We walked right in. The kitchen was gloomy and enormous, impossible to take in all at once. Pots and pans and ladles and rolling pins hung suspended like misshapen bats over a darkly gleaming butcher block table in the middle of the silent kitchen. The entire length of the southern wall was a precisely arranged grid of deep shelves and cupboards framing a walk-in pantry with a rounded arch entrance. I stared at the kitchen's two eight-burner stoves and trailed my hand along their sealskin black flanks as we made our way deeper into the room. Daniel stashed his knapsack in a low cupboard along the way.

"Why are you hiding it there?" I asked.

"If this bag was full of stuff from your dad's life would you want Gideon to know about it?"

"No."

"Well me neither."

We took a methodical approach to our search of the house, mindful that Gideon could have Buster chained up anywhere. From the kitchen we went down to the billiard room in the basement. We made our way up from there, scouring three gleaming floors of carpeted hallways and shining brass and high oaken beams and giant fireplaces that gaped like caves. We called out for Buster and assorted iterations of Icegrim again and again. We turned lamplights and ceiling lights and wall sconces on and off, opened and closed closets and cabinet doors. We rifled through an enormous armoire featuring dancing stags and wolves and rabbits and peacocks and foxes carved deep into the wood and peered under the great oaken desk that sat at the center of Stagg's magnificent library. We walked the length of the narrow servants' stairs at the back of the house and down the broad carpeted staircase in the front until we were down in the grand foyer again. All we had left to check were the four bedrooms on the second floor.

We peered through the foyer's massive chandelier of interlocking elk antlers to the banistered hallway above. It looked just as empty as the rest of the house.

"You think Buster's up there somewhere?" I asked.

"I don't know. If he is he's not awake. We would have heard him barking or walking around or scratching at the door, right?"

Daniel started up the stairs and I fell in behind him. When he reached the second floor landing he stopped, set his shoulders, and turned back to face me. "I hope your mom keeping the trunk a while doesn't cause problems for her with your dad. I didn't think that part through very well."

"It's OK," I said, although I didn't know whether it would be. "She's doing it for you, not your dad. Dad will see that." I hoped that saying it would make it true.

We searched the bedrooms together one by one. The only one we didn't enter was the one that had belonged to Stagg's daughter, Clara. As soon as we opened the door we saw it belonged to Clara still. It was a bedroom suspended in time. A dust-coated shrine of lavender lace and stuffed animals and storybooks about magical bears and turtles and panthers and cows. I was glad that Gideon had let the room be.

The other bedrooms featured an abundance of dark wood and tasteful decorations and natural light and were entirely empty of life. We turned the lights on and off in each room, taking note of the fact that the house still had electricity. Most of King County remained without phone and electric service due to the duster that had ruined Stagg's funeral. But not the long boulevard of streetlights and shops and houses connecting Greenheart's downtown district to the Great Man's mansion. It never lost power.

Did Gideon's *gifts* include the power to electrify the house we were standing in? The entire boulevard? We batted the idea around for a minute or two. It was not a conversation that settled either of our nerves and we still had one more room to check. The master bedroom.

We called through the door for Buster first, listening for anything on the other side. A footfall. A thumping tail against the floor. A low growl. Anything other than the oppressive silence of the house. So much adrenaline was pumping through my body I thought I might throw up. I was suddenly sure that the house had saved the worst for last. My gaze fell on the hallway's honey-colored wallpaper, looking for something to hold on to amid its procession of flower petals and curling leaves.

"Just let me know when you're ready," Daniel said. He tried to smile but it didn't take. I wasn't the only one scared about what might be behind the door.

The master bedroom was as museum-like as the rest of the house. The only movement came from an oscillating fan at the far end of the room. Its turning face ruffled the dark velvety curtains that adorned the room's three large windows. A faint click sounded every time the droning fan reached its right terminus and reversed direction.

As I moved deeper into the bedroom I found myself wondering what it would have been like to live in this house as Stagg had done. All those nights alone after the staff went home for the evening, just him and the ghost of his cherished daughter. Month after month, year after year, decade after decade. He never remarried, never even called on a lady in all his years in Greenheart so far as anyone knew. Wherever he went, he arrived and left alone.

Yet like pretty near every other man and boy in Greenheart I grew up wanting to be Stagg. Could you blame us? Who doesn't want to be the Great Man? The one that everyone admires. Who doesn't want to luxuriate in the kind of wealth that immunized you from worrying about the survival of your family. To have women look at you the way so many women around town looked at Stagg, whether they were married or not. And you couldn't even hate him for it. Or his wealth or straight white teeth or thick head of hair because everyone knew the man's heart had been forever broken by his daughter's grinding, relentless decline and death.

People said that the air out here still smelled of spring rain and fresh-cut wheat and newly plowed earth when John Stagg moved his daughter out to

Greenheart. They say the clean prairie air bought Clara a few more years of checkers and bedtime stories and grand birthday parties, the latter of which she delighted in planning for every nurse and housekeeper and stable hand in her father's employ. But the clean air and sunshine weren't enough to save her and one unseasonably warm day in early March she left the pains and sorrows of this cruel world behind to join Jesus up in Heaven. That's the story I've always been told.

Once in a while someone took a look at Stagg's money and businesses and fine clothes and big house and observed that good fortune smiled on some more than others. Those people were new arrivals to King County, mostly, or strangers passing through. People who didn't know what they were talking about. They weren't versed in the local lore. They didn't know that Stagg had been a constant presence at his daughter's bedside during those last brutal bedridden weeks, when she would cry out for hours from the pain. They didn't know how he would lose his voice reading her favorite books from childhood.

Two framed pictures hung from the walls of Stagg's purloined bedroom. One was a black-and-white portrait of a dark-haired girl standing in front of a pond fringed with tall cattails. She is no more than six years old and is holding a bouquet of wildflowers in her left hand. I had never seen a picture of Clara Stagg before but of course it had to be her. Once upon a time she had been a happy, healthy girl with dimples and bright eyes and a future bursting with possibilities. I wondered how many such days she was given before sickness stole it all away, first in wee drams and then in great plundering gulps.

On the opposite wall hung a large print in an ornate frame of gold filigree. The painting gave me a strange little shiver of déjà vu even though I was sure I had never seen the image before. The painting was of a gathering of animals dressed like businessmen at the edge of an autumn-touched wood. At the center of the scene stood an imperious-looking fox dressed in kingly robes, standing upright on his back legs. The fox was smirking toothily at a finely dressed rabbit who appears to be beseeching him for some favor or mercy. The rabbit's entire aspect was one of fearful supplication. The other animals—squirrels and hedgehogs dressed as plump bankers and lawyers and other citizens of means—were watching the exchange nervously from the edge of the forest. Underneath their waistcoats and cravats and glittering timepieces they were prey. Everyone in the painting knew it, the fox most of all.

Daniel joined me and studied the painting for a moment. "There used to be another picture hanging here. A couple cowboys watching their horses drink at a mountain stream. Gideon said he liked this one better. He had it in the trunk of his car and I never even knew."

"Me neither. He brought it with him?"

"I guess." Daniel reached out and tapped a brass plate affixed to the bottom of the frame. "He said he saw it hanging behind the register of a bookstore in New Orleans and had to have it." I crouched down to read the plate.

WILLIAM HOLBROOK BEARD
His Majesty Receives - 1885

"Gideon says it's whimsical." Daniel said. "I don't know about that. Looks to me like that fox is thinking about making himself some rabbit stew."

I turned away, unnerved by the sinister undercurrents pulsing through the artist's half-century-old brush strokes. A familiar snatch of memory came darkly bubbling out of that rushing black water, of petrified jackrabbits and sprays of warm blood and a voice that commanded the gaze of every damned jack, even the ones drawing their last through lungs punctured by their own shattered ribs.

"I keep having this dream about him," Daniel said. "Gideon. It's driving me nuts."

"What is it?"

"You know that magician trick where the guy pulls an endless handkerchief out of his sleeve? All different colors, silky scarves all knotted together at the ends?"

"Yeah."

"Well I keep having this dream that Gideon is pulling one of those endless ropes of silk out of his mouth. Handful after handful, using both hands, on and on. He looks like he could do it all day. It's creepy as hell. He keeps watching me out of the corner of his eye and smiling at me as he pulls the scarves out of his mouth."

"That sounds more like a nightmare than a dream."

"It feels that way too." Daniel's eyes cleared and he gave me a rueful smile. "You have to have had a dream about him too, right? I mean, how could you not?"

I thought of a deep sea diver caked in dust, staggering across a purgatorial plain. The baking sun an orange flare against the diver's jet-black faceplate. "I don't know," I answered truthfully.

I turned my attention to the big four-poster bed at the center of the room. The neatly made chenille bedspread was pale green with a medallion design at its center. The tapered bedposts looked like a quartet of cavalry lances pointed at the ceiling. Daniel said Gideon must have made the bed himself since he gave the housekeepers the day off.

Or he slept somewhere else. An unwanted image of Gideon and Miss Wells slithered into my head, both of them naked and panting and thrusting and clutching at each other. Whispering and groaning in each other's ears. I cast the thought away with a shudder of revulsion.

To the left of the bed sat an enormous nightstand, its surface area large enough to accommodate both a reading lamp and a tabletop cathedral radio far fancier than the one we had at home. I looked under the bed, then sat on the edge of the mattress and ran my hand over the gleaming curve of the radio top and the art deco embellishments of the front panel. The gold fabric screen of the speaker. Its triangle of polished knobs. A plate below the AM dial announced that the radio was a Philco.

I clicked the radio on and began looking for a station, only to get dead air up and down the dial. It was either broken or unplugged and I didn't care enough to check behind the nightstand about the latter. But when I stood up from the bed and began to walk away the sound of a single twelve-string guitar came floating out of the radio. The music gradually swelled in volume until a loping blues shuffle filled the room. I realized with a startle that I recognized the melody. It was a melody Gideon hummed on occasion back when he was driving us around the backroads of King County.

A man's voice settled in next to the guitar, singing in an eerie gospel-tinged tenor that made the hairs on my arms rise.

Rainmaker Rainmaker
   Give me a sign
   That your tongue speaks true
   Of powers divine

Rainmaker Rainmaker
   See the dust in my eyes?
   Bring me cold water to drink
   And rain clouds for my skies

Give me your razzle dazzle
   Your zim, zam, zuzz
   Come and chase these blues away
   That's what a rainmaker does

Rainmaker Rainmaker
   Shake, twist and shout
   You know you're the one
   Everyone's talkin' about

Rainmaker Rainmaker
   I pray you come soon
   Sing your midnight song to me
   I'll leave your money with the moon

The final mournful notes of the song faded out, followed by . . . nothing. No other music or advertising jingle, no news report or station call sign. No static. It felt like the radio was waiting for something.

Daniel stared at me. "That sounded like it was about Gideon."

I walked over to the radio and turned the knob off before it could come back to life and begin playing another song.

20

aniel and I checked every inch of the master bedroom and attached bathroom and found no canine bodies hidden in the enormous porcelain clawfoot tub or cavernous dresser drawers or behind the curtains. Everything was neat as a pin, just as I would have expected. Gideon liked to have things tidy and clean. You could see it in how he dressed. His finely tailored suits and silk ties. His spotless black Homberg hat with the silk hatband. His cache of dollar-sized lapel pins, exactly alike in appearance but for the enigmatic menagerie of images etched into their ivory surfaces. I'd seen six or seven of them since his arrival, each one emblazoned with a striking tableau. A fallen ram's horn. A lyre shaped like a tortoise shell. A gem-encrusted crown tangled in a lion's mane. Finely detailed totems of a badger's face and a rooster's claw and a hare's tall ears.

My eyes alighted on a handsome silverware box made of rosewood at the far end of the bedroom. It sat atop an ornately carved console table next to two battered ammunition boxes I recognized as the ones from the back of Gideon's cavernous car trunk. The ammo boxes looked alien and out of place in the room, like dried-out salvage liberated from some long-drowned ship.

"Hey Will?" Daniel said behind me, and for the first time since our arrival I thought he sounded nervous. "Gideon shouldn't be back for another hour at least but you never know with him. And once he's back he'll have me running around until showtime. You should probably hit the road. No sense in pressing our luck. I'm sorry we didn't find Buster. I swear it was him, though. He could have taken him into town with him I guess. Maybe he took him to a vet to get checked out? I don't know."

"Yeah ok." I said, pulling one of the curtains aside to peek outside. The front drive was still empty but for our car, its dusty black chassis baking in the early summer sun. "But I want to look around just a little longer." I nodded in the direction of the padlocked boxes. "Maybe there's a key to these around here somewhere. The padlocks look the same to me. One key might open them both."

"I've been wondering what the hell he keeps in those," Daniel said. "They showed up in the trunk one day out of nowhere a few days after I started working for him."

"I remember. They were in there when he moved out of the Zephyr. That was the first time I ever saw them."

"Hmmm. Maybe I should go back down to the library? I wasn't looking for a key in particular when I went through his desk the first time."

"Look for a safe too. Stagg seems like the sort of guy who would have a safe in his wall behind a picture or something. Seemed like. Not that we'd be able to open it."

"You think Gideon could get into that? Stagg's safe?"

"Do you?"

Daniel smiled. "I'll holler if I see him coming, you do the same. But Will—make it quick. You need to get out of here so we need to hurry." He ran out of the room and pounded down the broad staircase, the sound of his footsteps receding into silence.

I rifled through the twin nightstands on either side of the big bed, then worked my way around the room again. I pawed through drawers filled with neatly folded underwear and gleaming silver cufflinks and fancy tie pins and soft pairs of black and brown and gray socks. I browsed through the medicine cabinet in the wood-paneled bathroom, being careful to arrange everything exactly as I found it. If the shaving brush was a quarter turn or half inch off from where Gideon had left it he would notice, of that I was certain. I turned on the light in the walk-in closet and hurriedly patted down every jacket, shirt, and pair of trousers hanging inside. At the back of the closet I found four dark suits banded together by their hangers with a long black shoelace. Hanging from the shoelace was a butcher's tag with the word TAILOR scrawled on it.

More out of frustration than anything I returned to the table by the window and studied the ammo boxes more closely. Both were scarred with the glyphs of hard years of travel, but when I hefted one experimentally the box held together as if it were carved from a single block of wood. Without a key their contents would remain a mystery to us. We couldn't very well take an ax to them. At a minimum, Gideon would never trust Daniel again. His complicity in such vandalism would be a given.

Opening the boxes with an axe would give Gideon other information as well. He would know just how suspicious we had become of him. And who knew what was in the boxes anyway? The fact that they were padlocked—and that Gideon had taken the trouble of bringing them up to his room—hinted there might be valuable cargo within. But there was no telling what someone like Gideon might haul around with him on his travels.

I turned my attention back to the flat silverware case and was suddenly sure didn't contain silverware. Otherwise it would be down in Stagg's dining room with the fine china and wine glasses. The box was made of rosewood and looked more like it might safekeep a set of flintlock dueling pistols or a German bayonet plucked from a gory battlefield. Or a shiny set of ivory pins nestled in black velvet.

I reached out with trembling hands for the lid and it opened right up, as if it didn't want to give me a chance to reconsider. Inside, in the center of a bed of coarse black-and-gray wool rested a single lapel pin. Like the other pins I'd seen Gideon wearing, it was a half-dollar-sized circle of ivory set in a silver frame. But the polished ivory in this pin was a blank surface, untouched by blemish or etching.

I picked up the pin and felt a little bump along its fine edge. It was a locket, not just a lapel pin. Probably pilfered or won in a game of chance by Gideon on his travels. Were the other pins lockets too? And why was this one stored separately, away from the rest? Where did he keep the rest of them?

That's when understanding clicked into place. This was the only one

Gideon owned. A single locket with a multitude of faces. I fiddled with the fine catch along the locket's otherwise seamless edge until I felt it click. The face of the locket opened of its own accord, the ivory moon breaking and swiveling away in two pieces to reveal a single shining key.

I emptied the key into my hand and tossed the locket aside, but stopped short just before my hand grasped the first padlock. A sort of paralysis seeped into my bones, crystalline and cold. A sick dread that if I opened the ammo boxes another invisible gear deep in Gideon's glittering machine of artifice would click into place. Opening the boxes was a point of no return.

But what other choice did I have?

"Will, come on!" Daniel's voice, echoing up the stairs. "There's no key anywhere! Not in the library at least. Come on! You need to get out of here."

Daniel's voice shook me out of my lethargy of queasy fear. "Get up here!" I called hoarsely. "I found the key!"

I opened both padlocks quickly, the key slippery in my sweating hands. Daniel burst into the room and ran to my side as I opened the lid on the first box. We peered inside cautiously, wrinkled our noses at the stale air uncoiling out of its depths.

This was a different kind of treasure chest than the one Daniel's father kept. This one was a rat's nest of flotsam and jetsam hauled out of some strange twilight sea where Blackbeard and Long John Silver still plied their trade. Dully gleaming baubles and apothecary bottles. Matted pelts and beaded feathers. Teeth and bones and torn pieces of fabric. All tossed together in a black-grey dressing of grime and straw and dried out flower petals.

Daniel took a deep breath and rummaged through the contents with one hand. Cautiously, as if there might be a mousetrap or worse hidden inside. He brought out a rusty tin from which he took two yellowing dice and an ancient-looking pack of playing cards. He began flipping idly through the cards, then paused. He pulled two cards out and held them up to the light. The Queen of Hearts and the King of Diamonds, but with their eyes gouged out into ragged little holes. "Every face card is like that."

I peered inside the box and saw a dirty pouch the size of a small purse slumped in one dank moist corner. Tiny toadstools grew out of a packed black wafer of soil in the concave chest of the pouch, which had been fashioned from an old flour sack. The brand of the flour mill was still faintly visible on the front. It was one of those stylized lions that appear on family crests and the like, regal and gold and walking on its hind two legs. Underneath the strutting lion were the words ROYAL FLOUR.

I pulled out a bottle glazed midnight blue, cold, damp, and gritty. I peered into the glazed glass, searching for a glimpse of its contents. The bottle was stoppered by a wide cork connected to the neck by a metal harness of braided wire and hinges. The top of the harness was stamped with the image of a curved ram's horn lying in a bed of greenery. It was the same image I had seen on Gideon's lapel pin the day of the rabbit drive.

I tugged at the cork until it popped free and brought the bottle to my nose to take an experimental whiff. An unpleasant musty odor issued forth from the bottle and I held it away from us. That's when I spotted the inscription on the inside of the stopper:

The Horn of Bellin the Ram

I turned the bottle this way and that, listening to the faint hiss of shifting sand or salt or similar within. Daniel cupped one hand toward the bottle's open top and I poured a little out into his palm. It was grainier than dirt or flour, with little nuggets of gray and white pebble sprinkled in the coarse powder. We looked at each other and I shrugged. I didn't know what powdered ram horn was supposed to look like.

Daniel carefully poured the material back into the bottle, which I recorked and placed on the table between the two boxes. He gave a little unvoluntary spasm of delayed revulsion and rubbed his hand furiously on his pants leg. Then he calmed himself, set his shoulders, and reached into the box again. He brought out the ROYAL FLOUR bag, using a fold of fabric pinched between two fingers to avoid the malignant-looking mushrooms clinging to its moist flanks. He opened it and peeked inside, then pulled out a thick loaf of what looked like horsehair, mahogany dark but marbled with strands of grey. The loaf was held in place by a tight latticework of thick twine. The lines of twine pressed into the loaf like an iron maiden, keeping all but a few stray hairs imprisoned.

We plunged our hands into the contents of both boxes, pulling items out and holding them up to the light like pirates from *Treasure Island*. We found a rooster's leg shellacked to a mineral hardness, each splayed toe and spur a spearpoint. A small thick scroll of tabby-colored fur wrapped in catgut, the ends of it drawn together with a clasp from which dangled a small wrinkled nut. Daniel shook a ruby-colored bottle, tall and fluted like a vase for a single flower. We watched its contents swirl like smoke within. I found a pale white skull twice the size of my closed fist. The bones of its jutting jaws were still harnessed in a stained muzzle, the leather strips slack and loose over pearl-grey fangs.

Daniel pulled a big mason jar out of the other ammo box and wiped a circle of its surface clean with a corner of his shirt. The honey inside looked like it had come straight from the hive, liquid gold flecked with bits of comb. Suspended in its solidity was a slab of long thick tongue, curled and twisted like a fat eel. I rubbed my thumb over the smeared glass of the jar until we could read the words across the glass.

The Tongue of Brunn the Bear

"What is all this?" Daniel asked. "It's disgusting. It looks like garbage from a taxidermy shop. I don't get it."

A shiver of understanding ran up my spine like a ghost's trailing finger. "It's a collection."

"A collection of what?"

"I'm not sure," I said. "A trophy collection, maybe."

Daniel snorted. "He doesn't take very good care of his trophy collection. This is filthy. And weird. Who keeps the tongue of a bear stored away in a big jar of honey?"

That's when we heard the slam of a car door outside, followed by a familiar voice, the words faint but clear through the closed windows of the bedroom. "Well, look at this." Gideon's voice, faint but clear through the closed windows of the bedroom. We heard him bang the flat of his hand on the hood of our Model A. "I think we might have some unexpected company. Shall we go say hello?"

21

Gideon's voice ran through us like an electrical current and we fell into a frenzy of cleaning up. We stashed everything we had taken out of the ammo boxes back inside, though neither of us could remember which box contained the rooster claw and in the end we had to guess. Daniel swore up a storm under his breath as we closed the lids and swept ammo box residue—stray strands of hair and flakes of leather and dirt and skin and petal—off the table and into our hands with the underside of our shirts.

We could hear Gideon downstairs, his brisk footsteps and calls echoing through the house's first floor. He stopped at the foot of the stairs.

"Where are you boys?" Gideon called up. "Daniel, I'm not paying you to play hide and seek with your friends. And Will? I'm not paying you at all. So why are you in my house?"

"We're up here," called Daniel, his face going pale.

Gideon started up the stairs, clacking his rings on the banister, making the sturdy steps groan with his tread. We each grabbed an ammo box and raced to thread the U-shaped shank of a padlock through the twin metal eyelets and lock it into place. Our hands trembled as we carefully stacked the boxes by the window exactly how we remembered them, furiously scanning the glossy surface of the table for telltale scratches or scuffs.

Which left me with the padlock key, its serrations digging into my hot sweaty hand. The padlock key I had found in his locket, which had vanished from sight.

I had no idea where it was.

Gideon's footsteps reached the landing at the top of the stairs. He was no more than fifteen feet away from the bedroom door.

"Find it," Daniel whispered hoarsely and leaped for the open doorway. I fell to my hands and knees in an adrenalized fever, groping blindly under the bed and nightstand.

"What the hell were you doing in my room? Where's Will?" Gideon's voice was in the hallway but sounded shockingly close, like a window-shaking peal of thunder over my head. Full-blown panic pressed its thumbs into my throat, making me gasp for air. And that's when I straightened and saw the locket at eye level sitting right where I'd tossed it—into the open silverware box.

"His stomach is bothering him. I told him he could use your bathroom."

"You went inside my *bathroom?* I should put the belt to you right here and now, you insolent little whelp."

"We were looking for his dog. I told you before I thought it was Buster."

"And I told you before that you were wrong." An instant later the wall separating the hallway from the bedroom shuddered. Gideon had shoved Daniel into the wall and was coming in. He swung the door open just as I emerged from the bathroom, the toilet gurgling behind me.

"I don't believe this," he muttered. Gideon's pose of bemused aplomb had vanished. He strode up close until he loomed up over me and I flinched back instinctively in fear. I pictured my own severed tongue entombed in honey, like the one that once belonged to the mysterious Brunn the Bear.

"I—I'm sorry, Gideon," I said, cradling my stomach with one hand. "We were looking around for Buster. Daniel said you might have found him. But we didn't find him outside and I convinced Daniel we should look for him up here even though he said we shouldn't and then my gut started feeling all clenched up and—"

"I told you it might be Will's dog, run away or got lost," Daniel said, stepping back inside the bedroom. His voice was calm but his dark eyes were locked on Gideon's back and shoulders. He looked like he did back in church when Gideon's arsenic-drenched hymn was in full swing. Fully prepared to take a swing at Gideon if he came near him again.

"You said Isengrim *reminded* you of the Thorpes' dog," Gideon snarled over his shoulder. "Not that it *was* their dog."

"—and I brung Will here to see if it was so," Daniel finished defiantly.

Gideon ignored him. His gaze flicked around the room in search of evidence of tampering or theft or any other forms of mischief. His eyes passed over the table holding the padlocked ammo boxes and the rosewood case no more quickly or slowly than any other part of the bedroom.

He didn't buy our flimsy story. Did he think our hunt for Buster just devolved into the sort of snooping that curious boys have done since time immemorial? Or that we tried to take advantage of his absence to steal something? Gideon might believe that of me at least. He had cataloged many weaknesses in my character since April Fool's Day. He knew I had done worse.

"So like I said—"

"Shut up, Will," Gideon said coolly. "I'm not interested in hearing about which of your holes is causing you distress and why. Get out of my house."

"Sorry Gideon," I said again and started for the bedroom door. He didn't need to tell me twice. But as I passed by Gideon reached out and gripped the meat of my upper arm, his long fingernails digging into the muscle of my bicep. He leaned in close, his breath a hot bellows in my ear. "Only my friends call me Gideon, Will. And you're not my friend. Not anymore. You're something else now. Let's see if you can figure out what that is. You think long and hard on it. You hear me, boy?"

"Yes sir." My tongue was thick in my mouth, gluey with fear. He was restraining himself from hurting me. I could see in his eyes how badly he wanted to make me scream.

"Good. Now both of you get your asses out of here before I do something I regret."

22

Daniel and I clomped down the stairs, Gideon trailing silently behind like a prison guard itching for an excuse to send us to the infirmary. When we turned to face him out on the porch, though, the laugh lines at the corners of his wide mouth were back. "Just when you think you've seen everything. Last time I saw the two of you together you wouldn't have pissed on the other if he was on fire. How times have changed. I'm delighted to see that you mended fences."

"I told you, we were looking for Buster," Daniel said, sounding peevish. "I knew him too, you know."

"So I've heard. Then why doesn't he seem to know you?"

Gideon stepped over to the edge of the porch, brought his right thumb and forefinger to his mouth, and gave a piercing whistle. A few seconds later a medium-sized dog came shambling out of the slanted shadow of a small shed at the other end of the big yard. His fur was matted with dirt and he looked like he had lost a fair amount of weight but it was Buster all right. I knew it as soon as I saw him.

Buster crossed the yard toward us in a slow, palsied gait, flinching and blinking and snapping at the air around him. Pendulous lines of drool hung from his jowls, glistening like snail slime in the sun. He staggered to the bottom step of the porch and stood below us, shivering as a plague of fleas churned around his red-rimmed eyes.

"What's wrong with him?" I asked numbly. Upon hearing my voice Buster's head jerked and his whimpering entered a higher, keening register.

"Whatever do you mean?" asked Gideon. "That's not very nice. Don't you like Isengrim? Oh look at him now, I think you hurt his feelings."

Buster's whine disintegrated into a low teeth-baring growl at the sound of Gideon's voice. His tail curled further under his belly, its length trembling like a divining rod. He tried to skulk away but stopped after a few quick trotting steps, as if he had pulled the line taut on some invisible leash spiked into the ground. Buster whined and snarled impotently, turning around and around and around for some route of escape that didn't exist, snapping spasmodically at the tormenting fleas.

I felt a righteous anger flower in my heart, eclipsing even my fear. "I don't care what you call him, or what you've done to him to make him that way. That's Buster. That's my dog."

"He's right, Gideon," said Daniel. "Buster—"

Gideon silenced him with an upraised finger. "You don't have a dog in this fight, Daniel. Literally. You'd do well to remember that. Don't make me send you off down the road to look for your hobo daddy on the eve of the big show now. Who knows where he's dipping his wick tonight without you holding him down. Little Orphan Danny. Speaking of the big show, don't you have things to get ready for tonight? I want everything packed and ready to go in an hour."

Listening to Gideon berate a stone-faced Daniel, I realized their relationship was different than the one Gideon had cultivated with me. Gideon had swept me off my feet with his charisma and glamorous automobile and endlessly entertaining stories but he didn't need to be that way with Daniel. Gideon could treat him as badly as he wanted and Daniel would come back for more, as long as he got paid to do it. Or so Gideon thought.

My eyes met Daniel's for an instant. We both knew this was where we had to part ways. He was on very thin ice with Gideon and he had his orders. Any further hint of insubordination would land him on the unemployment line with me or worse.

Daniel walked stiffly down the porch steps without a word and headed for the garage, Buster skittering away from him like a crippled deer. "That's a good lad," Gideon called after him. "You must have got your work ethic from your dear departed mother. Everyone in Greenheart knows you didn't get it from your dad."

Daniel kept walking. He opened the trunk of Gideon's roadster, pulled the garage doors open, and disappeared inside. A moment later we heard the crashing sound of Daniel kicking or throwing something.

"Now then," said Gideon, his tone turning sardonic. "You claim that Isengrim is actually *your* dog? Do you have any evidence to support this ludicrous assertion?"

"Daniel knows that's Buster," I said, nodding toward the dog, still whining and twitching and snarling at the bottom of the steps. I wasn't sure how much longer I could keep my composure with Buster in such an awful state. "You heard him."

"Daniel's opinion doesn't interest me. He'd say and do just about anything to get back in your good graces, I expect."

My mouth worked soundlessly for a moment. "He knows my dog pretty well," I repeated uselessly. My heart was a thudding drum inside my chest.

"Oh, I'm aware. Just think: If things had broken just a *little* differently the two of you might legally be brothers today. Isn't that right?"

He smiled at my shocked expression. "Do you think you're the only gossip in Greenheart, Will? I wonder, between Daniel's father and your mother, who was the moth and who was the flame? That makes all the difference, you know. Your mother is a shrew but she's still a handsome woman. I expect Little Orphan Danny's father was the one who started sniffing around her first if that's any consolation. Who knows, maybe they'll find their way back to each other someday and you can be Danny's little brother after all. But I doubt it."

I spun away, face burning from Gideon's taunts, and watched Daniel carefully angle a folded easel into the convertible's trunk. He looked thin and unsubstantial out there, still more boy than man. No wonder Gideon's high spirits had returned so quickly. We were children. What could we possibly do to him?

"I have to hand it to Daniel," Gideon said, following my gaze. "He understands this world better than you ever will."

"You think so?" My voice sounded as if it was coming from a million miles away. We watched Daniel disappear back into the garage.

"Oh yes. Daniel understands that if you don't know who the mark at the table is, it's you. You on the other hand? You're always looking around the table. You're doing it right now."

"I want my dog back. Sir."

"Well, I'm not about to relinquish my beloved Isengrim without compensation, Will. I've grown quite fond of him. He plays fetch, rolls over, shakes hands, brings me my newspaper, all the things man's best friend should do. I don't know what's gotten into him today."

"What do you want? In return for Buster."

"Hmmm." Gideon placed his hand on his chin and began stroking it theatrically. "I've always found that cold hard cash can calm the stormiest of seas. It both greases the skids of understanding and acts as a poultice on the wounds of grievance." And then Gideon named his price and I knew without doing the math that the amount was exactly what he had paid out to me during my employment, down to the penny. Including the bonuses.

"I gave most of that to my parents," I said. He knew that already. He was toying with me. "It's gone. I can't get it back."

"Oh that's a shame. And the bonuses?" Gideon's unblinking eyes bored into me. "Did those remain our little secret, Will? Or did you betray me as you've betrayed everyone else in this town?"

"I want my dog."

"You can't have him. He's mine. Daniel's mine. Your father is mine. Everything of yours is mine, or will be soon enough. Your mommy too. Don't you see that yet? It's inevitable. Do you know what that word means, little boy?"

"I'm not scared of you," I blurted out through hot tears of impotence and hate and fear. He was whittling me down to nothing with the blade of his tongue, reducing me to a pile of curled shavings. I was feeling every cut.

"No?" Gideon's face split into a taunting grin. "Well, I'm not scared of you either."

23

I departed Stagg's place in a thoroughly demoralized state. Gideon was more unfathomable and frightening and invincible-seeming than ever. And I was just as weak and confused and powerless. I drove aimlessly around the outskirts of Greenheart, undecided about where to go or what to do. My first instinct was to run home to Mom but even in my agitated emotional condition I recognized that nothing good would come of that—and that disaster was a distinct possibility. She couldn't do anything about it if Gideon refused to give back our dog, not without Dad's support. But if Dad didn't rally to our cause and confront Gideon about the theft and abuse of Buster, I would never forgive him and neither would Mom. I didn't want to roll the dice on who Dad would stand with in that scenario. He was becoming a stranger to me. A changeling left by mountain trolls to replace the long-gone father of my childhood.

In the end I went to Reverend Rosbourne's house. I told myself that if anyone might listen to what I had to say with a sympathetic ear it would be him. Our pastor knew what it was like to tangle with Gideon firsthand.

The parsonage in which Rosbourne lived was a one-story brick bungalow tucked away at the back of a small lot adjacent to the church. He came to the door with a dishrag slung over one shoulder and his shirt sleeves rolled up to his elbows. He frowned when he saw who had come knocking but paused for only an instant when I asked if I could talk to him.

Rosbourne led me down the hallway to a small, sparingly appointed kitchen at the back of the house. We took seats at opposite ends of a small table shoved up against the wall, the tabletop bare except for a nearly empty sugar bowl. Somewhere at the front of the house I could hear the ticking of a grandfather clock, a big one by the sound of it.

Once I was there, though, I didn't even know where to start. And it was surreal to be sitting alone in our pastor's kitchen. Virtually the only words I had ever spoken to Rosbourne had been at the weekly conclusion of Sunday services, when our family took its place in the long post-service queue of congregants waiting dutifully to compliment Rosbourne on his sermon, impart important family news, or otherwise bend his ear before heading home. Every Sunday I followed my parents' lead and shook his hand when I reached the front of the line. And every Sunday I was treated to the same warm smile and the same gentle rightward tug of his handshake, pulling me to the left and releasing me downstream into the burbling eddies of the departing crowd. Dad and Mom called it his move-along handshake because there were more than a few folks at our church that could get pretty long-winded if they built up any steam.

"What can I help you with, Will?" Rosbourne asked. His face was a blank mask of politeness. The novelty of my visit might have lit a dim spark of curiosity in him but otherwise I got the sense that he was extending the conversational equivalent of one of those move-along handshakes.

I cleared my throat. "Thanks for seeing me, sir." A random memory popped into my head, of a church baseball game a few years previous when Rosbourne murmured from behind his umpire's mask that I was swinging late.

"How can I help you?" he repeated.

"Um, everyone says you were a professor back east before you became a pastor."

Rosbourne blinked in surprise at the question. "That's not quite right. I studied European history and literature at NYU. New York University. Medieval and Renaissance periods, mostly."

"Like Don Quixote?"

"Earlier than that."

"Shakespeare?"

"You're getting warmer. I joined the seminary when I was still a year short of getting my PhD." He shrugged. "I felt a calling and I answered it. I never became a professor if that's what you think. I gave lectures for a couple of semesters, did a little tutoring for groceries. That's it. What's this about, Will?"

The news that Rosbourne hadn't even been a professor was deflating. It made my visit feel even more like a fool's errand. I was still absorbing his depressing clarification when he spoke again, but this time in an unmistakably colder register.

"I understand you work for Mr. Starling. Gideon to his friends, of which he has made many. I've seen the two of you around town a few times. Thick as thieves by the looks of it."

I should have expected the cold reception. Rosbourne didn't trust me. Why would he? He thought I was one of Gideon's agents. He hadn't heard or seen me singing with him at the top of my lungs. He didn't know I didn't work for Gideon anymore. He didn't know Daniel had taken my place.

"I'm sorry I ever did, sir. You have no idea how much. I know it doesn't mean much but I quit. He says he fired me but I quit. I feel bad about working for him, sir. I shouldn't have done it. I wish I could take it all back. But we needed the money, sir. And he was different at first—"

"Of course he was. They always are until they get their hooks into you. That's how they operate."

"Yes sir."

I must have talked for an hour. He asked a couple questions to clarify one thing or another but mostly he just listened. I told him about meeting Gideon at the rabbit drive and how those glorious first weeks unfurled. How I reveled in every mesmerizing tale and mind-blowing anecdote he told me. How I hung on every word.

I told him about the secrets I shamefully divulged about friends and neighbors and people from church. I told him about the discord Gideon had sown between my parents and how his manipulations nearly destroyed my friendship with Daniel. I told him Gideon started asking me about him and the church a couple weeks after his arrival in town.

But I didn't tell him about Daniel's theory that Gideon was part of some wider "gifted" brotherhood of mind readers and clairvoyants and people who could talk to the dead. And I restrained myself from telling him that evidently every dog in King County was terrified of Gideon. I needed him to listen to me, not look at me like I was crazy.

I was preparing to fill him in on the afternoon's big discovery that Gideon had stolen my dog when the question that had been driving Mom crazy popped into my head.

"Sir, do you know how it is that Gideon is living over there in Mr. Stagg's house now? How is that allowed? Who gave him permission? Everyone says he just walked in like he owned the place and no one stopped him."

Rosbourne gave me a thin smile. "Some dispute came up about Stagg's estate back East. That's the story everyone's being told. Everything's tied up in legal knots due to some long-lost relation no one ever heard of who came out of the woodwork to contest Stagg's will. His lawyers are pretty fancy fellas, or so Mayor Sipe says. But Stagg's relations back East have money too. Sounds like the arguing's going to go on for awhile, as those things will do. At least the lawyers are making money. And Mr. Starling's happy and that's all that matters these days."

"But—I still don't understand, sir."

"Things have changed since John Stagg passed on, Will. Quickly too, almost as if his death was the starting gun for everything that's since come to pass. Starling has the mayor and town council and most everyone else falling over themselves to stay on his good side. I don't know why he's bothering with this thing down at the theatre tonight. He can name his price right now and if Greenheart can possibly scrape it together it will. He doesn't need the dog and pony show. Maybe he likes having his name on the marquee."

"That doesn't mean he gets to live in whatever house he wants."

"Sure it does. Right now in this town it does. Place yourself in Adrian Vrodegood's shoes. He's been Stagg's lawyer forever. That relationship made his practice the biggest one in King County and maybe three or four counties beyond. Vrodegood's the one responsible for looking after Stagg's house and other assets around King County while the lawyers fight back

23

East. But if the mayor and the town council come to you and tell you that Starling's going to stay at Stagg's house for a while, you're going to hand those keys over. Because otherwise Greenheart will lose him to someplace in Oklahoma or Kansas or Texas that's even more desperate than us. That's Starling's leverage. If you're Adrian Vrodegood do you want to alienate every client you have left in the county? Do you want to be the man who killed Greenheart by letting the town's last chance at rebirth get away? Because that's what they'll call you. And all because you refused to let Gideon move into an empty house? *What's the harm?"*

"Wow."

"Yes. Wow. Vrodegood and the mayor and the board cobbled together some sort of legal fig leaf justifying the rental agreement. But really they're just hoping none of the lawyers duking it out back East take notice."

The grandfather clock at the front of the house began announcing the arrival of the five o'clock hour. It sounded like one of those towering, coffin-shaped clocks. One made of gleaming oak or maple or cherry, with a spired crown and a face filigreed in gold and glass and slender black spearpoints. A clock from an N.C. Wyeth painting, standing sentinel over a pirate captain's booty-filled quarters or a sorcerer's secret library. I imagined the clock's long glass windowpane and the gleaming pendulum swinging inside the great hollow chest, counting days and years and centuries away.

It occurred to me then that I didn't know anything about the man sitting across from me other than he was a pretty good minister who had probably reached the point where he hated Gideon more than he loved God. I wondered what the grandfather clock meant to him. Why would he take the trouble of shipping it all the way from New York City to Greenheart on a minister's salary? Perhaps it was a treasured heirloom, deeply embedded in multiple generations of the Rosbourne family saga.

Or maybe the clock wasn't even his. Maybe it belonged to the church, a final bequest from a deceased parishioner. Maybe there was no one left alive who knew the story of how that great clock had come to reside in a modest parsonage in a dying town on the parched southeast Colorado plains.

Finally I got to the end. I told Rosbourne how Gideon had dognapped

Buster and treated him so cruelly. I told him how seeing Buster in such a fallen state broke my heart.

"Gideon gave Buster a stupid name too," I muttered. "Issgrin? Icegrim? It was something weird like that. He used it in a way that made it sound like a name he hadn't just made up."

Rosbourne sat back in his chair. "Look Will, I'm glad you're not involved with him anymore. Starling. I know that was a source of worry for your mother. I'm sorry about your dog too but I don't know what you think I can do about that. You need to talk to your parents about that situation."

I was only half-listening. Something had occurred to me when I mentioned the odd name Gideon had given to our dog. A shard of memory from the night Gideon and I parked in front of Stagg's mansion. It bobbed to the surface of my consciousness, jarred loose from deep fathoms of forgetfulness. A single word. "Have you ever heard of a place called Maberdice? Maperdice? Something like that?"

Rosbourne cocked his head at me, as if he was listening to the faintest snippet of a song he couldn't quite place. But after a moment he shrugged. "Sorry."

"I don't think it's a city," I added. "More like a house or a castle. A fancy one. The sort of fancy house that rich people like to give names to. Gideon talked like he used to live there. We were parked in front of Mr. Stagg's house one night and he said it reminded him of Maperdice or Maberdice, something like that. Except without the secret passages."

Rosbourne gave me a strange look and I felt my heart quicken in response. I wracked my memory for anything else to add.

"Oh! What about Bellin the Ram and Brawn the Bear? No! Brunn. Brunn the Bear, that was it. Bellin and Brunn. Have you heard of them?"

The blood drained from Rosbourne's face and he became very still.

"What does it mean? Who are they?"

He stared at me for a full ten seconds, then left the kitchen without a word. I listened to him trot down the hall and rummage around somewhere at the front of the house. He returned a moment later with a small stack of old books, many of them with embossed lettering on their flaking spines.

"It's usually pronounced Maleperduys," he said briskly. "Although it's been spelled and pronounced a lot of different ways over the centuries, and in a lot of different languages."

"What has?"

"The place Gideon referenced. Maleperduys." Rosbourne cleared his throat. "Ah, okay, let me see what I can remember off the top of my head, before I have to start looking things up. Maleperduys is a hideout—a lair, really—described in a collection of folktales that originated in Europe in the early Middle Ages, then spread across a good portion of the continent in subsequent centuries. Folktales about a trickster fox named Reynard. Maleperduys was Reynard's house. He had an Uncle Isengrim, who was a wolf—and his sworn enemy."

24

Rosbourne pushed the book across the table at me, tapping his finger on an illustrated plate that filled the right page. It was a fanciful depiction of a dapper-looking fox standing on his hind legs in the middle of a royal court of some sort, surrounded by a menagerie of robed goats and bulls and bears standing upright on their hind legs. The fox was nattily clad, with a fine-looking cape and a dagger at his hip. He was bowing before the throne of a regal if somewhat dissipated-looking lion upon whose flowing mane was perched a spiky crown. In his left hand the smiling fox held a feathered hat he had removed in a flourish of deference to the king. The lion's great paws, meanwhile, held out a necklace from which was suspended a round medallion, its flat surface faintly smudged with an indistinct image. He appeared to be bestowing it upon the fox as part of some ceremony of recognition or gratitude. All the other animals in attendance, though, looked saddened or scandalized by what they were witnessing.

Rosbourne gave me a quick rundown of how Reynard fit into the wider pantheon of trickster figures romping through faiths and lore and storytelling traditions of civilizations around the world. Loki and Hermes. Anansi and Tanuki. Nanabozho, the shapeshifting trickster of Ojibwa legend who fought Paul Bunyan for forty days and forty nights. Others too. Mercurial court jesters and thieves and intriguers, gaslighters one and all, armed with light fingers and clever musings and a thousand ways to kill you. Making mischief and merry among gods and mortals alike for generation after generation.

According to Rosbourne, stories about this Reynard character dated all the way back to the eleventh and twelfth centuries, when generations of French, Dutch, German, and English storytellers and bards breathed life into a cycle of breathtakingly cynical and bloody fables about the hardscrabble, deeply stratified Medieval world that all but the most canny or fortunate were struggling to survive. Collectively, the stories took the form of what Rosbourne called a beast epic—a long and dramatic narrative filled with animals who spoke, dressed, and behaved just like humans. Which is to say very badly.

The anthropomorphic world through which Reynard scampered was steeped in avarice and gullibility and the sweet satisfactions of getting away with it. The trickster spared no one who wandered into his field of vision— the powerful least of all. Indeed, Reynard took special pleasure in toppling those of high station from their great heights, from the dimwitted creatures who claimed noble lineage to the sanctimonious hypocrites who filled the ranks of the clergy. He liked hearing their screams when he sent them falling from their high perches.

The Reynard cycle evolved over the centuries, metastasizing into new forms in the hands of new generations of storytellers, but most of the grafts and mutations stayed true to the misanthropic spirit of the original tales. Chaucer even retold one of Reynard's stories in his Canterbury Tales.

And standing astride every tale like a snickering emperor was the gleefully amoral Reynard, whose appetite for mayhem and sport was matched only by his talent for narrow escapes and gusto for cruel trickery. Gimlet-eyed and silver-tongued, he was an unrepentant user of others, an arsonist at heart, and a libertine to his core. Self-interest and self-indulgence and sadism were his north stars.

And yet to hear Rosbourne tell it, Reynard was the hero of those nihilistic tales. They called him a rogue. He was admired for his slippery ruthlessness and his talent for deception. For his razor-sharp teeth and finely-honed dagger and liar's tongue and his willingness to use any and all of them on anyone. He was a hero for the cynics, of which there were multitudes in a savage Medieval world where the church and the lord of the manor always won.

In the Reynard stories, though, *he* always won. Always. His triumphs were cathartic for listeners who spent their entire lives with someone's boot on their neck. His diabolically stylish victories, combined with the venality and stupidity of Reynard's marks, somehow validated all the fox's raping and pillaging and murderous sleights of hand. It was only in the last century or two that those bloodthirsty tales were sanitized into bedtime stories and folktales for the little ones. A fox with more clever and refined Victorian sensibilities. More tea and crumpets than tooth and claw. But still and always the smartest one in the room.

"I want to read you one last thing," Rosbourne said, and began reading from a scholarly tally of Reynard's most famous victims from those blood-drenched fables. I heard him say the name of honey-loving Brunn, reduced to a state of anguished disfigurement by Reynard's trickery.

The Tongue of Brunn the Bear.

I heard the name of poor dumb Bellin, executed by the king after Reynard framed him for a murder that the fox himself committed.

The Horn of Bellin the Ram.

I heard other names called. Noble the Lion, monarch of the realm, who was so hoodwinked by Reynard's cunning lies that he made the fox his most trusted advisor. Isengrim the wolf, Reynard's greatest nemesis, whose children the fox blinded and whose wife he raped. Chaunticleer the Rooster and Cuwaert the Hare and Tybert the Cat, all of whom suffered grievously at Reynard's hand. One by one, I matched each name that Rosbourne read out of that book to something Daniel and I had pulled from Gideon's filthy ammo boxes. The rooster claw. The scroll of catskin. The pair of shriveled walnuts that had once been wolf testicles.

My eyes went blank as Reynard's brutalized victims came sidling up to my ear one-by-one, begging for a final move-along handshake to oblivion. Their longing for release whistled through the eaves of my bones, a ghost chorus of lamentation. The fox in the painting in Stagg's upstairs bedroom materialized behind my unseeing eyes.

It's true it's true it's true it's true Oh my God it's true
Gideon is Reynard
Gideon is Reynard
Gideon is Reynard
Gideon is Reynard
Gideon is Reynard
Gideon is Reynard

Is this what insanity was like? Believing that fictional characters walked among us? It was impossible. Which meant my mind had snapped in some awful, irrevocable way. I pictured myself as an old man, bumping along the damp hallway of a subterranean sanitarium echoing with shrieks near and far, like a call-and-response from different circles of hell.

It was impossible. But it was true. All those rabbits really *had* frozen in their death throes to stare at Gideon when his otherworldly voice first reverberated in their blood-filled ears. The dogs of King County really *could* smell the black-hole musk of him whenever he approached. Gideon really *had* spent time adventuring in all the exciting cities and mountains and palaces he had described in his lushly detailed and endlessly beguiling stories. He'd just done it under different names over the centuries, shedding identities like old snakeskin.

I felt a perverse urge to laugh but suppressed it. I was worried I wouldn't be able to stop. A whip-smart and manipulative talking fox from Medieval legend was moving among us in Greenheart and I was the only one who knew. I felt like a tiny boat at the bottom of four-story waves, hundreds of miles from land.

"Will? Will! Hey! Are you okay? Will!"

I returned to Rosbourne's kitchen in stages. His voice reeled me up out of the deep like a hooked fish. He had my left shoulder gripped in his right hand, hard. I dimly realized that he had been shaking me.

"Are you all right?" he said again, watching me closely over the top of his reading glasses. He released his hold on me. "You turned white as a ghost. Your eyes fluttered and you kind of moaned. I thought you were going to faint."

"Sorry," I managed after a few seconds. Once I was sure I could speak without breaking into sobs I took a deep breath and met Rosbourne's searching gaze. "Gideon knows those stories too. The ones you've been telling me. About all the things Reynard did to those other animals. He knows every single one of those stories. By heart."

25

Rosbourne flipped his attention from book to book, burying his nose in each one for minutes at a time. Not even a hint of a breeze came through the kitchen's lone open window. It was going to be warm in the theatre for Gideon's show that night.

Rosbourne took another book off the stack, flipped to the passage he wanted, and started reading. I counted seven books open on the table around him. The only sound in the entire house was that grandfather clock tocking away at the front of the house. I hadn't spoken in ten minutes and he hadn't noticed. The reverend was back with old friends.

Rosbourne had not responded to my alarming inventory of the contents of Gideon's ammo boxes as I had hoped he would. "Gideon did his homework, I'll say that for him," was his response. He admitted to being puzzled by the lengths to which Gideon was going to maintain his strange Reynard charade. "But there's a lot of things that puzzle me these days, Will. I'm trying not to lose too much sleep over them."

I cleared my throat and he looked up from the book he was reading. "I guess I'm going to head off, Pastor Rosbourne. Thanks for talking to me. Thanks for listening."

Rosbourne's expression softened. "I'm sorry Gideon stole your dog, Will. Truly I am. But like I said earlier, that's something for your parents to take up with Starling, not me. At least for starters. And then the police. Still not me."

"What about the rest of it? All that stuff we found in those ammunition boxes?"

"They don't prove what you seem to think they prove. He's got you all twisted up in knots with this Reynard nonsense. Will, whatever happened between you and Starling, my advice to you now is to steer well clear of him. Make it inconvenient for him to give you a hard time. However you got there you're on Starling's bad side now and that's not a good place to be. Having said that? Keep your distance tonight and you'll be fine. Starling's got bigger fish to fry."

I wanted to believe the reverend but he was wrong. He didn't understand. He hadn't felt the soul-lacerating purity of the hatred that radiated from Gideon in John Stagg's bedroom when he caught us snooping around. He didn't hear his low chuckle when Buster's ghastly appearance sent a wrecking ball through my chest. He didn't know how Gideon teased and pulled at the last fraying threads of Mom and Dad's marriage—then tugged harder.

Once upon a time I was the lucky boy who had been selected by Gideon out of all the boys in Greenheart to be his trusted sidekick. But the circumstances of our parting had triggered something in him. Something petty and vindictive. He had taken my withdrawal from his orbit personally and escalated it into a blood vendetta. Just as Reynard would have done.

I couldn't find the words to make Rosbourne understand any of that. Any more than I could make him understand that the jar we found really did hold the honey-pickled tongue of Brunn the Bear.

"I can't steer clear of him," I said miserably. "I have to stop him. You don't understand."

"What don't I understand? Stop him from what? Doing his little song and dance tonight? Who cares. And who knows? Maybe he'll make it rain for a month and earn every last dollar the town gives him. Wouldn't that beat all? Most likely, though, he'll be gone in another day or week and people can take a look around and see who can still look one another in the eye after."

"He's going to do something bad. Real bad. I know it."

"Well, you might be right about that. But if the people of Greenheart want to give their hard-earned money to a carnival hustler I guess they can. It's a free country."

Rosbourne settled back in his chair and rolled his neck around on his shoulders, making it crack. His eyes settled on mine. "Will, I've got a question to ask before you go and I want you to think real hard on it after you leave."

"Yes sir."

"Are you sure Gideon isn't just leading you around by the nose about all this Reynard business? He has you pretty spooked."

"No, I—"

"Hear me out. From where I'm sitting Starling has spent the last two months filling your head with lies and fantasies and tall tales about himself and now he's got you half-believing another one. It would be easy enough for him to get acquainted with my academic record at NYU, you know. Easy enough to turn that information into a trail of breadcrumbs for you to follow straight to me. Grist for the mill. All he does is add a few dusty props from a taxidermy shop, give you just enough time to sneak a peek, and *voila*. The person who knows more about what Gideon Starling has been up to than anyone else in Greenheart is off on a wild goose chase. Or a wild fox chase in your case. I'm sorry son but I think he's toying with you. With both of us. But I'm not playing. You shouldn't either."

"What if that's not what it is?"

"What?"

"What if it's not an act?" I said. "What if he really believes he's Reynard?" Even then, I couldn't give voice to what I already knew with every thrumming fiber of my being: Reynard the Fox was going to be striding across the brightly lit stage of the Greenheart Theatre later that night in all his cruel and resplendent glory.

Rosbourne tilted his head back and rubbed at his eyes. He gave me a hard-to-read smile, then retrieved a two-thirds empty bottle of bourbon and two chipped coffee cups out of a narrow cupboard at the other end of the kitchen. He brought the cups over to the table and splashed two fingers into his cup, then filled mine with milk from the ice box.

"What if Starling really and truly believes that he's Reynard?" Rosbourne said, repeating my question back to me as he returned to the table. "What if he actually thinks he's a talking fox from the Middle Ages carting around the remains of a bunch of other talking animals?"

He picked up his cup and tossed the bourbon back, closing his eyes to savor the burn. When he opened them again his eyes were fixed somewhere far away.

"Well if he believes that he's a madman, isn't he?"

And then he poured himself another.

III

Before the dawn he had loved and fed,
And found a kennel, and gone to bed
On a shelf of grass in a thick of gorse
That would bleed a hound and blind a horse.

There he slept in the mild west weather
With his nose and brush well tuckt together,
He slept like a child, who sleeps yet hears
With the self who needs neither eyes nor ears.
—John Masefield

It is only when you suffer that you really understand.
—Jules Verne

26

I reached the Greenheart Theatre with thirty minutes to spare but every street and alley downtown was already lined with parked cars and trucks. I had to retreat several blocks away, deep into a neighborhood, before I found a place to park.

The crowd milling outside the theatre was buzzing with excitement and nervous energy, replenishing itself with new arrivals as others churned their way inside to lay claim to good seats. The theatre's marquee had been turned on for what felt like the first time in months, adding to the festive atmosphere. The electric light illuminated the faces bobbing and moving and talking on the wide sidewalk below, burnishing them with the glow of occasion. The marquee didn't normally shine so bright, not with so much daylight left. But it seemed especially luminous that evening, what with still-powerless neighborhoods all around us.

Some of the people milling around on the sidewalk were pointing off to the west. I turned to take a look and stopped in my tracks. All across the western skyline, the day's last sunlight had been blotted out by a line of distant thunderheads. A blanket of mammatus clouds stretched from one end of the horizon to the other, their lightning-filled bellies spanning the sky like graveyard cotton candy. A thin, distorted blade of light cracked soundlessly out of the bottom of the line of the thunderheads. I wondered if I had imagined it but another one flickered across my retinas an instant later. An uneasy murmur rippled through the crowd. Beggars couldn't be choosers when it came to rainfall but no one wanted a gully washer.

I heard people around me saying they could smell rain in the air. They turned to each other with eyes newly bright with hope. If Greenheart's salvation was finally at hand in the form of Gideon Starling, an accompanying cannonade of thunder and lightning seemed pretty damned appropriate. The crowd made a collective decision to greet the approaching storm as a good omen.

I turned away and pushed through the press of people at the entrance, keeping my head down to minimize the likelihood of running into Dad. He was probably somewhere inside already—maybe even backstage with Gideon and other members of his inner circle. I imagined him somewhere deep in the bowels of the theatre on bended knee, polishing Gideon's already shining shoes. I pushed the image away. I didn't like thinking of Dad that way. Servile and compliant. At Gideon's beck and call. Besides, if anyone was shining Gideon's shoes it was Daniel.

I knew Dad would be furious with me for disappearing with the car that afternoon, Buster or no Buster. He had been working me hard since I had parted ways with Gideon. Mom had retaliated by making more of my favorites for supper. Dad saw what she was doing—she didn't bother hiding it—and that further pissed him off, though he never said a word. He just added a few more unpleasant tasks to my list of chores. Their passive-aggressive jousting left me feeling pretty whipsawed at the end of each day.

I squeezed through the doors of the theatre and into the crowded lobby. The space was a babble of bright voices and laughter and drifting cigarette smoke. Mr. Ellery emerged from the jostling crowd and made his way over to me, nervously stroking the brim of the frayed fedora in his hands.

"Hi Will," he said. "Quite a crowd, huh?"

"Hi Mr. Ellery. Yes sir."

"Did you hear about the hotel?" His smile of greeting disappeared. "It's closing fur sure. I didn't want to believe it but in my heart I knew this day was coming. I just knew. The lawyers finally broke up that logjam over Mr. Stagg's estate. That's what everyone's saying anyway. I don't know what's going to happen but all guests have to be out by the end of next week. Not that anyone stays there anymore. Two guests in the whole place last night.

A decade ago the Zephyr was turning travelers away. I don't know. Maybe somebody will buy it when things turn around here. You never know, right? Our luck has to change sometime, doesn't it?"

"I'm sorry," I said. Mr. Ellery sounded like someone who didn't have the faintest idea what his life was going to look like in a month. I thought about all the other men and women like him who were out there already, two or three or twelve furlongs ahead of him in their nomadic wanderings. I pictured them blowing across the continent, looking up at the black vault of heaven with homeless eyes. Searching the night sky for shooting stars upon which they could wish for another life.

"Don't worry about me, Will," Mr. Ellery said, as if he had read my mind. "I'll be fine. *We'll* be fine. Greenheart, I mean. All we need is a little rain. I guess that's why we're here, right? I know I shouldn't get my hopes up but I think this Gideon fella is something special, don't you? I could tell the first time I laid eyes on him, the very first time he come into the Zephyr. The very first time. I bet you could too. You could tell he was something special."

I didn't say anything. Mr. Ellery looked at me quizzically, then gave me a quick, unconvincing smile. "All of these bad times are going to seem like a bad dream, just you wait." He nodded to himself, as if he had cautiously stepped on a plank and confirmed that it would bear his weight. "You just have to keep the faith."

The words were out of my mouth before I could call them back. "I have faith all right. Faith that Gideon's not what you want him to be."

Mr. Ellery's smile vanished as if I'd slapped it off. I felt a stab of remorse at that, but it didn't cut nearly deep enough for me to issue an apology. I walked away without another word, leaving a dumbfounded Ellery behind, and joined the shuffling streams of people entering the auditorium. And just in time too. All but the last two rows were already filled on the main floor, and I could hear the thump and creak of footsteps over my head as the balcony filled up. Some folks were going to end up standing along the walls if they wanted to see the show.

I made a quick scan of the crowd for Mom and Dad, then retreated to a position deep against the back wall under the balcony. I closed my eyes and tried to calm myself as people shouldered past, hurrying to the seats that had been saved for them, the commotion around me growing louder and louder. White drifts of cigarette smoke wafted up from the crowd like breath from a hundred dragons.

I thought about praying but my mind refused to calm. Sometimes when I thought of God I imagined him as some wizened Rip Van Winkle, eyes clouded over with cataracts as he groggily fumbled for his ear trumpet. Other times He was a terrifyingly unbalanced family patriarch, volcanic and capricious like Zeus. There was the version of God that Rosbourne talked about too, compassionate and all-knowing, a Creator so devoted to our salvation that he gave us His only son. They all competed for my attention and consideration but none of them ever elbowed their way to the front of the pack. I gave all of them the move-along handshake.

The confounding mystery of Gideon's existence in our world, though, exerted a magnetic pull on my thoughts. The notion that Gideon's cruel chicanery was all part of God's inscrutable plan was too existentially bleak for me to confront, but a multitude of other possibilities took shape in my reeling mind. Had some witch or warlock beckoned Gideon into existence in some dark Germanic wood? Was he a refugee from the spiritual world in corporeal form, somehow made flesh by one of the gifted mediums or spiritualists Daniel had been going on about? Or did he hail from some other plane or dimension of existence, one thinly overlaid with ours in time and space? A place where the myths and fairy tales and ballads and stories humans have spun for each other across millennia are somehow alive and breathing? Some of them at least. The ones with lasting power. The ones that dig roots deep into the psyches and memories of towns and provinces and nations and continents until they become part of the cultural bedrock.

I thought about what it would be like to switch places with Gideon. To step out of this cruel and dreary world and into the green forests and resplendent palaces and bawdy tavern halls described in the Reynard cycle. Or any other of the worlds to which I'd been transported over the years by radio programs and movies and books and time-wasters and the brilliant storytelling of Gideon Starling himself. Magical worlds peopled with intrepid heroes and diabolical villains who carelessly tossed mortals about in the course of their archetypal adventures. It would be perilous to live among such high-flying creatures. To be courted and discarded and manipulated and forgotten and avenged in accordance with the needs of the central plot, of which you were decidedly not an indispensable part.

Maybe Gideon discovered a gateway between his world and ours. A locked door that finally opened on the millionth try. I imagined him strapped into a glittering machine that traveled not through time but across planes of existence, enabling him to come and go as he pleased. Or maybe he had become trapped here somehow—fallen through a dark rabbit hole or stuffy wardrobe closet or ghostly fog bank or other magical means of conveyance—and can't find his way back. It was a grim scenario to consider. The Reynard the Fox described by Rosbourne would be incandescent with rage at such a fate. To be imprisoned forever in a world where drab humankind reigns and the only animals that talk are parrots? It would bring out the worst in him. He would gnaw his own leg off to get out of a trap like that.

Finally my thoughts returned to the diver. He had paid me another visit the previous night. He left me sweating and panicky and sure I was the last person on earth when I resurfaced in the ticking dark of my bedroom. I retraced every detail of the diver's approach across that pulverized moonscape. The familiar horizon line of desolation that encircled me. My frantic efforts to save the convulsing diver from whatever was strangling him. The way his empty Mark V diving helmet faceplate yawned open in the orange gloaming. The nightmare had the feel of prophecy to it. But what was it prophesying? What augury lay hidden in its dust-caked entrails?

I don't know how long I replayed that clacking nightmare reel in my head. I don't know whether Gideon started on time or made everyone wait forty-five minutes. All I know is that I was still thinking about that diver when the house lights dimmed.

And the worst night of my life began.

27

The auditorium went dark and the stage lights came up on a wall of heavy red velvet curtain. A swell of excited whispering rippled through the crowd and a moment later Greenheart's mayor, Theodore "Teddy" Sipe, walked out from the wings to the standing microphone to a smattering of polite applause. His son Conrad was a classmate of mine. He would have been one of my most enthusiastic tormentors if word had ever got out about my crush on Miss Wells.

Mayor Sipe knew enough to keep his remarks brief. Nobody was there to see him. He informed the crowd that after a great deal of careful deliberation, he and the town council had unanimously voted in favor of securing Gideon Starling's rainmaking services. He said that Gideon was offering a full money-back guarantee that his application, which would take eighteen days to complete, would generate five years of moderate, predictable rainfall that would enable Greenheart to turn back the clock to yesteryear's oceans of wheat. That got people talking with their neighbors pretty good for a minute or two.

Sipe glossed over the various ways the town and its citizenry were going to have to twist themselves into financial knots and deeper strata of debt to meet Gideon's steep price—then shut down the rising mutters of dismay by emphasizing that they had all gathered together that night at Mr. Starling's specific request: he wanted to show them he was worth it. They could judge for themselves whether to put their trust—and their future—in Gideon's hands. Nothing had been signed yet. Sipe must have said that three or four times. He told us that Gideon insisted on waiting until after the evening's program so that we could withdraw the contract if we wished.

"And so without further ado," he concluded, "please join me in giving a big Greenheart welcome to my good friend and yours, Mr. Gideon Starling!" He looked to his right and began clapping his hands with performative enthusiasm as Gideon strode into view, waving and grinning at the burst of spirited applause his appearance elicited. He exchanged a vigorous handshake with the mayor and the clapping and cheering intensified, filling the theatre.

Sipe scurried offstage and Gideon stood up there alone, smiling at familiar faces in the front rows as he waited for everyone to settle down. He looked perfectly at ease. His suit was crisp and spotless and fit him like a glove. The pin on his lapel twinkled like an ivory coin under the stage lights. Even from the back of the auditorium I could see that Gideon was scanning the sections closest to the stage as the applause rolled on. His gaze lifted to take in the back half of the house and I hunched deeper into the shadowed underside of the balcony. I closed my eyes and became still, like a rabbit frozen by the shadow of a hawk passing overhead.

I counted to five and opened my eyes again. Gideon was staring right at me, lips peeled back in a smile that I could tell was just for me. The sight of his chess-bishop eyeteeth turned every capillary in my body to ice. I had never dreamed that it was possible to be so terrified.

He released me then, his gaze moving on to complete his sweep of the packed auditorium, but I had seen the blood pledge in his eyes. He was coming for me. I might have bolted from the theatre then and there if I had trusted I could make my legs work right.

Gideon took the big bullet-shaped microphone out of its cradle and brought it up to his face as the thick black cord coiled itself docilely at his feet. He started off by thanking everyone for coming and asking if everyone in the back could hear him. From there he pivoted to name dropping, thanking Sipe, various council members, and other prominent business owners, church and other community leaders, and farmers scattered across Greenheart and King County for their inspiring faith and patriotism and community spirit and inspiring example. He identified every one by name. He even thanked Mrs. Brennan, our church organist. I felt a rising queasiness in my stomach as I braced myself for Dad's name.

But it never came. Gideon downshifted instead into a subdued but stirring paean to the stories of hardship and fortitude he had heard since his arrival in Greenheart. The shout-outs were over. He had wrapped them up without ever saying the name Tom Thorpe. He must have rattled off forty names or more but he never said that one.

That meant something and it wasn't but a moment until I had a working theory. It was a parting gift for me from Gideon. He was leaving me with an embittered, humiliated father, stripped of his membership in Gideon's innermost circle of supporters due to a disloyal son.

Gideon's tone turned admiring as he told us how our bravery and strength in the face of great sorrows and setbacks—the *great* heart of *Green*heart, he called it—convinced him that we deserved a second chance. Not a hand out but a hand up, just as he had provided for other deserving communities in Nebraska and the Dakotas.

He said he had some people he wanted us to meet. Gideon pointed stage right and a moment later two nervous-looking couples walked onstage and lined up next to Gideon on a welcoming tide of applause. The men had guileless wind-weathered faces and the women were pretty but not too pretty. They were all wearing what we recognized as their Sunday best because they were wearing the same sort of clothes we wore on Sundays. One of the women wore a look of wavering self-control and finally broke ranks to give Gideon a big hug. He gave her a fatherly pat and gently guided her back to her smiling husband's side.

That couple was from Romeo, Nebraska. The other hailed from Votteler County, South Dakota. The farmer from Romeo spoke first. He cleared his throat and said his name was Allen Fether and that he and his wife were God-fearing people who had traveled a great distance to bear witness to Gideon's many wonders. He was followed by his South Dakota counterpart, a farmer named Edgar Tarr. He told us he and his wife had been on the verge of pulling up stakes and heading back to live with her parents in Baltimore before Gideon came to town. He said leaving would have been the biggest mistake of his life. Their wives took turns at the microphone to deliver similarly heartfelt testimonials, their shining eyes going tender when they spotted the hopeful expressions of fellow farmwives in the audience.

Each of the four stepped forward and back to the microphone at regular intervals, seamlessly handing the baton of the narrative back and forth. The men spoke of once-barren fields thick again with golden seas of wheat. Of emaciated livestock returned to good health and chugging tractors and new family cars with full gas tanks and patch-free tires. The women told us how wonderful it was to eat roast beef on Sundays again, and to be able to buy clothes and shoes that fit their growing children. To be able to buy them Christmas presents again. Gideon had saved them and he would save us too. They told us to call anyone in Romeo or Votteler County when the phone lines were back up and working and they would tell us the same.

The couples gave Gideon firm handshakes and chaste farewell embraces before floating offstage to loud applause. As soon as they disappeared, though, every eye returned to Gideon, who began pacing back and forth at the front of the stage as he talked. He briskly summarized his years of study at Europe's finest schools of meteorology and his lifelong passion for scientific inquiry and discovery. He whisked us through abbreviated discussions of barometric pressure and drought patterns and water tables and the bundle of natural laws and weather systems that had worked hand-in-glove to turn King County into a golden land of ripe wheat in the first quarter of the now blighted century. And then he told us why our fields had withered and died.

Features darkening with anger and indignation, Gideon told us how the great stinking factories and squalid slaughterhouses and towering tenements of America's overcrowded cities were polluting the heavens above us—"Yes, even all the way out here!" Gideon declared. He painted a picture of deadly vapors and sickly stenches spiraling into the atmosphere from every city sewer and chimney and stockyard, rerouting seasonal air currents and sterilizing swaths of the atmosphere that Almighty God Himself had set aside for the incubation of spring rains and summer cloudbursts.

Gideon shook his head and glowered with anger at the unfairness of it all. He told us that he knew firsthand the discouragement and impotence and fury festering in our hearts. He understood what it was like to watch the hard-earned fruits of all your sacrifice and toil blow out to sea. To wonder if your prayers are being heard.

"Well, I'm here to tell you that they have been heard," he declared. "Because I know how to fix what's broken up there." He pointed to the ceiling and an instant later an audible rumble of thunder rolled over our heads, as if on cue. The theatre's dimly glowing wall sconces rattled in response. I could see the question forming in the wide eyes of the men and women around me. I could feel it in my own thudding heart. *Did Gideon do that?*

Gideon told us that bringing regular rainfall back to Greenheart and the rest of King County required precise and exacting recalibrations of complex weather systems, but that it could be done with the right tools.

"Now I've had the pleasure of getting to know quite a few of you over the last few weeks, at least a little bit, and I think you've gotten to know me a little too," Gideon continued. "You've welcomed me into your parlors and kitchens and stores and fields and told me about your lives and what you have at stake out here and I appreciate that more than I can say. Truly I'm honored. And in return for your honesty and hospitality I've shown you my charts and tabulations and blueprints. I've explained how my cloudseeding process works. Earlier tonight I even arranged for you to hear from a few of the people I've been able to help. But talk is cheap at the end of the day, isn't it? Seeing is believing." A sly smile danced on his lips. "So is it time we got to that? The proof of the pudding is in the eating, wouldn't you agree?"

The crowd roared approval, the sound swelling until it filled the theatre. Gideon grinned and placed the big microphone back in its cradle, then carried the entire stand over to the far side of the stage, the thick black cord trailing behind him like an endless rat's tail. He left the microphone stand at stage left and returned to center stage, whereupon he held his right hand out straight at chest level and slowly lowered it. The stage lights dimmed as if in obedience to his hand and a fresh burst of excited chatter ran through the auditorium. Everyone was on pins and needles, including me.

The lights dimmed until the entire hall was bathed in a dusky sunset hue. The sconces lining the auditorium walls glowed like ingots of molten amber, then flickered as another ordnance of thunder exploded over our heads. A few small children started crying. A heavy metallic clacking sound pierced the air somewhere above my head, up on the balcony, and the white beam of a single spotlight pierced the darknes. Gideon basked in the circle of light, his wingtips poised at the edge of the orchestra pit. The town hall trappings of the gathering had been entirely cast aside. Gideon was turning it into something else entirely.

"Ladies and Gentlemen!" Gideon's voice filled every corner of the darkened theatre. He hadn't needed the microphone at all. "I'd like you to put your hands together and help me welcome to the stage a familiar face to many of you! A stalwart member of your fine community who will be assisting me with the evening's closing ceremonies—and she's pretty easy on the eyes to boot! Please welcome Greenheart's favorite schoolteacher, the one and only Miss Helen Wells!"

28

I was too stunned by Miss Wells's appearance—and the sight of the ammunition boxes she carried in her hands—to join in the obligatory applause that rose up around me. Miss Wells was with Gideon now? Could that be true? I flinched away from the bleak thought and some of its more miserable possible implications. The torch I once carried for Helen Wells might have no longer held heat but that didn't mean I wanted to watch her keeping company with a psychopathic fox.

The audience continued to clap as Miss Wells set the two ammo boxes down on their marks, ten feet apart and about fifteen feet behind where Gideon stood. But the applause died away when she joined Gideon downstage and everyone got a good look at her. I heard the first titters of stifled laughter and scandalized whispers filter back through the rows to us. A low roiling that spread through the hall like mustard gas. Something was wrong with Miss Wells.

She was dressed in a sleeveless, low-cut black dress filigreed in tassels and sequins. The dress shimmered like diamonds on stage. She wore a matching black headband, striking against her ash blonde hair, from which sprouted a starburst of shiny black feathers. Gideon had dressed her like a flapper, one of those legendarily loose and liberated party girls who used to haunt the speakeasies and jazz clubs of the big cities that Gideon had just finished excoriating. I had watched flappers dance and smoke and drink and flirt across the big screen of this very theatre on many a Saturday. Flappers were exotic and alluring and made me think about sex a lot. But I knew what people around Greenheart thought about flappers in 1936. Dressing up like Zelda Fitzgerald had been a mistake.

Her garish makeup was even more jarring than her costume. Whatever stage makeup Gideon had applied on himself gave him an appearance of natural vigor and good health. By contrast, Miss Wells's features were almost clownishly painted. Her lipstick gleamed blood red against the white powder caked on her face and the twin bruises of plum-colored rouge on her cheeks. A racoon's mask of black eyeshadow framed her frightened, pale green eyes.

I couldn't make sense of what I was seeing. Didn't Miss Wells know how she *looked?* I glanced around at the people lining the back wall around me, first to my left, then to my right. The only people who weren't enthralled by the events unfolding onstage were three men in frayed overalls stationed down the way a little, in one of the doorways between the lobby and the auditorium. They were taking turns checking on the approaching storm outside. I watched as two of them silently switched places.

When I looked back to the stage I saw just how sad and scared and utterly alone Miss Wells looked up there. I watched her brave attempt to smile at some people in the front rows. I saw the way she dropped her eyes and looked away when she saw the way they looked back at her. Their puritan frowns and narrowed eyes and leering snickers. Her face crumpled for a moment, then quickly recomposed itself into the same expressionless mask she donned the morning Gideon visited our church.

Whatever Gideon had told Miss Wells to get her out onstage had been a lie. He had dolled her up like a tart and forced her out into that blinding light for the sole purpose of punishing me. Because he knew she meant something to me. Humiliating her was another twist of the knife in my guts.

Miss Wells would never be able to teach in Greenheart again. Not after this. I blinked away sudden tears of shame and impotent fury. No one in that packed house was speaking up for her. Not even Mom, who hated Gideon and had always liked Miss Wells. Not even me, the person who first spoke her name into Gideon's ears.

But I didn't understand why she was standing up there and taking it. Why didn't she just walk off? Why didn't she just cram that sequined headband in

Gideon's big mouth, curse out the entire theatre, and walk away? He wasn't holding a gun to her head.

But she just kept standing up there, straight-backed and expressionless, her mannequin gaze fixed on some distant point in the darkest corner of the balcony. I wracked my mind for possible explanations. Gideon threatened to leave Greenheart high and dry if Miss Wells didn't help him. He promised her the money for a new life far from Greenheart in exchange for a guest appearance in his big show. He threatened to kill me or someone else in Greenheart—someone I didn't even know, a dear friend or secret lover—if she didn't knuckle under to his demands. Other possibilities far more awful to contemplate came flooding through in short order. Wave trains of fear and jealousy and dread crashed down around my ears, blotting out even Gideon's ringmaster voice.

What if Gideon was forcing Miss Wells to do things . . . sex things . . . to spare Greenheart from his wrath? What if he was going to make her leave Greenheart with him—or even marry him—in return for sparing the town from whatever razor-toothed trap he had set? What if she knew he was magic of the most blackhearted kind? What if he threatened to treat her like the children of his Uncle Isengrim and eat her alive? My knees weakened with relief when Gideon finally dismissed Miss Wells. She walked offstage quickly, head down, to limp applause and isolated catcalls.

Gideon strolled back to his perch on the edge of the orchestra pit and looked us up and down. "Now then. This is the part of the program where I am dutybound to caution everyone that what you are about to see may be upsetting to those with delicate constitutions. Episodes of fainting are not uncommon, and I've seen grown men moved to tears—tears of hope for the future—by what you are about to see. So please attend to your mothers and wives and children and neighbors seated next to you and comfort them if they become overwhelmed or excitable."

The theatre rustled with uneasiness at the words of warning but no one left. They had come this far, after all. And whereas Gideon's tone struck my ears as laden with mockery—a burlesque of respect and concern for our welfare—no one else appeared to hear his words that way. Everyone around me was a trembling tuning fork, begging to be struck again.

"I hope you will keep an open mind about what you are about to see," Gideon declared. "It may leave some of you a little shaky in the knees. But that's ok because that's how you *ought* to feel when you witness one of God's miracles. I don't say that lightly. I say it because I have felt God's divine hand at work in me these past years. I tell you, good people of Greenheart, I have felt it!"

A good number of men and women scattered across the theatre immediately rose to their feet to applaud. A genuine, unscripted response? Maybe from a few, but I guessed they were mostly plants in the audience. The same tactic Gideon had used to crowbar his way into our hymn at church. It was effective, I had to admit.

Gideon's followers got the ball rolling but in truth it didn't take much encouragement to get most of the sweltering crowd up on their feet. Could it be true? Was Greenheart's long nightmare of drought and dust and hunger finally at an end? Everyone wanted to believe the answer was yes so much.

A few pockets in the crowd remained seated, refusing to play along, but they were badly outnumbered. Some of the people standing and clapping became angry at the ones still in their seats. They loomed over them, snarling and staring. I hoped no one was doing that to Mom. I hoped Dad wasn't doing it to her. Most of all, though, I hoped that whatever spell Gideon had cast to bring our congregation over to his side wasn't also working its way through that packed auditorium.

"And now," Gideon's voice cut through the rising crowd noise like a whetstone-sharpened scythe, silencing all others. "Let's give you a taste of what God has in store for you, shall we?"

The last of the stage lights winked out dramatically, right on cue, and the sound of excited, half-hushed voices swirled through the dark hall. The only illumination in the entire theatre came from the honey-colored sconces set at regular intervals along the auditorium's back and side walls. All we could see of Gideon was his silhouette, a deeper black in motion across the darkened stage. Even from the back of the hall I heard the clanking echo of the padlocks when he dropped them onstage. The creak of the boxes as he opened them.

Gideon's silhouette positioned itself between the boxes and slowly raised its hands, as if it were a maestro bringing an orchestra to life. The interiors of both boxes flickered with faint light and a fresh shiver of excitement ran through the crowd. But their whispers and exclamations subsided into mute wonderment when the lights brightened and coalesced into angled beams of warm yellow-gold rising out of the containers. Each column was composed of hundreds of tiny luminous flakes of molten light that came out of the ammo boxes in dense swirling clusters and lonely strays. The columns of light crossed several feet above Gideon's head, bathing his upturned face in a golden glow. He was flushed and sweating and appeared to be talking or singing under his breath.

Another peal of thunder exploded like artillery fire over our heads, rattling the wall sconces and stirring the crowd out of its semi-mesmerized state. The spiraling golden flakes began rising out of the boxes in thicker clots— and more quickly too, as if the light was being *pulled* out of the boxes by some invisible net-wielding fisherman. An icy fingernail of revulsion traced down my spine. I knew what was in those boxes. What I was witnessing was a desecration. A grave robbery.

Above Gideon's head the two luminous rivers of light melted into a seething whorl of grey cloud that pulled in dirty skeins of cigarette smoke with each sluggish rotation. Every flake of light vanished into that expanding cloud, sending up faint flares of illumination before disappearing into the murky depths. Cries of amazement and fear and religious ecstasy rang out across the theatre as the cloud filled the stage over Gideon's head. Several people fled for the exits, some arguing furiously, others silent and ashen-faced.

The sky detonated with a thunderclap that sounded like an anarchist's bomb, the kind that blows up horse carriages and train cars and parliamentary buildings and stock exchanges. The boom made everyone jump and the wall sconces on the left side of the hall winked out, further reducing visibility. I sensed more than saw people next to me look up at the dark underside of the balcony, listening for some telltale crack or other harbinger of impending collapse.

The echo of the thunderclap lingered strangely, reverberating in air that smelled suddenly of ozone. I could hear children crying, frightened by the thunder or the increasingly hallucinatory quality of Gideon's presentation. For a moment I allowed myself to hope that Gideon might have overplayed his hand. That Greenheart would recoil from this spectacle. But then someone yelled *Look!* and people started pointing and we turned our attention back to the stage as one.

Gideon stood under a light, steady drizzle of sweet, precious rain. The mass of cloud above his head rotated clockwise in perfect harmony, clumps clinging to the underside like grey-black sacs of spider eggs. His fine suit was drenched and streaks of brown ran down his wet face from the pomade in his hair. He looked tired. But his eyes sparkled as frenzied applause erupted from the sea of dark faces at his feet. Exclamations drifted in from the lobby as well, followed by shouts of joy and wonder.

It was raining outside too.

Gideon muttered something under his breath and the churning gray cloud over the stage began to break apart and evaporate, taking the rain with it. Within thirty seconds the only evidence that the otherworldly cloudburst had even taken place was a soaking wet Gideon and a rain-slicked stage.

When the house lights came back up Gideon was still basking in Greenheart's adoration. He leisurely shrugged out of his dripping suitcoat and folded it carefully over his right arm as the applause rolled on and on, then strode downstage until he was back at the edge of the orchestra pit. "Well?" He looked out over the stupefied crowd and chuckled. "Do I get the job?"

29

Less than an hour later it was all over. Sipe returned to the stage after Gideon's showstopper of a finale carrying a frozen rictus of a smile and a large towel. The mayor managed to give Gideon's hand a vigorous shake and thank him for his "very impressive display of your system and its capabilities." Gideon left the stage to thunderous applause, the wet towel tossed around his shoulders like a cape.

Sipe looked a lot more scared than when he had introduced Gideon but he still had a job to do. In short order he returned the evening to its nominal town meeting trappings. He advanced the agenda with pre-arranged resolutions and seconded motions and whatnot that passed in a series of voice votes, all of which went heavily for Gideon.

Not everyone stayed. Some people quietly slipped out of the theatre and into the rain-slicked streets before the voting began, too frightened or dismayed by the foregone results to remain. I only heard fifteen or twenty voices call out no when Sipe put the questions to the crowd. One of them was Mom's. I wondered how her defiant, heartbroken voice sounded to Gideon backstage. Music to his ears, no doubt.

I slipped out of the theatre while the last of the votes were still being arranged. The parked automobiles and trucks lining the street gleamed with the freshly fallen rain, making them look like new. Rainwater from the marquee dripped down onto the sidewalk in a dozen different places. Off to the west the fast-darkening sky was aglow in gaudy purples and reds and golds. I looked up and down the empty street, cogitating on the possibility that for all my dire predictions of doom, Gideon might actually fulfill his end of the hard bargain he had made. If Greenheart ultimately received what was promised, even at extortionist prices, where was the grift?

My mind skipped on to other matters. Such as the question of where and how Gideon had become a genuine rainmaker. A conjurer of storms. Because Reynard the Fox never displayed a capacity for spellcasting in any of the satirical tales Rosbourne recounted. Reynard wasn't a sorcerer or magician or warlock in any of those old beast epics. So how could Gideon control the weather now?

I didn't know where to go. I didn't know what to do. Mom had known Gideon was bad news from the start but she couldn't help me now. And I was dreading my next encounter with Dad given his apparent expulsion from Gideon's inner circle.

I almost didn't recognize the two farm couples when they emerged from the dark alley on the north end of the building. They didn't look like farmers anymore. The men wore expensive-looking suits. The women had changed into stylishly patterned dresses and colorful hats. All four of them were carrying small suitcases. One of the men had several suits flung over his shoulder, the hangers bundled together by a single black shoelace with a dangling butcher's tag. I couldn't make out the writing on it but I knew what it said. Those were John Stagg's finest suits, earmarked for tailoring to accommodate Gideon's long-limbed build. The sacking of Greenheart was already underway. The people packed inside the theatre just didn't know it.

I watched the four of them disappear down Depot Street in the direction of the train station. I had no idea where the tickets they purchased would take them, but I knew it wouldn't be Votteler County, North Dakota, or Romeo, Nebraska.

"You and Daniel aren't the only people who work for him, you know."

I turned to the familiar voice and found Miss Wells standing in the half-shadows at the corner of the building, smoking a cigarette. She had changed into a simple, modest dress that I recognized from school and scrubbed all the garish makeup from her face but I felt as if I was looking at a stranger. I told myself it was the smoking.

"Hi Miss Wells." I nodded at the cigarette. "Is he making you do that? Smoke, I mean?"

Her eyes locked on mine, unblinking. Cold. "No, Will. This is a vice I discovered all by myself, thanks. I've always been careful, you know. People don't like schoolteachers who smoke. Bad example for the children. Not very ladylike. I know not to do it in front of anyone, least of all my students. I have to sneak around like a kid myself. Well not anymore."

A knot of guilt twisted in my chest as I watched her take another drag. It was me who had unleashed the tornado that had laid waste to her life. Who said her name to Gideon that night. Who said she was pretty. She would never know why he had singled her out for destruction. Not unless I told her.

I was seized by a sudden memory of my run-in with Gideon after my return from Colorado Springs. Of how he had leered and brought his wriggling fingers to his nose in a suggestive pantomime of sniffing, as if he knew all about my secret lust for Katherine. I wondered if the big dog we spotted lurking in the shadows that night hadn't been a dog at all. Maybe it had been a freakishly large fox. If Katherine's name had ever reached Gideon's ears from my lips he would have gone after her too. I was certain of it. The closeness of that call flushed through my body like ice water.

"Can I ask you a question?" Miss Wells asked, her expression shifting to one of genuine interest.

"Yes Ma'am."

"Do you think he's crazy? I'm only asking because you probably know him better than anyone in this town. You worked for him when he first came to Greenheart, isn't that right? You helped him get in."

A low flush of shame rose in my cheeks. "I did. I'm sorry. You don't know how sorry, ma'am."

"Those lovely folks you saw heading for the train station aren't Gideon's only other employees," Miss Wells repeated, returning to the subject with which she had opened. "Who do you think's been tying John Stagg's estate up in knots these last weeks? Who do you think the mysterious cousin is, the one with all those lawyers suddenly demanding a big piece of Stagg's pie?"

"Gideon."

"Gideon." She said flatly as she shook out another cigarette. "I should probably get going," she murmured to herself but lit up anyway. "Gideon told me to be ready at midnight. I don't want to keep him waiting, do I?"

One of the lobby doors opened down the way and then another. People started filing out, some talking excitedly, others looking weary to the bone. Everyone was finally going home. Miss Wells' eyes turned skittish at the sight of other people. She looked poised to bolt.

"Why do you have to go with him?" I cried. She was going to her doom. How could I warn her about Gideon in a way that didn't make me sound as if I'd gone mad? "Why are you doing that? Please don't. Please don't do that."

Her expression never changed. "That was part of the deal we made," she said patiently. It was the same voice she used to help us figure out math problems at the blackboard. "I only have to go with him to California. He said he wants company for the drive. Someone to talk to. He told me I was interesting. It's been a long time since someone's told me that. He promises to let me go when we get to Los Angeles. And in return he'll spare Greenheart. Although after tonight I'm less inclined to care what happens to this town one way or the other."

"Spare us from what?"

"From what he has planned."

"Which is what?"

"He won't say."

"You can't trust him. He's a born liar, Miss Wells. And he's a lot worse than that. Reverend Rosbourne thinks he's a rapist. And a murderer."

A shadow of uncertainty crossed her face at that shameless shading of the truth, but then her eyes turned flinty and she flashed a savage smile. "Gideon says I'm between the devil and the deep blue sea. That's how Gideon described my situation the other night. That's pretty apt, don't you think? That's where he likes to put people, isn't it."

"Don't go with him."

She took another puff on her cigarette and raised her face to the night sky. "Who knows whether he even comes by to pick me up. He might decide to just leave me here. That would be crueler, I think. To abandon me here. He can always find someone else to listen to him on that drive. I don't know why he singled me out in the first place. I'm nothing special. There's prettier women than me around here."

More people were coming out of the theatre now, their animated voices dropping to hushed whispers when they saw Miss Wells. I sidled out of the light cast by the marquee and joined Miss Wells as she withdrew deeper into the shadowed alley. I didn't want to be spotted by either of my parents, even though they were probably worried sick about me. Neither of them had seen me since Daniel and I had taken the car earlier that same day.

Miss Wells swiped the back of one hand across her eyes and made a sound that was half-laugh and half-sob. "I'm going to go now, Will. But before I do, I want to say something. I'm glad you and Daniel patched things up."

"Yes, ma'am, we did."

"He told me backstage, before the show. You shouldn't be too tough on him about working for Gideon. These are hard times, especially for boys like him. And you worked for Gideon too, remember."

"I remember."

"Good friends don't just grow on trees."

"I know. Yes, ma'am."

"One other thing. Daniel asked me to do something for him. He asked me to grab the lapel pin on the suit coat Gideon was wearing tonight."

"He did?"

"Yep."

"Did you do it?"

Miss Wells's eyes glinted with satisfaction. "I did. It was easy. His coat was hanging off a chair in the dressing room, dripping all over the floor. No one else was around and Gideon was changing his clothes. I gave the pin to Daniel before I left." Her tone turned speculative. "It's only a trinket, I know. Maybe Gideon won't even miss it. But Daniel seemed pretty excited when he saw it."

"I think he'll miss it."

"Really?" She allowed herself a small smile. "Good. One other thing. Daniel asked me to find you after the show. He practically begged me. That's the only reason I'm still here."

"What is?"

"To give you a message."

"What is it?"

"He said he hopes you remember your semaphore alphabet."

30

Gideon's great black shark of a car rolled up from the end of the boulevard to Stagg's long curving driveway, its headlamps sweeping across the silent grounds like twin searchlights. I was sequestered deep in the shaggy pines at the far end of Stagg's property so the beams never approached my hiding place. Even so I hunkered behind the widest, shaggiest boughs I could find, remembering well how his eyes had pinned mine at the back of the dark theatre earlier that night.

Adrenalized fear pulsed in me like a fever. How had it come to this? Daniel and I were going to try to stop Gideon from making off with the money he had pried out of Greenheart earlier that evening. And if we couldn't do that, I was going to at least stop him from doing whatever he had chilling on ice for the town. The successful execution of the trick or con was only rarely the end of a Reynard story. Not according to Rosbourne. There was usually a final clever, ironic, or brutal twist at the end. A mordant coda of cruelty or black humor to give the story's denouement that special Reynard flavor.

Who else was there but us? Gideon had eliminated every other potential threat. He had neutralized Rosbourne, bent the city council to his will, and written Stagg out of the proceedings entirely. Powerless holdouts like Mom had subsided into sloughs of grief and disillusionment. Daniel and I were the last ones standing.

Gideon's rainmaking ceremony down at the theatre had made it clear that the graveyard contents of those old ammo boxes were vitally important to him. They reminded me of the lightning-haired Tesla coils that powered the laboratory in *Frankenstein* where Doctor Frankenstein raised the dead.

But the padlock key inside Gideon's locket—the same one Daniel now had in his possession according to Miss Wells—would be useless in a matter of hours. Gideon and his boxes would more than likely be gone in the morning, at which point the loss of the key would be no more than a nuisance. Gideon could take the ammo boxes to any locksmith and get the padlocks replaced.

Perhaps Gideon had some sort of symbiotic relationship with the locket? Maybe hammering it to pieces would weaken him somehow. Maybe even kill him. It was a thin reed on which to rest any hopes but at least it seemed like the sort of exotic folktale vulnerability someone like Gideon might have. Or perhaps the locket had sentimental value for him, like the story-drenched buttons and bullets and baubles he liked to pluck out of his vest pockets. Could it be a memento from the land of his birth? Whatever the nature of Gideon's relationship to the locket, it was just barely possible that the threat of its loss or destruction might convince him to spare Greenheart—and even return the money he had extorted from the town. As plans go it was equal parts desperation and fantasy but from where I was standing it was the only play we had left.

But I didn't have the locket. Daniel did. And the idea of sneaking into Stagg's place to find Daniel, retrieve the pin from him, and sneak out again— all without attracting Gideon's notice—felt like a suicide mission now that I was hidden away on the grounds.

I watched from deep in the black pines as Gideon stepped out of the driver's seat, shut the door, and strolled to the back of the roadster. Daniel appeared at the back of the car from the other side and Gideon opened the trunk. He stood back and watched with his back to me as Daniel lifted both ammo boxes out, one in each hand. Gideon's voice came floating across the dark yard, the sound carrying in the night air. "And make me a drink!" Gideon bellowed as he clomped up the porch stairs and followed Daniel inside. "You know what I like. Make one for yourself too! Revelry awaits!" The front door slammed shut, cutting Gideon's laughter off like a cleaver.

All was still again but for the night wind rustling through the trees. Long rectangles of paned light materialized on the ground around the house as electric lights flicked on inside. A cool gust of breeze pushed through the pines, my sweat-filmed body going clammy at its touch.

When Daniel marched up Stagg's porch steps and went inside with Gideon, he did it knowing full well that he was in the company of a man who could bring lightning and thunder and rain down from the sky. What he didn't know was that Gideon was *also* a murderous talking fox from another dimension or reality or plane of existence. I decided that on balance I was grateful for that. Even Daniel's courage had its breaking point.

I stepped to the edge of the pines to reconnoiter, a confetti of dead wet pine needles adhering to my sweaty neck and arms as I pushed through the heavy boughs. I studied Stagg's moon-washed barn and stable and garage and the pinprick lights of far-off farmhouses, then tracked the boulevard that ran from Stagg's place all the way down to Greenheart's town square and the Greenheart Theatre's still-glowing marquee. The boulevard was emptied of people now but was still lit up like a carnival midway on the edge of a great black sea.

Satisfied that my perimeter was secure, I turned my attention back to Stagg's moonlit house. Eight windows lined the side of the house facing me, four on each floor. Unlike the brightly lit first floor, the second-floor windows were dark. I focused my gaze on the dark window in the top left corner and moved right until I reached the end of the row, then dropped to the bank of windows below to complete the circuit. I spent five or ten seconds on each window with every clockwise rotation, looking for signs of life. Nothing moved. Every window looked like an empty stage set.

Minutes ticked by, the cool of the night starting to set in. I tried to remember everything Rosbourne had told me about what made Reynard tick in those Medieval tales. In truth he didn't sound very complicated. He was the archetypal trickster. Besotted with his own cleverness. Delighting in the gullibility and misfortunes of his marks. And addicted to the thrill of the hunt from the tip of his pointy black nose to the end of his thick bushy tail.

This had to be a big night for him. No matter how many times Reynard pulled it off, a flawlessly executed con or duplicitous gem of trickery had to feel good. I imagined him inside, tossing back shots from the bench of Stagg's grand piano and making Daniel sing along. Recounting favorite moments from the triumphant campaign just concluded. All we could do was hope his guard went down a little when he took his victory laps because Gideon would tear Daniel limb from limb if he discovered the locket in his possession. For all I knew he was inside the house snapping Daniel's fingers like twigs at that very moment. If Daniel was screaming, would I be able to hear him way out here? I told myself that I would . . . but what if he was moaning or sobbing in pain instead? Or bound and gagged as Gideon did unspeakable things to him?

Such were my tortured ruminations when a low, menacing growl issued out of the night behind me, very close.

Buster.

I twisted around to look behind me and found Buster standing stiff-legged on the fringe of the shelterbelt, the hackles on his wet knobby back shimmering like river stones in the moonlight. He was twenty feet away, maybe less. His eyes were rooted on mine even though I stood deep in the pines where the moon and stars could not reach. I wondered what he was seeing when he looked at me.

He filled the space between us with another low, rolling growl and I felt myself falling away into that special black hole of fear that comes with the prospect of long and sustained physical suffering. I didn't want to experience the agony of a shredded arm or leg from any dog, let alone my own. But if Buster's low growls turned into barking? That would be much worse. Gideon would be out on the porch in a flash and if he caught me he would introduce me to horizons of suffering I never knew existed. I imagined my tongue floating next to Brunn's in its tomb of honey.

Buster wasn't in as bad a shape as he had been that afternoon. His ears were up and alert, not matted against his skull in fear. He wasn't twitching or whining or cowering. He wasn't poor, miserable Isengrim anymore. Understanding came to me in a flash: Buster's level of misery correlated directly with his proximity to Gideon. That's why he was out here at the edge of Stagg's property, far from the house where Gideon lived and slept and ate. Growing scrawnier by the day as he strained at the far end of whatever invisible rope Gideon was using to keep him tied to the place.

I wondered where Gideon had kept Buster stashed before he commandeered Stagg's mansion. Most likely in a crate or cage in an abandoned farmhouse at the end of a forgotten road. Given just enough food and water to keep him alive until Gideon's big reveal.

"Hey Buster." My voice sounded shockingly loud in the shelter of those hulking pines.

Buster stopped growling.

"Hey Buster," I said again, lowering my voice to a whisper. If Gideon somehow heard me from all the way inside the house . . . well, so be it. There was nothing I could do about that. "You've had some rough times, boy, I know that now. But we're going to take good care of you when this is all over, I promise you that. Me and Daniel. Yep, he's here too, he came back. We both did. We came back for you, Buster. We're not going to let him hurt you anymore."

The dog remained frozen in place, a statue in the moonlight. I said his name again and felt a thrill of excitement when he cocked his head at me. Just a little, in that quizzical way dogs do. Then Buster turned to the west with the same fixed stare he had been using on me. He raised his nose and sniffed the air. His ears flattened down against his head and an instant later he bolted, vanishing around the pines to my right without a sound. He reappeared a moment later on the other side of the trees, a silver-flecked silhouette loping across Stagg's moonlit lawn. I watched him disappear into the open left bay of Stagg's three-car garage.

Unnerved by Buster's spooked departure, I peered from my black-boughed hideout to the west, as he had done before running off. All I saw was the same three widely spaced farmhouse lights in the far distance. I exhaled heavily, going limp with relief—until an awful throb of panicked realization hit me square in the chest.

I was supposed to be watching the windows.

I turned back to the house and there Daniel was, leaning out the last window on the second floor, a semaphore flag in each outstretched hand. His ramrod straight arms pointed the flags outward like arrows on a clock face, snapping them precisely from position to position. The flags shimmered and flashed as Daniel moved them around the clock, frantically spelling out letters in the semaphore code we had learned together.

I feared I might no longer remember them all but the first few letters came easily and the rest of the code fell into place after that. I watched Daniel spell out the same word over and over again for the better part of a minute as he stared blindly out into the night.

G L O V E B O X

G L O V E B O X

G L O V E B O X

And then he brought the flags down and disappeared, shutting the window behind him. If Buster had distracted my attention for another thirty seconds I would have missed Daniel altogether—and wouldn't have to grapple with the terrifying message he had sent.

Daniel wanted *me* to grab the locket and take it inside. He wanted *me* to sneak past Gideon while Daniel kept him occupied, go find the ammo boxes, and use the key tucked away inside that locket to open them up. And then he wanted me to spread their contents far and wide and find out if Gideon could conjure rain and thunder from a couple of empty boxes.

An enervating numbness washed over me at the thought of entering that house. Even the pounding of my heart felt distant somehow, as if it was hammering away in someone else's chest. Visions capered at the edge of my mind, a cacophony of shrieking and sobbing and wailing that could have come from John the Revelator. It was one thing to fear death. It was another to fear the sort of gruesome, agonizing death that Reynard the Fox was fond of bestowing on his enemies, of which I was now one. The night was starting to feel like it was building to that but I didn't know how to stop it. Not without abandoning Daniel altogether and I wouldn't do that—couldn't do that. Not unless I wanted to wake up every day of the rest of my life filled with self-loathing.

The wind rose then, swaying the treetops overhead. I tasted grit in the air. Another gust of wind shouldered through the tall pines and a mist of flying dust stung my arms and cheeks. I felt static electricity building around me, remaking the night air with its alien energy, another dark magic all its own. A moment later the twinkling farm lights on the western horizon vanished, as if God Himself had pulled a big black window shade down on that end of the world.

The faint rumble of a speeding truck reached my ears over the rising wind. It was a truck, barreling up Hurley Boulevard out of downtown with headlamps blazing. And right behind the truck a rolling fogbank of churning black dust that looked a thousand feet tall. The light of the theatre marquee vanished, swallowed up by the oncoming tide. Seconds later the boulevard's streetlights winked out two by two, as if the storm hid pole-wielding lamplighters in its choking depths.

The duster overtook the speeding truck at the end of the boulevard and a second later I heard the truck engine short out followed by the faint crunch of metal and breaking glass. The duster rolled forward, as implacable and uncontrollable as the spinning earth over which it passed.

I was directly in its path.

I thrashed my way out of the pines and sprinted for Gideon's car. I was only halfway there, the fast-rising wind thrashing through the trees, when the crest of the oncoming duster blotted out the sky and took the moonlight away. Angling to keep the parked roadster between me and the house, I opened the driver's side door, pushing hard against the rising wind. I wedged myself in the opening between the door and driver's seat and lunged for the glove box. A second later the locket was in my trembling hand, smooth and cool to the touch. I put it in my pocket, backed out of the car, and quietly shut the door, then sprinted for the back of the house, praying that the kitchen door Daniel and I had used earlier that afternoon was still unlocked.

By the time I reached the back corner of the house I was flying blind, eyes shut tight against an enveloping blackness of stinging, swirling dust. The wind alternated between low hissing moans and banshee howls, ululating up and down in unholy scales as it hurled dirt and straw and slivers of wood against every inch of my exposed skin. A pin-sharp tumbleweed thistle planted itself in the flesh of my left eyebrow and I wondered if a tornado was spinning away somewhere out there in the roaring dark. I imagined locomotives and tractors and farmhouses suspended hundreds of feet above my head in the roiling blackness, tumbling this way and that in the Great Bowler's hands, waiting for just the right moment to hurl them down on my head.

Eyes shut tight against the storm, I used my left hand to keep my shirt collar bunched up around my nose and mouth as a makeshift screen against the suffocating dust. My right hand was my anchor, I kept it on the house at all times. I knew people wandered off and died in black blizzards, some of them just yards from lifesaving shelter. I had heard all the sad stories, Mom and Dad both made sure of that. Dad used to tie one end of a long rope around his waist and the other around one of our front porch posts so that he could go to the barn to tend to the animals during dusters. Amos and Andy were good-natured but big, built for the plow, and they got pretty spooked in bad weather. Dad wouldn't be the first to meet his maker because of a horse that lost its head in a storm. I remembered how hard Mom hugged Dad after he staggered inside at the tail end of one fifteen-hour duster. The next night I dreamed that someone came out of a black blizzard and untied Dad's rope from the porch post, then led him away while Mom and I slept.

The duster was everywhere, a howling aria of annihilation. I coughed and gasped behind my shirt, never letting my right hand leave the wall lest I get pulled out to sea. The storm scratched against a long bank of windows over my head like a thousand hissing cats but the sound came as a relief because it reassured me about my progress. I had reached the kitchen windows. A moment later my questing hand finally brushed against a familiar door and I staggered inside, coughing low and hard into my elbow, mouth dry as an old wasp's nest. I needed water.

31

T he quiet of the gloomy kitchen was a disorienting sonic whiplash after the Niagara of dust raging outside. I coughed into one hand and wiped at the grit caking my eyelids with the other until I was able to go still and listen for approaching footsteps. All I heard over the storm outside was a faint, watery echo of big band swing music blaring from somewhere deeper in the house. I crept through the silent kitchen, all darkness but for a lone wedge of light spilling in from the hallway at the far end of the room. I calmed myself as I recalled the layout of the house. The phonograph player was at the other end of the house, tucked away in a corner of Stagg's spacious library. Which meant that's where Gideon was. Probably.

I opened my eyes, took off my shoes, and tiptoed to the faucet. I grabbed a glass that was drying upside down on the counter and filled it to the brim, twice. I gulped down both glassfuls and carefully put the glass down just as I'd found it. I crept to the other end of the kitchen and put my shoes in the same cupboard Daniel had used to hide his semaphore flags earlier that day. The cupboard was empty when I opened it, which meant Daniel must have stashed the flags under the bed or inside the closet of whichever room he had used to send his signals.

I disappeared up the first steps of the pitch-black servant's stairs, my stockinged feet slippery on the wood. My destination was the master bedroom. Would the ammo boxes be there? I had no idea. I had watched

Daniel carry them inside the house at Gideon's direction—he wasn't about to leave such valuables in an unattended car overnight—but where they ended up was anyone's guess. For all I knew they were sitting downstairs just inside the front door for easy repacking in the morning.

But Gideon's bedroom was where I had last seen the boxes and I had to start somewhere. So I groped blindly up the servants' stairs, grimacing in the dark with every creak of the steps. I could have ascended more quickly and quietly with the light on but unlike the top of the stairs the bottom didn't have a door. Any illumination from the staircase would spill into the kitchen, an obvious indication of an intruder if Gideon were to visit the icebox or pantry.

It was unnerving to ascend in such utter darkness. An awful thought came to me: What if Gideon had done something to the stairs? Cast some sort of protective hex or enchantment on them to punish overly curious children? What if I was doomed to climb the stairs forever, groping blindly for a door that never comes? Another possibility leapt to mind, one equally horrifying to contemplate. Opening the door at the top of the stairs to find myself in the world of Reynard the Fox, where animals talked and schemed and feasted and fought and humans didn't exist.

I climbed the stairs slowly, listening to my heart pound, until a faint stripe of horizontal light appeared in the dark. I gave a great sigh of relief. Another three steps up and my right hand felt hard wood. I took a moment to collect myself, then opened the door and stepped into the dimly lit upstairs hallway. Every door along its length was closed but one. The grand prize—Gideon's bedroom—sat at the far end of the hall from me, closest to the main staircase. Lamplight spilled out of the room from the open doorway, cleaving the wide landing. I counted to sixty, watching the entire time for someone to step between that light and the doorway. No one did.

The hall's only other illumination came from an old oil lamp tucked into a corner of the landing, strategically placed on a small table to cast light on the landing and staircase both. The lamp looked like a little sister to one we had seen on the mantle of the gargantuan fieldstone fireplace in Stagg's library. Golden flecks of dust floated around the lamp's glowing glass chimney as it hissed its one-note song.

As I took my first halting step down the hallway toward Gideon's bedroom the first faint fiddle notes of an Irish jig came wafting up the stairway. The record player had been turned up loud so that the dancing fiddles, guitars, flutes, and drums could be heard above the duster's white noise din. It was a sprightly melody, redolent of an older world of cobblestones and thatched roofs and flagons of mead and high-stepping maidens.

I made my way down the hall to Gideon's bedroom, pausing every two or three steps to stop and listen. Gideon's voice came drifting up the stairs, faint but audible whenever the music quieted. He was talking to Daniel somewhere at the other end of the house. My relief at being able to place Gideon so far away was overwhelming, knee-weakening in its intensity. I pictured him lolling in one of the room's several stuffed leather chairs, a glass of whiskey or brandy in his hand. Tapping cigar ash out on one of Stagg's beautiful rugs. He would not be in a hurry. There was a duster raging outside. No one was going anywhere soon. Not even Gideon unless that roadster grew wings. And if there was one thing Gideon had in spades it was time.

By the time I reached Gideon's bedroom door an iron spike of dread was wedged up through the thick of my chest. Because suddenly I knew: the ammo boxes were behind that door. Daniel would have seen to it, one way or another. His semaphore message came with an implicit pledge that I would be able to get my hands on the ammo boxes. If he didn't get them back up to where we found them I would have been flying blind.

I pushed the bedroom door open and there the boxes were, sitting on the table by the window like before. Dust motes tumbled through the amber light of a tall, electric-powered floor lamp that stood behind a sleek chair dressed in burgundy velvet. The light's warm glow turned the dust on the chair's cigarette-burned arms to gold. Even John Stagg's sumptuously appointed bedroom was not impervious to the dust. It always found its way in.

I took a brief look around the bedroom, wary of a Gideon trap. But everything looked unchanged from before with the exception of a fruit crate crammed with liquor that had been liberated from the overturned cart at the foot of the bed. The crate sat neatly next to Gideon's two leather suitcases. He was preparing to light out, all right.

I sprinted across the bedroom to the ammunition boxes and opened my hand to study the locket a final time. Etched across its ivory surface was an intricate, finely detailed carving of a grinning fox. Just as before, the ivory face of the locket opened to reveal the key hidden within. But when the locket opened a screaming howl of pain filled the air. The keening sounded uncannily like that of a screaming child for about five seconds, then abruptly metastasized into a vicious volley of canine snarling.

I emptied the key into my left hand and unthinkingly hurled the locket through the open bathroom door, revolted by its otherworldly properties. It was the worst possible place I could have thrown it. The locket skipped like a stone across the bathroom's marble floor and fetched up along the baseboards under the big white clawfoot tub. Its furious barking and howling echoed off the tub's porcelain belly and the black- and white-tiled walls, a bomb of sound that punched through the duster's wailing and carried out to the hallway.

An instant later the propulsive Irish reel playing downstairs was obliterated in a shattering explosion of wood and glass and metal. A sick understanding settled deep into my being, followed by a spasm of nauseating terror. Gideon had armed the locket with some sort of alarm. Of course he had. An added precaution in response to our earlier snooping. He was three steps ahead of us as usual. I had been a fool to think we could ever match wits with him.

The sound of the record player's destruction hung in the air for a heartbeat, then gave way to a strangled cry of agony—Daniel—followed by the sound of Gideon's footsteps pounding down the first floor hallway toward me, obscenities streaming out of his mouth like artillery fire.

Gideon was coming to put me down for good.

32

I grabbed both ammo boxes and sprinted into the bathroom, then slammed the door behind me and wedged my back against it. I braced my stockinged feet against the base of the cabinet across from me as the locket's crazed howls and snarls filled the bathroom. I hoisted the nearest ammo box into my lap and jammed it between my trembling thighs. My hands were shaking badly but the flickering bulb above the mirror gave me just enough light to guide the key into the padlock. I clicked it open as I heard Gideon burst into the bedroom on the other side of the door.

"Where are you, you little *shit!*" he screamed, his words slurred with rage.

I removed the padlock and opened the lid and thrust my hand inside at the same instant the bathroom door splintered inward, half stove-in by the crunching force of Gideon's blow. The violence of the impact threw me forward and I rolled up in the far corner between the toilet and the enormous tub, its great sloping curves held aloft by huge silver lion's paws. The locket continued its savage barking and snarling from somewhere under the tub.

Gideon gave the battered bathroom door a final kick and it crashed to the floor, taking down a wall shelf in the process. Several bottles of cologne fell along with Gideon's shaving kit and shattered, filling the bathroom with powerful vapors. An instant later Gideon strode through the threshold like an avenging angel, broken glass crunching under his feet. In his right hand he hefted a gleaming brass fireplace poker, its heavy spike and hook sheathed in hard crusts of black soot from years of tending fires.

Gideon's slicked-down widow's peak was no longer combed back against his scalp or pomaded to within an inch of its life. His thick hair had become a bushy, unruly mane. Dense white stubble shadowed his cheeks and ran down into the neck of his shirt.

When Gideon saw me cowering between the toilet and the tub, his murderous expression mutated into a baleful smile. "Ah, there you are. What am I going to do with you? You just keep turning up like a bad penny, Will. Maybe I should flatten you on the railroad tracks."

Gideon stepped deeper into the bathroom, twirling the fire iron as if it were a gentleman's cane. He nudged at the ammo boxes half-buried in the door's wreckage with one foot, tsk-tsking and taking inventory as Stagg's mansion groaned and creaked around us. He retrieved the locket first, squatting down on his haunches at the other end of the tub and using the fireplace poker to drag the howling piece of jewelry out, neat as you please. He closed the locket and stroked its ivory face. It instantly fell silent, as if he had put it to sleep.

"Well, that proved to be a sensible precaution, didn't it?" he said drily. "You never know when you're going to get a visit from the Hardy Boys." He rummaged through the wreckage around him with the poker until he found the padlock I had opened. The key was still inside the padlock's mechanism. Gideon lifted the padlock up with the poker's fire-blackened spearpoint and dangled it in my face.

"So close and yet so far," he mocked, then pulled the poker back to deposit the padlock and key in his free hand. But the grin he gave me was unable to find firm purchase on his face. Even in my terror I recognized he was a little out of sorts. We had surprised him.

Gideon removed the key from the padlock and placed it back inside the protective cocoon of the locket. He gave the curio an affectionate pat for my benefit, then stuffed it into one of the front pockets of his trousers.

"You're Reynard the Fox, aren't you?" I raised my voice to be heard over the storm. I don't know what came over me. I suppose I just wanted to know I was right before he began carving me up or eating my liver or whatever he was going to do to me.

A low growl of laughter came out of Gideon as he set the first ammo box by the doorway to the bedroom. The one I never even had time to open. "Where did you hear that name?" he said in a low teasing voice. "That's a very old name. I haven't heard someone say that name in a long time."

"Are you?"

"I know you've been whispering in Daniel's ear. Who's been whispering in yours?"

"Reverend Rosbourne says—"

"Reverend Rosbourne! How is my fellow fabulist these days? Still licking his wounds from Sunday, I imagine. I'm afraid your holy man is due for another disappointment tomorrow. I don't expect there will be a lot of folks in the pews to pass the collection plate around, do you?"

"Are you Reynard?"

Gideon ignored me and devoted his attention instead to the second ammo box at his feet. He used the fireplace poker to skillfully lever the box into an upright position. But as it rocked into place the hinged lid of the box swung open for just an instant—long enough for Gideon to see it was open.

He wheeled on me with murderous speed, swinging the poker like a cavalry sword. The blow broke the radius and ulna bones of my right arm— approximately one half-second after I shattered the heavy glass jar hidden behind my back against the side of John Stagg's silver-clawed tub. And freed the soul of Bellin the Ram from centuries of tortured imprisonment.

Or so I like to think.

The eruption of shattered glass and powdered ram horn ripped a howl of anguish from Gideon. He slammed into me with one broad shoulder, crunching me against the bottom of the wall with a force that cracked two of my ribs and made the entire bathroom shake. He slammed my skull against the porcelain floor so hard I almost blacked out, then pulled me to my feet by my hair. I cried out involuntarily when he bumped the broken arm I had cradled against my chest. Gideon silenced me with two short, brutal punches to the stomach that left me doubled over and gasping for breath, sure my lungs would never work again.

He threw me out of the bathroom and across the polished hardwood planks of Stagg's bedroom floor. I fetched up next to one of the room's two great iron-finned radiators, directly underneath twin west-facing windows. I lay there in a fetal ball and took stock of my much-degraded physical state. My cracked ribs were a torment but they were nothing compared to the pain radiating from my broken forearm, which was already swelling and going black and purple. Or the collapsed bellows of my lungs, which had me gulping like a fish in the bottom of a boat.

All I wanted was for the pain to stop and Gideon was only getting started. He was going to make me suffer. Grievously, just as Isengrim and Brunn and Tybert and so many others who displeased Reynard had suffered at his hand.

An instant later the bedroom windows under which I lay crumpled shattered inward, shockingly loud, and showered me in broken glass. The gaping mouths of the window frames frothed with clouds of black dust that poured into the bedroom, the invading wind tossing the crushed velvet curtains to and fro. A powerful gust slammed the bedroom door shut, trapping the swirling dust and sand in there with us. I inhaled a mouthful of airborne dust fine as talcum powder and dissolved into another hacking cough that made my entire body vibrate with pain.

Gideon emerged from the bathroom brandishing the poker in his left hand but stopped in his tracks when the room's electric lights flickered. He glared at the table lamp nearest him as if daring it to go out. "Not yet!" he roared at the lamp.

"What did you do to Daniel?" I gasped as I struggled to my knees. "This is all my fault, Gideon. Everything. Listen to me. It was all my idea. Don't take it out on him."

"Only my friends call me Gideon, Will. You know that."

"I fooled him about all this, just like you fooled everyone in Greenheart. He's not that smart, Mr. Starling."

"Now we both know that's not true. He's smarter than you, that's for damn sure. Now up you go." Gideon pulled me up by my hair once more and marched me out of the bedroom to the second-floor landing. We stood there at the top of the stairs for a moment. His long fingers were still twisted in my air. Pulling hard on my scalp.

Gideon turned my head so he could be sure I saw his smile. "Would you like to know how Daniel's faring? Why don't you go down and ask him yourself?"

Whereupon he threw me down the main staircase.

My crash down the stairs left me with a badly sprained ankle, bloody nose, and black eye to add to my catalog of injuries. But none of those compared to the spectacular pyre of pain radiating from my already shattered arm. I lay sprawled at the foot of the staircase like a marionette with its strings cut. My half-concussed, terror-numbed mind only dimly registered the sound of something heavy toppling over upstairs. It sounded like God was moving furniture around in the dark.

I was still slumped at the foot of the staircase when I heard Daniel. His voice was faint, audible only in brief interludes when the storm's howling relented. But he was insistent and the third time I heard him calling out I could not pretend otherwise. He was telling me not to worry about him. To run away if I could and to hide if I couldn't.

Stagg's library was down the hallway on the left. I used the wall at the foot of the staircase to push myself up until I could stand, my ruined right arm held close against my chest the entire time. The sound of slow sardonic clapping filled my ears as I took a long shuddering breath. I felt rather than heard the tread of Gideon's footsteps coming down the stairs behind me and a moment later he was standing at my side.

I took a sidelong glance at him and instantly wished I had not. Gideon looked like the picture of health. To all appearances my release of Bellin's remains hadn't injured Gideon in the slightest. I didn't understand. When I had broken the jar of powdered ram's horn Gideon had responded as if I had committed the foulest of crimes but it didn't appear that he had suffered any ill effects from its loss. The black blizzard was still rampaging out in the dark too, blotting out the rest of the universe.

We might as well have stolen Gideon's thermos for all the good the key did us. It had all been for nothing. We were going to die in that house.

But still I heard Daniel calling. And so I dragged myself forward, lurching across the grand foyer and down the wide hall in the direction of the library. Gideon fell in beside me, adopting the strolling gait of a man walking through a green park on a sunny day. Framed portraits of Stagg's dead and distant relatives rolled by us like scenery from a demented carriage ride in the hallway's deepening amber fog. The ceiling lights blinked and dimmed as I shuffled forward. I thought about how complete the darkness would be when the electricity finally gave out. Something heavy thudded to the floor over our heads again. I heard the muffled sounds of breaking glass and cabinet doors banging open and closed. The storm was taking a wrecking ball to John Stagg's fine house.

"You're getting warmer," Gideon taunted, nudging me onward.

Airborne dust scratched at my eyes like steel wool as I lurched through the open doorway of Stagg's library. I felt Gideon's gaze on me, expectant. I blinked away the grit as I surveyed the room's long walls of bookshelves and upholstered leather armchairs and hulking desk. Every exposed surface was veiled in a pollen-like coating of dust. The bashed-in remains of the phonograph player lay in a heap of broken wood and twisted metal a few feet away from Stagg's enormous floor globe. It spun lazily on its creaking axis, round and round on the buffeting wind, as if the ghost of a bored child was in the library with us.

I turned to the other side of the room and saw a figure slumped against the wall next to the yawning black mouth of the fireplace. A lone oil lamp blazed on the fireplace mantle, illuminating the terrible tableau. Gideon had pinned Daniel's hand to the mantle with a jagged spear of metal from the wrecked gramophone. Daniel's entire forearm shone like wine-red paint in the lantern's lurid spotlight. He looked as if he had lost a game of Pinfinger stolen from the ninth circle of hell.

Daniel opened his eyes and mustered a wan smile as I burrowed up under his right arm with my one good shoulder. I firmed him up against the wall so he could stabilize his mangled hand and keep his arm from being pulled clear out of its socket.

"I told you to run away," Daniel murmured. He looked intently at me for a moment, as if reassuring himself that it was really me, then slumped back against the wall and closed his eyes again.

"And leave you to have all the fun?" I said. "Good job playing possum, by the way. We've got him right where we want him."

Daniel chuckled slowly and opened his eyes again, blinking in the orange murk. His face was cadaver pale and beaded with sweat. When he turned his neck to get a better look at me a fresh bolt of pain came lancing down from his crucified hand. He writhed against me for a moment but the chuckle never went away. It strengthened instead, turning into a full-blown laugh that got him saying ow ow ow ow over and over. The next thing I knew I was laughing and grimacing in pain right alongside him.

Gideon took a savage swing with the poker, obliterating a nearby tabletop crowded with framed photographs and pottery. He aimed the blow so the shrapnel pelted us. Something sharp—a shard of wood glass metal porcelain stone—skated across my flinching cheek and opened a fresh seep of blood.

Gideon loomed in closer, his eyes an unearthly tangerine in the dust-clouded light of the hissing lantern. It perched at the far left end of the mantle like a tiny sun, casting a golden nimbus of light over the proceedings. "Why don't you ask me how much I took from them?" Gideon roared as he loomed in closer, raising the poker high.

"I don't care," I said. "I really don't."

He gave the poker a thoughtful twirl. "I don't believe you," he decided. "I think you secretly want to know. How could you not?"

He was wrong. I didn't care because it didn't matter. His haul wouldn't be an astronomical sum, we couldn't give him what we didn't have. But between the money surrendered and assets offered as sacrifice it would be enough to cripple us forever. He was leaving Greenheart in the desert with four broken wagon wheels, an empty water barrel, a team of dead oxen, and a lot of hungry mouths to feed. He might as well have stranded us on the moon.

"Why are you even out here?" I cried out, my frustration boiling over. "I don't get it. We're in the middle of nowhere and we don't have anything to take. Not anymore. We're already poor! Why aren't you fleecing millionaires in Los Angeles or New York or Denver? Why aren't you selling out Madison

Square Garden or the Royal Albert Hall?"

That's when the electricity finally cut out for good, leaving us with only the oil lamp for light. Gideon didn't miss a beat. He was a fox after all. He could probably see in the dark just fine. Maybe he staged the timing of the power outage for maximum dramatic effect.

"The money is secondary, Will. Surely you know that by now. I have plenty of money. Gold and diamonds. Sticks and stones and bones too. It's the game that keeps me coming back." A Cheshire cat grin materialized out of the gloom. "And the opportunity to further burnish my legend. To write another chapter in the greatest story ever told. Have you ever won a treasure sweeter than another man's pride? His dignity and self-respect? You can't put a price on that kind of booty, my boy."

He was rubbing it in. Taking his victory lap. And that's when I remembered something Rosbourne had told me about the beast epics through which Gideon had roamed. The old Reynard stories often closed with the fox recounting to toadies and victims alike the precise manner in which he had triumphed, whether through shameless falsehood or ingenious betrayal or savage act of violence. Reynard the Fox loved that part. The vainglorious victory lap.

If I wanted to know Gideon's story, maybe all I had to do was ask.

<h1 style="text-align:center">33</h1>

I had so many questions I wanted to ask, though. How had Gideon washed up on the shores of this world in the first place? How long has he been here? Could he go back and forth between our worlds as he pleased? And then there were the questions I knew I would never ask because I wouldn't give him the satisfaction of telling me the answers. What was the point of finding out in my last moments on this earth about the extent of my father's complicity in Gideon's schemes? Or that Gideon planned to kill or marry or enslave Miss Wells when they reached Los Angeles?

I had to be careful. Gideon would not submit to a barrage of interrogation, no matter how inclined he might be at the molecular level to preen and talk. Nor would he answer questions that asked him to revisit unwelcome setbacks or embarrassments, even if I framed them as stepping stones in a grander narrative arc of redemption and victory. He would dismiss the former questions as stalling and the latter as inhospitable soil for self-aggrandizement.

So in the end I limited myself to two questions I had pondered many times since I first dimly apprehended Gideon's supernatural state of being and blackhearted ways. Two questions I thought Gideon would probably enjoy answering.

The first question: "Why me? Why did you pick me?"

He barked out a short laugh and the hair on my arms and the back of my neck stood up in response. It was the first time his laugh hadn't sounded human. "You keep surprising me, Will. Do you really want to know?"

"I just asked you, didn't I?"

"Mind your manners, whelp."

"Yes. Yes, I want to know."

"Pure chance," he said, drawing the words out. The reflection of the blazing oil lamp danced merrily in his eyes. "I wonder . . . does that make you feel better or worse?"

Gideon tucked the fireplace poker under one arm and settled in next to me against the wall. He leaned in confidingly. "I remember the morning like it was yesterday. I drove into town on a Sunday morning in March and the street in front of that big church of yours and all around the square was lined with parked cars and trucks. I could hear the faint sound of people singing inside and the sound of Mrs. Brennan's organ," he smiled. "She's a peach, isn't she? Anyway I soaked in that scene and I knew in that instant I had found a worthy canvas for my next masterpiece. And when the service ended and the people began to spill out I felt like a child on Christmas Eve, waiting to unwrap presents from Santa. Would you like to know why?"

"Tell me."

"Because I knew I was about to lay my eyes on my Trojan horse. The one I would use to get inside Greenheart's gates."

"Me."

"You. It makes the game more challenging, not knowing what raw materials I'll have to work with. But that's the point. It keeps me sharp. A poor craftsman blames his tools." He gave me a wink. "Words to live by."

"But why me? There were lots of people from church you could have picked."

"True. But you were the first one to sneeze. Just think if someone else leaving that church had sneezed before you. Just one second earlier, that's all it would have taken and you would have been spared. Or if I'd chosen some other identifying characteristic. First redhead. First man with a mustache in need of a trim. First girl with a blue ribbon in her hair. First person to mention the weather. I've done them all, or so it seems. At this point it's become a little tiresome but what are we without our little traditions? Our lovable little ceremonial tics and habits and superstitions?"

33

"So you didn't see anything special in me at the rabbit drive."

"Not in the least."

Gideon tilted his head at me, his long teeth gleaming in the shadowed slash of his mouth. "I learned quickly enough, however, that selecting you was a stroke of luck. You were so willing to share! What a geyser of information you turned out to be when it came to your friends and neighbors! Long cons take time but you made the prep work a breeze. Don't get conceited about your contributions, though. I could have made anyone work. Some beaten down sodbuster down to his last nickel. A desperate mother scrounging for pennies to keep her family fed. Your mom. Your dad. It wouldn't have mattered. Well, your mother would have been . . . problematic. That would have been interesting. It would have been fun to break her, don't misunderstand me. Oh that would have been a great pleasure indeed." He smiled. "But we'll never know how that version of this story would have gone, will we? Not in this world. Because the lucky soul who sneezed was you, and so a completely different story evolved. I'm glad it wasn't Stagg who sneezed. Could you imagine? Everyone around here was kissing his ring already. That would have been too easy. Like shooting fish in a barrel."

"Because you can do magic, can't you?" It was my second question and I hated the trembling wonderment in my voice when I asked it. "Real magic. Like a witch or a wizard can do."

Daniel shifted beside me, then gasped in pain as his impaled hand jostled against the jagged blade of metal pinning him to the mantle. He looked blearily at me through eyes glazed with pain and exhaustion and blood loss. "What are you talking about? Are you—"

"I'm talking about magic, Daniel. The real thing. Gideon knows how to do it. I . . . " I watched Daniel's eyelids flutter shut again and turned back to Gideon.

"I don't understand that part," I said. "Reynard didn't have magical powers in any of the stories Reverend Rosbourne told about you."

Gideon smirked. "No, that's true, I never had such abilities. Not back then. That's one way in which this life is better, I'll grant you."

"So how? If you couldn't do magic in your world, how can you do it in ours?"

Gideon gave the fireplace poker a couple desultory swings, his expression turning contemplative. Papers and maps that had been swept to the floor by the duster's invading winds swirled round his feet, then slid past and disappeared into the dark again.

"Do you really think I'm the only one?" he asked, his tone turning impish. "What are the odds? That I'm the only one?"

"What are you talking about?"

"I run across others like me on occasion, you know." Gideon said. "Other visitors. Remember Huay Chivo? I told you about him. That Mayan spirit from the Yucatan? Ate a hundred goats in a single sitting? I ran into him in Mexico City back in aught five, he was running security for a couple casinos down there. Skinny as a rail, he was. Didn't expect that."

"I remember him. You telling stories about him."

"Nice to know you were listening."

"He's an evil stupid goatman or something."

Gideon smirked. "You know perfectly well what he is. You remember every word. In any event, that's who I went cliff diving with down in Acapulco. He's calmer now that he travels a bit. He had to get out of the Yucatan."

"Who else?"

Gideon shrugged. "Some I see more than others. Some travel in pairs. Not my cup of tea, that. Most of the ones I know about are like me. Pretty solitary when you get right down to it. It all depends on how innately sociable you are, though, doesn't it? What pastimes you choose to pursue here among you mortals. How you're going to pass the centuries. Some try to turn over a new leaf here. Make a new start. That never works. You are who you are. Your fundamental nature always asserts itself in the end. You know that as well as anyone, don't you, Will?"

"Who else? Who else is here?"

"Oh I probably run across Rumpelstiltskin more than anyone on my peregrinations." His grin widened at my stricken reaction. "Oh Rumples is always up to something interesting. He was a slaver down in South Carolina for a time. I bet that's not in your history books, is it? Ha. Or in your fairy tales for that matter. Rumples owned a fleet of slave ships that made that Middle Passage run from Africa to Charleston, year after year after year. Five ships, each one able to stack more than three hundred jingle-jangling slaves-in-waiting in their bellies. Some of them weren't jingle-jangling their chains by the time they got to Charleston, of course, but sharks need to eat too, right? He had a soft spot for the pickaninnies, Rumples did, and that's a fact. He'd pluck three or four lucky boys or girls from every ship and take them out to his plantation to cook his meals and wash his clothes and scrub his floors and empty his chamber pot for a few years until they got too old."

"What did he do to them then?" As soon as the words came out of my mouth I wanted to take them back. I knew the answer would be monstrous.

"When they weren't cute anymore?" Gideon ruminated on the question. "Turned out to the cotton fields or sold off, I expect. I never thought to ask. In any case, all good things come to an end, even for Rumples. He lost four ships in a single storm trying to squeeze out a second run too late in the year. I don't know what he's up to now, though I heard he moved to Spain. Something lucrative, I'm sure. Rumples likes his money and he's got a nose for it. He always lands on his little feet."

"Will, what . . ." Daniel asked sleepily, then grimaced as a fresh wave of pain came radiating down from his crucified hand. I shifted to better prop him up against the wall, fighting my own exhaustion as well as the sawblades of pain pulsing out of my broken arm and busted ribs and throbbing skull. I wasn't sure how long I'd be able to keep Daniel shored up against the wall before I gave out.

"Who else?" I asked. "Who else is here?"

"Hmmm, let's see. I met Noah once out on Vancouver Island. He smelled like fish."

"Really?"

Gideon laughed his new barky laugh. "No, I was just pulling your leg about that one. Oh they come and go. We tend to gravitate to the tribes and languages and places we know. Our places of origin. Like Chivo does."

"But you're not American. You came from Belgium or France or England or Spain or wherever. Countries in Europe."

"What of it? That's where you and yours came from. America is the Great Melting Pot, haven't you heard? I feel right at home here, Will. And there's always so much going *on.* So many opportunities for mischief. It was a perfect destination for an extended holiday. I've only been here for a century or so and I still haven't seen everything! It's a big country and I'm not done looking at it."

I heard no guile in his tone, no traps lurking behind his words. He liked it over here, sneaking and rampaging through the hurly burly dreams and mythologies of the awakening American colossus.

"Do you want to know a secret?" Gideon's eyes glowed like amber moons in the grainy lamplight. We could have been talking under a fog-shrouded lamppost at the end of the world, a thousand miles from another living soul. "Something I've never told anyone before? I can tell you, Will, because you're not going to be around to tell secrets much longer. You know that, yes?"

"I know."

"Just making sure. Hmmm. You look white as a nun's leg. Did I give you a fright?"

"I'm fine." I kept my voice steady but those had been hard words to hear. I realized that until that moment I had harbored a secret hope that Gideon might spare me in the end. That all those days and nights I spent spellbound by his stories and laughing at his jokes and keeping him company might be enough to stay his hand. That he would remember in the end that I was just a boy.

Other times I wondered if he might spare me from death out of malice—so that I might suffer the fury and contempt of whoever came staggering out of Greenheart after Gideon finally moved on. Men, women, and children struck dumb by this latest disaster in their star-crossed battle to survive. Some of them would be catatonic with hopelessness. Others would be out for blood and I recognized that Daniel and I were obvious stand-ins if Gideon chose to maroon us among their vengeful ranks. Still and all, the yearning for clemency had slithered through my mind like a silent black eel. A bloody beating and a life of shame-filled exile was better than no life at all.

But that's not what Gideon had in store for me. He wanted me to know that I was nearing the end. That I was going to spend my last minutes of this life trapped in a grief-haunted mansion with a murderous talking fox and a best friend who was bleeding out in my arms.

"You know who I would love to meet?" Gideon said, his tone turning both confidential and salacious. "Besides Becky Sharp. I would *love* to meet Snow White. Can you imagine? A roll in the hay with that Bavarian wench? I always picture her as a virginal milkmaid to some pallid poet with a castle in the Alps. Or the trusting, doe-eyed granddaughter of some jowly Canadian lumber baron with a bad ticker. Good girls like her can't stay away from men like me. That's just as true here as it was back home."

"What—"

"I know, I probably shouldn't get my hopes up. If I ever cross paths with her she'll probably have bred a dozen little trolls who remind her of those seven degenerates who were always following her around. I can hear them now, sniveling for food or toys or a diaper change or a hug. She probably collects Green Stamps." He brought up a heed-me finger. "Nonetheless, I'd look her up if I caught wind of her. You never know. Or perhaps I'll meet someone more exotic. Diasporas are expanding in every direction. It's exciting, isn't it? The next one I meet might hail from the mountains of Peru! Or the teeming cities of the Orient. I think I'd like that."

"Have you ever come across someone like her?" I asked. "Snow White? Here in our world, I mean? Someone who's like you, but good and kind instead of . . . what you are?"

It was a question I had spent a fair amount of time thinking about. The notion that if our world contained Grendels perhaps it contained Beowulfs as well. I didn't even need Beowulf or the Three Musketeers or Tarzan or anyone so heroic to come to my rescue. A Phileas Fogg or Friar Tuck would do just fine. I would have been happy to hitch my star to someone for whom things always somehow worked out in the end.

"Can the good ones get in too, do you mean? The ones with hearts of gold? I've wondered that myself. Perhaps one slips in once in a while. But I've never actually met one of them. I don't think they last long when they do." His smile widened to reveal his gleaming eyeteeth. "This world would eat most of them alive."

Gideon reached out with the fire iron and placed the black spearpoint under Daniel's chin. He lifted his sagging head with the poker, then leaned in close and gave him a sniff. "Out like a light," he pronounced. "You should thank me. It will go easier for him that way. That's not usually my style, you know."

"I know."

A fresh gust of wind pushed through the room, sending the big globe in the corner spinning anew. It moaned and creaked in the dark as it rotated on its axis, filling the room with its spectral song. I imagined the ghostly hand of John Stagg at work, pushing the globe round and round as he watched our final act unfold. Did he even care about the ending now that his part was done? Now that he'd been written out? Did he hope that I would avenge him? That I might somehow triumph over the depraved grifter who had poisoned him in his own home? Were ghosts capable of experiencing catharsis? I hoped if Stagg was watching that he was keeping his expectations low. Gideon didn't write happy endings for anyone but himself.

"I wish I could make you understand your role in all this," Gideon said. "You should be honored, really. But how could you know? You haven't the slightest inkling of the scale of the canvas upon which I work. You are like a child looking up through a small skylight at a dusting of stars who believes he's seeing the entirety of the universe in that little box above his head. You haven't been *anywhere.* You haven't seen *anything*! Until I took you under my wing the highlight of your short and entirely unremarkable life was ogling your cousin at your uncle's funeral. Now *that's* sad. At least now you'll have one interesting story to tell in the next life, if there is one. You're welcome."

Gideon drew himself down until he was at eye level with me, and for the first time I could smell the centuries of rotting meat on his breath. "I'm working from a palette of memory and experience you can't possibly fathom, Will. And an understanding of humankind you even now only dimly apprehend. How did Hobbes put it? Man is a wolf to man. Smart fella. He understood the savagery of life. But dwelling on that is boring, don't you think? Do you know what gets me out of bed in the morning? Watching the endlessly amusing folly and striving and hypocrisy and dumb hope of your kind. I watch and wait for inspiration to strike."

"Inspiration," I repeated, and all at once the spell of bone-weariness under which Gideon had placed me fell away. "You haven't had an original thought in your life. We *made* you. We told you what to think and how to act and what to say and you've been doing it ever since. Us. Human beings. You're our puppet, not our puppet master. You should be on your knees worshipping *us*. We *created* you."

Gideon's gaze hardened into a murderous glint. "Careful, boy. I can always make it worse for you. Always. You have no idea. Galeazzo gets the credit but the Quaresima Torture Protocol was a yawn until I got to Milan. I opened his eyes to what was possible. I can show you precisely what I mean if you'd like."

"You still haven't told me how you can do magic," I muttered, dropping my gaze. Let him think he had cowed me once again. Let him think his threat of torture had done its work. Gideon wouldn't answer my questions if he was angry with me. And I wanted answers before I died. I wanted to at least finish the puzzle. I wanted to see for myself the picture it made.

"You wouldn't believe me if I told you."

"Try me. *Sir.*"

Gideon smiled and took a couple more slow, swashbuckling swings of the poker through the air, back and forth, the blackened point arcing dangerously close to my already battered face.

"You ruined every spell." Gideon spoke matter-of-factly, but an almost childlike frown of disappointment flashed across his face. "Every last one of them. What a shame."

"What are you talking about? The duster's still blowing. You're still human."

"I've always been able to control my lycanthropy, Will. It's not so hard to do. I don't have to use a *spell* for that. And I stick out like a sore thumb around here when I'm my true self. I still have fun with it once in a while, though. The transformation. It always feels good to get back in that old skin."

"The duster's still blowing," I repeated impatiently.

"You're not listening, chum. The storm's running on fumes. You cut the juice. The propellers aren't moving. The stars will be shining overhead in a few hours." He shook his head sadly. "It was going to be a humdinger of a storm, Will. A lot of folks around here have been hankering for some Book of Revelations smiting and I aimed to satisfy their itch. But instead of a humdinger of a storm it's just going to be a dinger. Still, I expect people around these parts won't soon forget it. Them that's left."

"Them that's left," I repeated.

"That's right. As I was saying, I'll have to recast a number of the spells you ruined. Start over from scratch. That will necessitate some travel abroad to replenish my stock of certain essentials. Or it might be invigorating to ride lean for a while, as I did once upon a time. Simplify, simplify, isn't that what Thoreau said? Perhaps I'll follow the lead of so many of your countrymen and become a vagabond. I like the sound of that. Ride the rails to the Big Rock Candy Mountain. Live by my wits without the crutch of magic, as I used to do back in the old days. Back before I met Morgan le Fay."

A low growl of laughter came rumbling out of Gideon's chest as my face drained of color. Gideon had told me all about Morgan le Fay. She had been both protector and nemesis of King Arthur and the Knights of the Roundtable, depending on the tale and the time period in which the story had been forged. A powerful enchantress and skilled healer who had studied at the side of Merlin himself, she eventually became drawn to the dark arts of necromancy and internecine court intrigues. At least that's how the men who told the stories came to tell hers.

I tried to form a picture in my beaten-down mind of how Morgan le Fay would appear here on Earth but didn't know how to make my conception of her essential *being*—mercurial and ruthless and magical and dizzyingly sexual, yet forever haunted by her unrequited love for Lancelot—take shape in my mind's eye. Would she pine for Lancelot even here? Would she spend her days and nights lost in old books that told of his bravery and beauty? How would someone like her get by in this world, whatever her fearsome powers? It wasn't that long ago that we were burning witches at the stake.

But Gideon didn't find Morgan le Fay at a witch burning. He found her on Christmas Eve 1688 in London's Bethlem Royal Hospital. Better known as Bedlam, the most notorious insane asylum in human history. A night watchman had found her unconscious and with two broken wrists on the London docks three years earlier. When she awoke and told the authorities who she was they splinted and bound her hands and locked her away in the deepest bowels of the hospital. Physicians and nurses provided grotesque treatments of leeches and blistering to cure the madwoman of her ravings of Camelot. When they plunged her into ice-cold baths she told them through chattering teeth that someday she would pluck all their eyeballs out and eat them like grapes. Only a handful of Bedlam staff even knew she was down there in that godforsaken hole.

The lamp on the mantle sputtered and coughed, dimming even further as it drew down its last dregs of fuel. The swirling darkness advanced, probing the retreating light like an army laying siege.

"Poor Morgan," said Gideon, pouting out his lower lip like a sad clown. "She was the loneliest girl in London Town."

And then one day a handsome new physician came to see the madwoman. He had been called in to replace the doctor charged with her care after his mutilated body was found bobbing in the polluted waters below London Bridge. The new doctor told Morgan that he knew she wasn't insane. He told her he would help her wreak vengeance on everyone on the Bedlam staff who had tormented and wronged her. He promised to arrange her release in his care and return her to Camelot—just as soon as she taught him how to cast a few spells and hexes. A little black magic to prove she possessed the powers she claimed. Morgan agreed, though the instruction would be excruciatingly painful for her still-healing wrists. The pain would be worth it. She was familiar with the need to sacrifice for knights in shining armor.

And so it was that Reynard the Fox learned enchantments that made cars run forever in any kind of weather and lockets bark out alarms and flowers disintegrate overnight and electricity run through dead wiring and rain darken the ground and thunder shake the heavens and dust storms fill the lungs of blind, bawling cows. In a matter of weeks the doctor's wiles and flattery had her gifting him greater power than she ever intended—and more than he ever dreamed of. In no time at all the handsome physician had a big bag of black magic slung over his broad shoulder and grand plans to wreak havoc with it.

"Morgan always did choose poorly in matters of the heart," Gideon sniffed.

"So that's how you did it. You cast her spells to make everyone do what you want. To sing your terrible songs. To believe your lies."

Gideon reached out and gave my blood-specked cheek an affectionate pat. "Silly boy. They're not *her* spells. They're out there for anyone to find, as are the requisite materials. If you look hard enough and in the right places. But I didn't need magic to convince all those people in your church that I was singing a better song. That was the *easy* part, Will. They all wanted to believe *so badly.* As did you, my darling little Judas. You practically—"

"You were telling me about how you stole magic from Morgan le Fay."

"So I was," Gideon acknowledged breezily. "Well poor Morgan was a wee bit distraught when I finally bid her adieu, as you might imagine. She *begged* me to release her from her imprisonment! Oh you should have heard her, she was promising me the moon. But I had everything I needed from her and I liked her right where she was. I left the staff with explicit instructions to keep her in a straitjacket and heavily sedated for the rest of her days. I recommended a lobotomy. For everyone's good, really."

"You're a monster."

Gideon waved the accusation away. "I'm mischievous. And don't worry about Morgan, that bitch is fine and dandy. Unfortunately. She got out of Bedlam."

"How? When?"

"Nineteen months after I left her, give or take. The night before she was scheduled to undergo trephination to bring her disordered humors back into balance and cure her madness."

"What?"

Gideon smiled. "They were going to drill a hole in her head. She had to have sensed it was coming somehow. She always did have a flair for the dramatic."

"You all do."

Gideon barked out a laugh of genuine pleasure in an uncanny timbre that made my teeth hurt, as if I was biting down on tin foil. "Touché," he said, the word reverberating oddly in the gloom. "In any case she's still on the loose out there somewhere. Still looking for me. Nineteen months wasn't much of a head start. Not when you don't know the clock is even ticking. That vengeful bitch needs to find another hobby."

"And you can't go back." It wasn't a question. It was another thing I had wondered about and now knew. Gideon was still on the run from Morgan le Fay because he had no way to return to his own world of talking beasts and simpler times. "You're stuck here with us. You fell through a trapdoor and now the door might as well be a million miles above your head. And she's after you and she's never going to stop. That's why you're way out here in Greenheart instead of New York or Washington or London or Paris. Isn't that right, Reynard?"

Gideon's lips curled up in a terrifying canine snarl and for an instant I thought he was going to rip my throat out then and there. But the lamplight at his ear gave another little moth-wing flutter and as if it were a signal Gideon subsided back into his usual unflappable self. He nodded in the direction of the sputtering lantern.

"Look at how long we've been talking," he said softly. "Where does the time go? I really should be running along while the car outside still has some magic in its belly. A moment's indulgence, please, as I make final preparations for departure. Don't worry, Will. I won't forget to say goodbye."

34

Gideon disappeared down the hallway, whistling a happy tune. We both knew I wasn't going anywhere. Where was there to go? I closed my eyes as I shored up Daniel's limp heavy body against the wall with my own black and blue one and seconds later an undertow of exhaustion pulled me down down down through fathoms of unconsciousness.

> *Where is the diver*
> *Where is the diver*
> *Where is the diver*
> *I see the diver*
>
> *. . .*
>
> *I see the diver*
>
> *. . .*
>
> *I see the diver*
> *a smear of face this time*
> *behind the caul of dust—*

I came awake with a jerk to a midnight world starred with a single blazing light. Another oil lamp, shining like a miniature sun in Gideon's high right hand. I recognized it as the one from the table on the second-floor landing outside Stagg's bedroom.

My return to consciousness felt like yet another cruelty. It was the closest

I'd ever been to seeing the face inside that helmet. The features were just coming into focus, the dusty faceplate finally clearing. If I had stayed under just two seconds longer I felt sure I would have at least gone to my death knowing who had been hiding in there. I wanted to scream with frustration but my ribs hurt too much to do anything more than sigh.

"Boo." I blinked and peered up through the lamp's amber light in the direction of the voice until I found him in the murk. He looked more like a fox than a man now. Every inch of exposed skin was covered in a light coat of dense fur and his ears had migrated up the side of his skull and reshaped themselves into big furry triangles pointing to the sky like radio towers. The bone and cartilage in the bottom half of his face had been refashioned into a long snout bristling with sharp teeth. He was fast returning to his Reynard state. He looked pleased by the prospect, to judge by the mad glimmer in his eyes. That old familiar body must have felt like the closest thing he had to a home in our world.

The wind was still whistling in and out of the mansion's blown out windows, rattling picture frames as it raced up and down the hallway. A sound came floating into the room from the grand foyer, faint and strange, and after a moment of dazed puzzling I placed it. Stagg's great chandelier of antlers, clicking and clacking in the midnight dark like a mountain giant's wind chime. It made such a forlorn sound that it gave me a shiver. Maybe the ghost of John Stagg was still hanging around, I thought deliriously. Maybe he was using the antlers to type out a final telegram of condolences, writing in a tongue I would soon come to know myself.

It was only then that I registered what Reynard held in his other hand: a rusty gasoline can on which was emblazoned a leaping red Pegasus. He had poked me with the gas can's long metal spout to rouse me from my passed-out state. He swung the can back and forth gently, like a child with a milk bucket in a nursery rhyme. It bonged against the side of his leg with each metronomic pass, its hollow echo a counterpoint to the moaning wind.

bong

bong

bong

empty

empty

empty

The realization came slowly and then all at once when the fumes from my gasoline-soaked feet and lower pants legs filled my nostrils. He was using the empty can to sound out a Morse code of doom. A great black gush of terror flooded through my body at the smell. He was going to burn us alive as if *we* were the witches. The awful unknown fate I had felt circling over my head for weeks, its monstrous silhouette drawing closer with every tightening orbit, had finally revealed itself to me and somehow it was worse than any of the hundred horrible fates I had imagined for myself.

"Can you even die?" I cried out, my voice breaking in anguish and rage.

Reynard snickered and scratched at his whiskered chin with a sabre of nail. "I'm kind of curious about that myself, Will," he said. "But it's not anything you need to trouble yourself over, is it?"

He nodded toward the front door. "Well, my chariot awaits and it's been one hell of a long day. I quite enjoyed our time together—even if you did put a turd in the punch bowl at the end. You and Danny boy there gave me a run for my money. It's been awhile since anyone's done that. Uncle Isengrim himself never tested me so. Rest assured you will live on in the stories I tell in my future travels. Goodbye, Will." And with that he dropped the empty gas can at my feet and casually tossed the oil lamp back over his shoulder.

The lamp arced through the air and shattered on a coffee table between two overstuffed sofas, igniting a roaring fireball of flame that lit up the entire south end of the room. The smell of gasoline wasn't just coming from my soaked feet. Gideon had emptied the last of the gas can's contents around the room, wetting the dust-choked carpet and drapes and furniture for incineration. The velvet drapes at the room's far windows were already ablaze, hungry flames surging. I watched them lick at the ceiling and make the wallpaper blacken and curl and ignite. The house of Greenheart's Great Man was going to be our funeral pyre.

Or at least Daniel's. Reynard had left me with a choice. Stay with Daniel and perish in agony or abandon my best friend to die alone in the most horrific way imaginable. And in so doing, sentence myself to a life of shame and grief and self-loathing for failing him. I was between the devil and the deep blue sea. The place where Gideon's victims always found themselves eventually.

I squinted into the heart of the fire, blinking away specks of flying dust and ash generated by the oxygen-sucking flames. Reynard was still standing there, watching me. He wanted to see what I would do before he left. Would I stay or run?

The black smoke boiled and twisted around us, and I fell into a fit of hacking coughs that made me cry out in pain. If Mom and Dad survived Reynard's obliterating duster would they ever learn how I died? Would they ever find our charred bodies? Or would my parents and Daniel's father go the rest of their lives wondering what became of us? The questions poured over the crumbling gunwales of my mind in icy sheets, swamping me in black seas of hopelessness.

And that's when it happened.

A final magic trick that outshone every one that had come before.

The diver from my nightmare, materializing out of the gloom behind Reynard.

He was obscured by the room's chaos of churning black smoke and wind-tossed papers and my own watering eyes but the diver's Mark V helmet cut through the murk, aglow like a spectral meteor in the firelight. As he stalked closer I noticed he was dressed not in his sun-cracked diving suit but rather in a long skirt and plain shirt. The base of the huge brass diving helmet sat atop a threadbare blanket wreathed around the diver's neck to form a makeshift seal against the storm's choking gales of dust. I recognized the blanket as one we kept in the back of the car to help ward off the cold of winter drives. The edge of the heavy breastplate had settled deep into the diver's left collarbone, staining blanket and shirt alike with blood that gleamed like engine oil in the room's eerie light.

I saw that the diver carried a rifle at the same instant that Reynard's eyes—

still locked on mine, still waiting for me to cut and run—widened with the realization that someone was standing behind him. Someone he wasn't expecting because that's not how Reynard stories went. He snatched up the fireplace poker from its resting place against the wall and turned with killing speed, raising the iron to strike as if it were Excalibur itself.

The rifle went off with a thunderous boom that obliterated every other sound in the world. Even the fire seemed to subside for an instant as the bullet tore through Reynard's voice box and sprayed leprous black spots on the wall behind him. Reynard dropped the poker and clutched at the wound in his throat with both hands, staring in disbelief at the apparition standing before us both. His mouth worked soundlessly as blood bubbled out of him, coating his tongue and lining the crevices of his big teeth. He looked like he was trying to smile.

The diver reached up, unlatched the helmet's flame-glittered front face-plate, and opened the circle of glass to reveal my mother's pale face. She drew in great gulps of hot polluted air that made her cough and gasp but her furious, red-rimmed eyes never left Reynard. Nor did the barrel of the rifle, which I now recognized as Dad's Savage 99. Mom kept it resolutely trained on him, ignoring the flames all around us. She followed his every movement with eyes that shone with horror at what they were witnessing.

Reynard pressed his hands against his throat in a fruitless attempt to staunch the endless scarf of blood fountaining through his fingers, into his fur, and down his shirt front. Then he lurched away from the wall and lunged at Mom with a fearsome speed that froze my heart.

Mom was ready for him. The second bullet caught Reynard in the meat of his right shoulder and spun him backward into the fire. He went up like a roman candle, his fine clothes and fur igniting instantly. He threw his head back as if howling in pain but all his ruined larynx could squeeze out was a panting, gurgling sound.

I didn't trust what I was seeing. Even after Reynard's head became a medusa of fire and he fell to his knees in the middle of that raging inferno. Even after he collapsed and his unmoving form blackened and cooked. I couldn't take my eyes off him, though the heat and smoke baked my throat with every ragged breath I took. It had to be a trick. Reynard was going to rise up and walk out of the fire any second now. Any other outcome seemed impossible. He was Reynard the Fox.

"Will!" Mom's adrenalized voice was suddenly pressed up close to my ear, shouting to be heard over the devouring flames. I dimly realized that she had discarded the helmet. "Oh my God what did he do to you? Will! Will, listen to me! You have to help me with Daniel, we don't have much time! Will! Honey, you need to hold him up just a little longer! Just a little longer, I promise!"

Mom dragged a coffee table over to the great fieldstone fireplace until it was positioned in front of Daniel. She jumped up on the table and tore a strip of cloth from the thin blanket unraveling around her neck, then wrapped it tightly around the end of the spear of metal Reynard had driven through Daniel's hand. She gritted her teeth, wrapped her hands around the twisted metal spike, and pulled on it with all her might, one foot braced against the wall next to Daniel's head as she snarled and cursed and screamed. When the spike of twisted metal finally came free from the mantle I thought for an awful moment that Mom was going to fall back into the fire herself. But she recovered her footing and leaped to Daniel's other side, helping me support his weight.

Mom helped me hurriedly strip out of my gasoline-soaked pants and then we carried Daniel out of the burning house and into the night. My cracked ribs and broken arm made me involuntarily grunt or cry out with each lurching step down the porch steps. The fire behind us cast the stable and garage in coruscating waves of coppery light.

Mom steered us toward the open bay of Stagg's garage, which promised both a safe distance from the lung-baking heat of the fire and shelter from the storm. We collapsed with Daniel just inside the door. Mom turned a strip of cloth from the hem of her skirt into a tourniquet around Daniel's upper arm, then wrapped his mangled hand in another strip of cloth by the light of the fire.

I watched her tend to Daniel off and on but my eyes kept wandering back to the final death throes of the Great Man's home. Flames surged out of the windows of both floors as if God had placed the sun itself inside. I could hear things crashing and collapsing deep inside, even over the fire's mindless bellowing. I didn't feel relieved or vindicated or triumphant at the knowledge that Reynard's body was burning to a crisp inside that inferno. I felt numb.

"Where's Dad?" I finally thought to ask. "Is he . . . ok? Did Gideon . . . hurt him?"

"He's fine, honey," Mom said in a tight voice. "He's back home. Passed out on the bed, last I saw him. For all I know he's still there snoring the night away." Mom raised her head and looked me in the eye. She was already taking stock of what a life without him might look like. "Your dad's fine, Will. We'll go find him in the morning."

"You came to Stagg's all by yourself?"

"All by my little old self," she said. "When I got back from Gideon's show and saw you still weren't home, and then found your dad the way he was . . . I didn't know what to do. For about five seconds. Until I remembered where you and Daniel were headed earlier today. I crashed the truck down yonder trying to outrun the storm."

"I saw."

"You did?"

"You got pretty close before it caught you."

"Thank God for that driveway. I couldn't see a thing but I could feel the flagstones under my feet. I had to get on my hands and knees a few times to make sure I hadn't wandered off the drive."

"The helmet was a good idea."

"Between what we saw earlier tonight and what happened at Stagg's funeral it seemed like it might be a handy thing to have. Good thing Daniel left his father's trunk at the house this morning. I never would have made it without it. God is it really the same day?"

I looked down at Daniel's face, scarily pale beneath sand-pocked smears of blood and ash. "Is he going to live?" I asked, and held my breath for the answer.

"I think so. Yes. But we need to get him to a doctor as soon as it gets light.

I'm worried about infection. I don't know if he's going to keep that hand. Gideon did a number on it."

She looked at my broken arm, which I was keeping cradled gingerly against my chest. "I'll make you a sling for that as soon as I can, honey."

I turned back to watch the reflections of the flames dance across the hood and windshield of Reynard's roadster. My mind emptied of thought. I watched expressionlessly as a section of the mansion's roof collapsed and the first exploratory flickers of orange fire reached through the glowing hole a moment later. The fire climbed steadily higher as the minutes ticked by, filling the night sky with thunderheads of smoke and airborne embers that winked like fireflies. I just kept watching.

Mom was placing the sling she had fashioned for my arm over my head when we heard it: a low whine coming from somewhere behind us, deep in the vast pits of shadow at the back of the garage. Mom and I exchanged glances and ducked away from the garage's open bay doors to let the firelight pour in. It was Buster, crouched under an old work table. He stared at us for a long moment, his unblinking eyes glowing like discs of burnt orange fire.

Then his tail started thumping on the floor and his ears perked up, like a dog just waiting for his name to be called.

Epilogue

The official death count across King County was two hundred and three souls when all was said and done, though some of the missing not included in that tally were ever well and truly accounted for. The authorities waited a year to give an official number because bodies turned up for weeks after the duster, some of them within yards of life-saving shelter. They found Mayor Sipe fifteen feet from the bottom step of his back porch with his mouth and eye sockets filled to the brims with dirt. They said it looked as if the duster had placed coins on his eyelids to keep them closed.

Most of downtown Greenheart went up in flames that night too, burned to cinders by flames that lit up the pre-dawn sky. Legend has it that just before the duster hit, Mrs. Brennan spotted a blazing lantern perched in an open window at the back of the theatre, as if it were waiting for a stiff wind to knock it to the prop room floor.

Neighboring counties were left miraculously untouched by the storm. The duster materialized at the western edge of King County, leaped and spread eastward, and then churned in place over our heads all night long, pulverizing Greenheart into dust like a monstrous pestle.

The mass exodus from Greenheart in the weeks following the storm included the dead as well as the living. The bodies of John Stagg and daughter Clara were exhumed from Greenheart's cemetery grounds and shipped back east by relatives who no one ever heard from again. They left their gravestones behind. The two of them remain buried side by side in a Philadelphia cemetery to this day.

Reverend Rosbourne played a major role in organizing Red Cross camps and getting search and rescue efforts up and running. But when those operations began wrapping up he moved on like everyone else. He became the pastor of a small church in Iowa, where he worked until Pearl Harbor. He promptly requested a leave of absence from the church and enlisted as a chaplain in the U.S. Army. When the war ended he returned to that same little church in Iowa and shepherded it into a thriving community of faith. Along the way he married a widow and helped raise a son who grew up to become an astronaut in the Apollo space program. This was all according to the obituary Mom sent after Rosbourne was felled by a stroke in 1967. The obituary noted that our old pastor had been part of the D-Day invasion at Normandy. I imagined him crashing through the icy Atlantic surf onto the terrifying killing zone of Omaha Beach, Holy Bible clutched firmly in hand. Ministering to the wounded. Praying over the fallen. Fortifying the spirits of the terrified. Reynard never broke him, Omaha Beach wouldn't have either.

I never saw or heard from Miss Wells again. No one did to my knowledge and believe me I asked around when I got older. But no one ever found her body either.

I hope she didn't wait around for Reynard that night. I hope she got away. I hope she built a life somewhere that was grand and full of laughter and love and people who treated her well. I hope she did a lot of singing with that thin joyful voice of hers. Mostly I can't bear to imagine her any other way.

Katherine and her parents were still in Colorado Springs when Mom and Dad and I fetched up on the shores of Aunt Ruth's house. My aunt put a brave face on about it. She called us a dust bowl Swiss Family Robinson and doggedly insisted it was all a great adventure. We spent a year there licking our wounds and I saw a lot of Katherine during that time. We dutifully tried to recreate the explosive magic that had burned between us during the week of Uncle Leonard's funeral but found ourselves pumping a dry well. It wasn't the same for either of us. It was with mutual relief that we became friends instead. Close friends, even. One night I told her a little about Gideon, though I know she didn't believe most of it and I was careful to never say his real name. I never forgot the power he attached to names. Katherine and I still exchange cards at Christmastime. Even after all these years the arrival of one of her cards stirs up memories of how it felt to be fourteen years old and achingly infatuated with the girl sitting on the porch swing next to you.

Daniel and his father bounced around for a few years, fighting to keep a roof over their heads the same as us. Then World War II strapped the economy onto a rocket ship and everything changed. Uncle Sam wasn't interested in Daniel and his mangled hand so he helped his dad scrounge up the down payment for a rundown property that became the first of a chain of roller-skating rinks and bowling alleys sprinkled across the upper Midwest in places like Milwaukee, Detroit, Duluth, and Muskegon.

Grant Ballantine died of a heart attack shoveling snow in his driveway in 1959. Daniel sold everything off within four years and retired. He became a homebody, content to marinate in the simple pleasures of family life. It was the treasure he had always wanted most of all. Years later, after their kids moved away and got settled on their own, he and his wife Margie traded the Windy City for Florida, where Daniel became an avid fisherman of those warm coastal waters. He was a better fisherman with one hand than most are with two. Daniel remained my best and truest friend. He had nineteen grandchildren—sixteen more than me—when he died last December of brain cancer. I miss him every day.

Mom and Dad parted ways without evident rancor in 1946, the same year I graduated from college. In the end there was just too much bad history wedged up between them. Dad had gone all in on Gideon and busted bad and there was no coming back from that. He understood. Not all broken bones heal back stronger at the break.

Dad landed a good union job with General Motors and became a Red

Wings season ticketholder down at Olympia. In time he married again, acquiring three adult stepchildren in one fell swoop. I run into them every year or two around the holidays and everyone is perfectly nice.

I think he had a good life with them. When Dad thought about the best possible version of his life, though—the one he most wished he had lived—I think it was still Mom at his side, just in another world or place or time that came with second chances. Dad passed in 1972, three days before my daughter's high school graduation.

Mom lived to the ripe old age of ninety-two and it was only at the very end that she experienced any pain or confusion. She was strong and kind and opinionated, suspicious of rationalizations and wishful thinkers, outspoken on occasions when she thought it necessary. She lived frugally and read lots of books and grew her own basil and never showed any inclination to remarry, although I know she had offers. She was a patient grandmother to my children and a friend and ally to my wife. Her later life was calm and quiet and revolved around the walking schedules of a succession of beloved dogs and the weekly gatherings of two book groups. It all seemed to suit Mom just fine.

I never found out whether Mom and Grant Ballantine had a torrid ongoing affair or a one-night earthquake or something in between. Or nothing at all. Maybe Dad's overactive imagination conjured it up out of thin air. Daniel and I learned to talk about my dad's suspicions as we got older and he didn't know anything either.

If Mom and Grant Ballantine were ever lovers, though, they didn't leave a paper trail. At least not that I've found, though I'm still working my way through Mom's mountainous correspondence with Aunt Ruth and the many friends she acquired at church and the Post Office, where she worked for twenty-six years. I often wonder how I'll feel if I ever come across an incriminating letter or postcard from Grant Ballantine, or a flurry of cryptic references to GB in Mom's handwriting.

Mom's big problem was nightmares. Not at first. Later, long after she and Dad split up. They were bad ones, impervious to any sleep aid or other medication. Mom stayed with us for a month after our son was born and three times she woke us in the middle of the night with blood-curdling screams. Each time we raced to the guest room and turned on the lights to find her sobbing in bed, eyes wide with terror. And each time I held her close until she stopped trembling and crying, knowing all the while that we were thinking about the same thing: the full-page black-and-white photograph on page 35 of the April 1, 1954 issue of *LIFE* Magazine.

* * *

I've pulled all-nighters staring at that photograph. I've done it three sheets to the wind and high as a kite and stone cold sober and the message it contains never changes. The whispered promise leering in its pixels. I can hear what it's saying. Mom can hear it too. That's why it upset her so.

The picture didn't get under Daniel's skin the way it did ours. He refused to engage with it at all. That would mean peering into the abyss of its implications. He looked at *Dust Bowl Trinity* once and to my knowledge never looked at it again. He said it didn't matter. He said that he intended to keep his head on a swivel like always but that he wouldn't spend his days living in fear or his nights pondering terrifying what-ifs. He didn't want to talk about whether Reynard or Spearfinger or Iago or Baba Yaga or Loki or some other blackhearted golem of fiction-made-flesh was prowling this great seething world of ours. Toying with us mortals, battering and discarding us as they pleased. Laughing at us behind our backs and taking their pounds of flesh with impunity.

Daniel refused to engage when I speculated it might be Reynard or another of his ilk hiding behind the face of one of the calculating politicians and preening entertainers and malevolent sensations that paraded across our television screens as the decades rolled implacably on. He said that talking about that nonsense was a waste of time. *Let it go,* he said. *Let the past be the past.*

I had to remind myself that Daniel had been dead to the world when Reynard cast off his Gideon mask. He didn't hear Reynard talk about Morgan le Fay and Rumpelstiltskin and his own demented artistic sensibilities and his unquenchable appetite for the hunt. He never saw the volcano flare of madness in Reynard's eyes when I guessed he was marooned on this world—and that Morgan was hot on his trail, tracking him like a bloodhound across continents and centuries. Daniel never saw the black tips of the furred fox ears sprouting from the top of Reynard's skull. Or the way his lips peeled back on his long snout when he smiled to reveal sharp teeth flashing like daggers in the murk.

Daniel never got the full Reynard experience. Not like Mom and I did.

The photograph became another Gideon puzzle to solve. Another padlocked box to open if I could only find the right key. I fashioned a strange little warren of a library for myself in the years that followed, full of rabbit holes that went deep deep deep.

I acquired dog-eared copies of *Alice in Wonderland* and *One Thousand and One Nights* and *Daemonologie* and *Uncle Remus, His Songs and His Sayings*. Rare editions of Lang's Coloured Fairy Books and assorted translations of the Brothers Grimm and Malory's *Le Morte d'Arthur.* Moldering stacks of Sweeney Todd penny dreadfuls and a pristine set of Jean de la Fontaine's *Fables* and a water-swollen edition of *The Facetious Nights of Straparola*. Folktales and mythologies starring shapeshifters and skinwalkers and various anthropomorphic tricksters—foxes and coyotes and cats and wolves and spiders and ravens and rabbits—from around the world.

I became an authority on odd little nooks and crannies of history. I pored over heavily footnoted tomes that spoke of political intrigue and espionage in Germany before the Great War and the ship-owning slavers who turned Charleston into a cancerous pearl and the men who braved the Roaring Forties with Sir Francis Drake and the perpetual conniving of Charles the Bad—most particularly the accounts of his fiery end.

I collected studies on sociopathic personalities and mass psychosis and personality cults. Botanical guides that detailed the poisonous properties of certain species of mushroom. True crime thrillers about deranged serial killers, the margins of several filled with my frantic scribbling. Fantastical accounts of mesmerism and mind-reading and weather control and speaking with the dead. Tracts and meditations and peyote-fueled visions about free will and predestination and the nature of man and the miracles of God. Essays that waxed philosophical on the ways in which the stories and myths we tell ourselves become the warp and weft of our existence. And three long shelves of books on Reynard alone, ranging from lavishly illustrated editions recounting his exploits in poetry and prose to dense scholarly treatises on his blood-soaked oeuvre.

What did all of those years of study and sleuthing get me in the end? Not much. Bread crumbs that disappeared into impenetrable woods of myth and conjecture. Exhausting excavations that turned up naught but bitter-tasting reminders of Reynard's mordant wit, such as my discovery in 1959 that the surnames of the two farm couples he had trotted out onto the Greenheart Theatre stage a quarter-century earlier—Fether and Tarr—had been lifted from an old Edgar Allen Poe story about a gullible traveler's failure to recognize that the mental asylum at which he is dining has been overthrown by its insane patients. Or maybe the two men on our stage that night really had been the Tarr and Fether of Poe's story, fallen through the same trapdoor that claimed Reynard. The notion became another heavy stone on my heart.

Mostly Reynard was invisible. Everywhere and nowhere. A strobe flash in a hall of mirrors. In all those years I only found him once. A stray paw print, still faintly legible in the shifting sands of time, made years before he ever darkened Greenheart's door. A paw print that proved I wasn't crazy. That he actually *existed.*

I found it on a battleship-gray microfiche machine deep in the bowels of the Detroit Public Library. I was looking at the November 1, 1928 edition of the *Atlanta Daily World,* a Black newspaper that had begun publishing only a few months earlier, because it included an article about Blind Willie McTell and his historic recording session for Victor Records. The session where McTell put down his first ever recording of "Statesboro Blues" and a fistful of other legendary blues songs. The session that Gideon once told me he had witnessed firsthand.

The article includes an admiring quote about McTell from an Atlanta nightclub owner and promoter named Bernard "Bernie" Casanova: *Those songs he put on wax the other day are just a taste. Ralph didn't even get his best song in the can. The stylus skipped halfway through and Ralph had to scrap it. Rainmaker Rainmaker, it's called. Wait til you hear that one. No one sings the blues like Blind Willie. Are you kidding me? He grew up a blind Negro boy in a world of Sea Island cotton fields and the Klan. Who knows the blues better than someone born between the devil and the deep blue sea?*

To this day that's the only reference to "Rainmaker Rainmaker" I've ever found. I've never come across a mention of it in any session notes or oral histories, let alone an actual recording. It's as if the song never existed. But I still remember every note and word.

A grainy photo of two men accompanied the newspaper article. According to the caption it was taken on the street outside the Victor Records recording studio in Atlanta on the evening of October 18, 1928. Neither of the men are McTell. The white man on the left is identified in the caption as Ralph Peer, a legendary talent scout and music engineer who recorded McTell's songs that long-ago afternoon. The lean black man standing next to him, arm wrapped around Peer's big shoulders, sports a homburg hat with a feather in the band and a finely tailored suit adorned with a round lapel pin that shines like a tiny full moon against the dark fabric. He has a pronounced widow's peak hairline and is grinning so widely into the camera that his oversized eyeteeth are visible. The caption says the black man is Bernie Casanova, the music promoter who was quoted in the article.

The name is different. So is his skin color. I still recognized the smile.

It's all in the basement now. What's left of my collection anyway. The last of the books and other materials that I just couldn't bear to donate to the library or take down to the used bookstore. The last of it is packed away in four or five slowly softening cardboard boxes that have sat undisturbed behind Christmas lights and board games for going on six years now.

I knew I had to stop obsessing. I knew the *LIFE* photograph and what it portended had taken over my life. Dana threatened to take the kids and leave if I didn't get help and still I couldn't stop. It was Mom who finally got through to me. She told me that if I wasn't careful I was going to throw my family away for Reynard just like Dad did back in Greenheart.

Those were the words that finally got me to stop.

* * *

The magazine photograph Mom showed me that long-ago afternoon is *Dust Bowl Trinity*. It was taken by Gretchen Larsen, a comely chameleon who effortlessly straddled the worlds of photojournalism and art for more than four decades, jumping back and forth between gallery exhibitions in glittering cities around the world and Pulitzer-winning photojournalism assignments for *LIFE, The Atlantic,* and *The New York Times.* By 1954, when *LIFE* published *Dust Bowl Trinity* and ten other photos from an upcoming retrospective of her Depression-era work in Mexico, Cuba, and the American Southwest, Larsen was regarded by all but the most stubborn contrarians as one of the great American photographers of the twentieth century.

Back in 1936, though, Larsen was just another anonymous young photographer trying to survive the Depression. According to legend she was looking at bus schedules in Santa Fe when the first horrific reports from Greenheart trickled out to the wider world. She hitched a ride on the first Red Cross relief truck out of town and reached Greenheart's smoking remains a full day before anyone else with a functional camera, let alone the expensive rig she hauled along with her.

She took *Dust Bowl Trinity* and several other famous shots featured in that *LIFE* spread from high atop the soot-streaked bell tower of our church, which had been miraculously spared from the previous night's horrors but for the loss of all eight of its prized stained-glass windows. Larsen used a climber's harness of sorts to attach herself to the bell tower's highest ramparts, then spent the better part of three hours clambering around up there like a steeplejack, documenting the carnage radiating out in every direction. Clicking away as the shadows stretched and deepened with the day's dying light. She didn't come down until long after nightfall had drawn down the curtain on our obliterated world. Some people say they heard her carrying on a conversation with herself while she was hanging up there in the dark.

Dust Bowl Trinity looks like a photo negative of a Gustave Dore engraving. One of his biblical ones, piled high with wrathful storm clouds and desolate battlefields and looming crosses and haunted ruins. That's what Greenheart looks like in *Dust Bowl Trinity.* Like the kind of place where swan-winged angels and bat-winged demons periodically clash in their eternal war for dominion. And every time those squadrons of angels and demons depart they leave behind an empty stage, swept clean of human life by the furious beating of all those wings. In *Dust Bowl Trinity* it looks like Larsen missed them by ten minutes.

There's so much to see it's hard to take in all at once. In the upper left corner of the photograph dense shafts of sunlight punch through a battalion of black-bruised clouds. They unfurl in bands of brilliant white columns that slant almost parallel to the ground, their fiery glow illuminating a frozen sea of pewter-colored dust below. When the sunbeams reach the center of the image, though, they vanish behind locomotive-black clouds of smoke spiraling off the cindered bones of two buildings in the foreground: the Greenheart Theatre and the Zephyr Hotel. Here and there, rifts in the black smoke provide glimpses of a boulevard filled with stranded cars and burned storefronts. And further in the distance yet, floating at the end of the boulevard just to the left of the drifting towers of black smoke, the remains of John Stagg's once-grand home.

The mansion's two massive stone chimneys occupy the precise center of *Dust Bowl Trinity,* like the hole in the middle of an LP. They thrust like devil's horns out of the smoking rubble of John Stagg's home, profaning the day's last golden sunlight. The garage, stable, and other outbuildings huddle around the ruins like reluctant mourners at an open-casket funeral. Beyond the outbuildings a vast sea striped in black and white stretches to the knife-edge horizon, the lee of every motionless swell scalloped in the darkest obsidian.

* * *

I could tell something was wrong over the phone. Mom sounded out of sorts in a way I'd never heard before. But when I questioned her all she said was to come over right away. She was waiting for me at the kitchen table when I walked in the door. The glossy magazine in front of her was already open to page 35.

An overwhelming sense of déjà vu fell over me when I saw the photograph that day because I recognized the land in which it had been taken. It was the land my nightmare diver called home. It was uncanny. The icy fingertip of recognition that ran down my spine was so paralyzing that I didn't even notice what was missing from the image. Not at first. Not until Mom tapped one agitated finger on the center of the full-page spread.

"Where's Gideon's car?" she asked in a small, trembling voice. She was on the verge of tears. "Where is it, Will? Where did it go?"

The question made my bones vibrate with fear because she was right. In *Dust Bowl Trinity* the top of the looping driveway upon which Gideon's roadster had been parked throughout that terrifying night is an unbroken blankness of white. His car is gone.

I couldn't make sense of it. I had watched the reflection of the flames coruscate up and down the roadster's sleek black skin like an aurora borealis from hell for hours over the course of that endless night. I had watched its wheel wells drift in with dust and spiky clots of Russian thistle. Gideon's car had been half-buried in dirt when we staggered out of the barn and down the ruined boulevard into town at dawn. Yet by the time Larsen took her camera to the top of our church steeple later that same day the roadster had vanished.

In *Dust Bowl Trinity*, though, you can see where it went.

Larsen's high vantage point revealed the secret hidden from more earthbound eyes. A faint sidewinder pattern of disturbance in the otherwise blank expanse of desert stretching behind the funeral pyre of Stagg's once grand estate. A paired set of furrows originating at the top of Stagg's driveway and curving away to the western horizon, forsaking streets and roads and highways for empty country. The furrows mark the land like the ghost ruts of some nineteenth-century wagon train. Or the fast-disappearing tracks of a coal-black roadster convertible with a spark of magic still buzzing in the battery and a thermos of cold lemonade bouncing on the front seat.

About the Author

Kevin B. Hillstrom is an author and academic book editor who writes on subjects ranging from wilderness paddling to the political history of environmental and health care policy. He lives outside Lansing, Michigan.

You can connect with me on:

- https://www.kevinbhillstrom.com
- https://www.instagram.com/kevinbhillstrom